Other Titles by Edie Ramer

Raining
Love & Murder

LOVE & MURDER, BOOK 4

Edie Ramer

Blue Walrus Books

Published by Blue Walrus Books

ISBN: 978-1-939328-29-8

Cover design by EJR Digital Art
Copy-editing by Blue Otter Editing
Proofreading by Judicious Designs

Published in the United States of America.

One

"YOU'RE CUTE, CHUCK." Her face wreathed in smile lines, Angie Hornbuck leaned over her kitchen table to pat Chuck's cheek, as if he were four years old instead of thirty-one. "But you're just not a businessman."

Chuck Pascal's smile fell. He glanced away from her, at her paintings on the walls of the room and on the tables. Every spare space. And this was her house. Her studio was filled with her paintings, too.

Though Angie looked like someone's tall, thin grandmother, her paintings were fiery and vital. From April to September, she opened up her studio two days a week for tourists. Like other local artists, she also sold her paintings through galleries.

"Angie, I don't know how this can be anything but a good thing," he said. "The Trouble Bay Art Mart won't take any more of a percentage than the galleries charge, and it's going to be much bigger. It's—"

"A giant flea market." Her long witch's nose pinched. "I can't imagine how that will work out."

He opened his mouth but was stopped by her pursed lips and the sound of her fingers tapping the table. As if he were the idiot child she was trying to humor but she just wished he would leave.

"Okay, I get it." He stood.

"Oh, now I've hurt your feelings." Her hands flat on the table, she pushed up to her feet. "I wish I could help you. I always did like a handsome man." She reached up to pat his cheek again. "But, Chuck honey, to be honest, I'm at the age where I just don't like to try new things. I've been doing this a long time, and I'm established. My paintings have been featured in *Reader's Digest*."

"That's the reason I came to you first."

"Maybe you think the art mart sounds like a great idea, but to me, it sounds like one of those discount superstores." She eyed him sadly. "I like you. I really do. You're so cute, and if I were younger... Well, I'm not younger, and I just don't do discount art."

"Angie, it's not a flea market." Even as he spoke, he knew it wasn't going to change her mind, but he needed to defend his project. "*You* set the prices, and we don't change them. It's the same thing as putting your paintings in a gallery, except more people will come."

"Maybe more will come, but they'll be the kind of people who are looking for bargains instead of art." She shook her head. "It's just going to be a waste of my time, and, to be frank, I don't think it's a good idea to have my name associated with it. Maybe someone else could make it work, but I don't think you're that person."

Her words were belly slams.

"We're doing just fine in Trouble Bay," she continued, "and we don't need a flea market for our artwork. I hate to see you throw away your money. Better to stick with the B and B now that your mom has found a man good enough for her. Even if he is Jewish."

He took a step back from her. "If you change your mind, let me know."

As he turned for the back door, she said, "Everyone in town is worried about you jumping into this crazy thing. You know we all love you."

He didn't answer. If this was love, then kill him now.

THE MEMORY OF that bad time, before the man had found him, never disappeared from Dog's mind. The time when his human family had pushed him out of the car, then sped away without him. Dog had followed the smell for a long time, until he couldn't smell it anymore. Even after that, he'd kept looking. For a long, long time he'd looked everywhere for them. Kept trying to catch their scent. Running and running. Smelling and sniffing. Sad noises coming from his throat.

He'd never found them.

Confused, his heart breaking, he didn't know what to do. Food smells finally drew him to a restaurant. They wouldn't let him in the front door but he smelled food in the back of the alley, too. A tall boy would sometimes throw him scraps of food before throwing the rest of the food in the giant food holder. *Dumpster*, the tall boy called it.

Dog still continued to search for his family, but every night he would come back to the alley, though the weather got cold, and sometimes snow came down. He found a place that blew hot air on him, and he huddled by it, one side cold and the other hot. Changing positions all night and sometimes during the day.

He lost hope, but still he searched, because he didn't know what else to do.

One day, the man stepped into the alley and spotted Dog eating.

A bone in his mouth, Dog backed away. Snarling.

This wasn't the first man who tried to take away his food. One man had even pointed the loud thing at him. The thing that made a big bang and made a window shatter and left a bad smell in the air.

But this new man hunched down, like a dog trying to make itself smaller. Showing Dog that he wasn't a threat. "Don't be afraid," the man said. "There's enough for both of us."

Dog snarled under his breath. He didn't want to leave. This alley was *his* place now. His home. And he could smell the man. His scent told Dog that he was living in alleys and eating scraps of food, just like him. That he had no home. That he lived from meal to meal. Just like Dog.

Dog's heart pounded hard, and he backed against the next building, pressing into it, hoping the man would think he was gone. Then he watched the man upend an old cardboard box and step on top of it, then bend over the big black dumpster. Opening the top and diving down so that it looked as if he'd fallen into the dumpster, where all the smells came from—the good smells and the awful smells.

The man came back up with a *whoop*, and in his hands was meat. *Food.* Wonderful-smelling food.

Dog wanted the food so badly that he shook with need. But his fear of humans, after too many betrayals and too many kicks and rocks thrown at him, made him wary.

People were bad. Other dogs looked at him as a rival for food. And cats...well, cats didn't bother him. He had even curled up with one or two on a few nights. Cats who weren't afraid of dogs.

But cats were loners and hunters, and they never stayed with him long.

He was a dog who'd had love—or who'd thought he'd had love.

The love had vanished in an instant, like a flower plucked from the ground, then thrown away.

He still didn't know what he'd done wrong. They hadn't yelled at him. He'd slept next to their beds. He'd barked at a skunk at night and scared it away. He'd licked the boy's face, and the boy had laughed.

Why? Why? Why?

Now his ribs were sticking out, and some days he dreamed about food and his old family, only to wake up and realize the family wasn't there anymore.

So he took the man's food, but he would never trust a human again...

"IF DAWN ACCIDENTALLY dies, the rights for her lyrics and music will revert to you," Grant Wellington said in his compelling preacher's voice.

In the hallway of Grant's Los Angeles mansion, Dawn Keighly froze. Vince, her sister's brother-in-law, stood next to her on the other side of the partially open door to his father's office. Not saying anything. Not rushing in to warn his father that she could hear him.

Dawn started to step forward, and Vince gripped her arm with his long one, holding her in place. Still not saying a word.

"I don't want Dawn to die," Sunny said, and her voice sounded weak. Soft.

"We all die sometime, sweetheart," Jarret, Grant's oldest son and her sister's husband, said. "It's not as if Dawn will disappear. None of us disappear, isn't that right, Dad?"

"Absolutely." Grant's voice rang out with all the conviction of a visionary. "She'll be in Nirvana."

Dawn turned her gaze to Vince, a dark-haired man with sharp features that made him look handsome in the way a black jaguar was handsome. He stared back down at her. Still not saying anything. Not needing to say anything. His silence and his stillness said it all.

He'd *wanted* her to hear this. When he'd led her here, he'd known they would be talking about her.

She was aware that Grant and Jarret wanted the royalties for the lyrics and music that belonged to her. Apparently they had thought that since Sunny was the singer, and her name was associated with the songs, she would have the rights. It was insane, but Grant and his followers had convinced a lot of smart people that the stairway to heaven started with Nirvana Now, the powerful religion that Grant had created out of the sheer force of his personality.

Or perhaps her sister's father-in-law had taken one look at Sunny's quieter and younger sister and had thought, *Easy prey.*

5

If so, that was a big mistake. A giant mistake. For a long time, she and Sunny had been on their own, and one of them had needed to see through bullshit.

Though she'd been only sixteen, two years younger than Sunny, when they'd fled their mother's house in Memphis, she'd taken on the role of the mom they'd never really had. At least, not a caring and loving mom.

With her songwriting and Sunny's singing and golden beauty, they'd done better every year, and the last two years, they'd been on the top of the charts and all the important lists.

But now Sunny had Jarret. Now Sunny didn't need her.

Her songs, though...apparently her songs were a different matter.

Dawn glanced at Vince, the highest-ranking lieutenant in Nirvana Now.

"You're the real talent, Sunny." Grant's words oozed into the hall as smooth as warm honey. "Everyone knows that."

"Your voice and your magnetic personality are the reasons the songs are so popular," Jarret said.

"You are beloved by your fans," Grant said.

"You are their angel," Jarret said. "You're my angel. I knew that the day I first saw you."

There was silence, and Dawn imagined Sunny's eyes filling with moisture.

"Once Dawn is in Nirvana," Grant said, "she'll be happy for you. She'll be grateful that you're getting the adulation you deserve."

"I'll pray for her." Sunny's voice wobbled, which wasn't like her. It was thick with tears and something else. As though her tongue were too big for her mouth.

Drugs? Were they drugging Sunny?

Dawn stepped back. She glanced at Vince, who was watching her, his dark eyes shadowed with his own demons and secrets. Her teeth clenched, she snapped around and hurried away. Sad. Angry. Afraid. Shaken.

Vince made no outcry, and no footsteps followed her. But

she felt his stare on her back, long after she raced out of the mansion, jumped into her car, and sped away as if a wild animal were chasing after her.

Lyrics from an old song, "We Gotta Get Out of This Place," sang in her mind.

She added her own lyrics: *Before they kill me.*

Two

"I KNOW WHAT you're here for." Eric, a short man in his mid-forties with a body like a fire hydrant, positioned himself in the middle of his studio. His original paintings were slanted against the walls. The lithographs of his bird-people paintings were stacked on one long table along with the framing supplies.

Eric glared at Chuck, who decided coming here had been a bad idea. Eric's pretty wife used to take care of the lithograph side of the business, but at the end of last summer, she'd left with a college student and—so gossip said—all the money in Eric's bank account. Eric had been in a lousy mood since then, and Chuck couldn't fault him for it.

"Not interested," Eric said.

Chuck didn't leave. "Look, I know that Jeanie—"

"This ain't got nothin' to do with my private life. Everyone in town knows you're the fun guy. Nothin' wrong with that, but you're just not the business type. Nothin's wrong with that, either. That's just the way it is."

Chuck twisted to leave, then turned around to face Eric again, bracing his feet. He realized he was copying Eric's stance, his head up like he was ready for a gunfight.

Damn it. This was silly. He still had his bulky parka on. It was snowing outside, and he hadn't even taken his knit hat off, though he'd stuffed his gloves in his pockets.

"I could tell you all my arguments," Chuck said, "but I

can see your mind is made up. It's not that you don't think my idea is good. It's me. You don't think I'm a go-getter."

"Chuck, you gotta admit, you aren't a go-getter. And that tent idea is just wrong. It cheapens our stuff."

"It's not a tent. It's a building."

"A *pole* building. One of those aluminum things."

"Forget the damn building. That's just another excuse. I don't get it." He gestured toward the lithographs on the table. "You set the prices, not me. Whatever doesn't sell, you'll get back. Any way you look at it, it's a win for you."

Eric scowled. "It's a waste of time, and I've already wasted too much."

Chuck turned and headed to the door. He would be better off talking to a frozen snowman than Eric. As he stepped outside, a blast of snow and cold hit him, but the below-freezing temperature wasn't as cold as the way he felt inside.

He'd thought this part would be easy. That these artists were his friends, and he would be helping them. That it was a win-win for the artists.

He'd never suspected, never even harbored a twinkling thought that they'd had such a low opinion of him.

His gut twisted. His teeth clenched.

Maybe they were right. Maybe he was a fool.

THE PARTIALLY EATEN grilled cheese wrapped in bacon and white bread had bite marks in it. It was midmorning in Milwaukee, and Todd could hear the traffic on the street. Earlier, a truck had driven down the alley, and he'd been glad that he'd folded up his cardboard shelter and had stuffed it by the side of the garage. As soon as the truck turned onto the street, Todd dived into the dumpster again.

He'd gotten lucky. The sandwich was even warm.

A small sound came to him. A whimper.

He looked over at the black dog on the other side of the

alley, watching him again. Some kind of lab mix. But skinny. Too skinny.

Too starving.

He could *feel* the dog's hunger. He could *feel* the dog's need.

Still holding the sandwich, Todd closed his eyes. This morning, he'd gone to the coffee shop a few blocks down, where he'd had eggs and toast and orange juice. He did get some money because of his PTSD. If he wanted to, he could even rent an apartment. A small one, but he'd still have a roof over his head, and four small walls around him.

That was the problem. Small walls made him want to punch them until his knuckles were bloody. He'd done that once. He didn't want to do it again.

His hand shook now, and he held back the hot rush of despair and fear. He didn't even know what had brought it on, it was just there, like lightning and thunder were there with some rainstorms. And snow was there with cold weather.

Stop. Stop, stop, stop.

Stop thinking, and do something.

Taking a deep breath, he held out his arm. His hand was shaking, but he kept it held out anyway. The dog with the hungry eyes wouldn't care that he was shaking. "Here, dog. It's all yours. Here, dog."

The dog stayed back, not trusting him.

His hands still shook. He'd given the dog food before, leaving it for him, but the dog never stepped close to him. Never trusted him.

Someone must have hurt the dog. Some human.

"Here, dog. I'm not going to hurt you. I promise."

The dog didn't move.

He sighed and stepped slowly across the alley. "We could be buddies," he said, his tone crooning. "I promise I won't hurt you. There's bacon in here. It smells good, doesn't it?"

The dog kept backing away, but his neck craned toward him, his nostrils quivering. Sniffing the bacon and cheese.

Todd ripped the remainder of the sandwich in half. The dog's muscles bunched, getting ready to run.

"It's okay. It's okay." Todd stopped, and bent forward. He set the torn piece on the cold and dirty alley, then stepped back. One step. Two steps.

He stopped, and stood still.

The dog looked at him. Looked at the sandwich. Stepped forward slowly, warily. His gaze shifted from Todd to the sandwich and back again with each step. When he snatched the sandwich up and gulped it down, he kept his gaze on Todd.

In seconds it was gone. The dog backed up.

Todd held out the other leftover piece.

The dog stopped.

"For you," Todd said.

The dog didn't move forward, but he didn't move away, either.

"For you," Todd repeated, still holding the leftover sandwich.

The dog shuddered.

"Okay. It's okay, boy." Todd lowered his hand slowly and set down the last of the cheese sandwich.

But this time he didn't step back. This time he waited.

The dog lunged forward, grabbed the leftover sandwich, then scrambled two steps back as he gulped down the last of the sandwich.

He stared at Todd for a long moment.

Todd stared back. The dog was like him in so many more ways than the people who walked by him on the street. They were both damaged. They were both alone.

They were both scared.

He turned back to the dumpster. The dog needed more food. Todd knew he wasn't much use to the world. Not anymore. But at least he could do this.

DON'T SLINK. DON'T hunch your shoulders. Don't act as if you're a fugitive. Don't act as if you're on the run. Don't give off the smell of fear.

Raine—as she called herself now—strode into the truck stop, wearing black-framed glasses and the navy puffer jacket she'd bought at a Target store in Utah, her steps steady, her head up. The warning Howie had given her before she'd left Los Angeles was still sharp in her mind.

So were the words of Grant Wellington, her sister's father-in-law. The man who wanted her dead.

A waitress with a big smile and bigger hair greeted her and led her to a booth for two. Raine smiled politely at the waitress as she added the days up in her mind.

It had been six days since she'd overheard her sister's father-in-law's plan to kill her.

Six days since hearing her sister agree with her father-in-law in her new, slurry voice.

Three days to change her appearance with a new haircut and glasses and paying for a new ID before leaving California in her business manager's seven-year-old sedan that Howie's housekeeper used for errands.

Three days since she'd left L.A.

Three days since her face had showed up on the entertainment news as pop singer Sunny Keighly's missing sister. A few had put *songwriter* in her description, but most just connected her to Sunny.

She could have gone to the police, but she had watched enough police shows on TV to know they needed proof. And who were they going to believe? The head of a popular church? And her own sister?

Or the quiet sister who stayed in the background?

It would be just another she-said/he-said case. Worse than that, actually. It would be *she said* against her own sister, her brother-in-law, and her brother-in-law's father. Three against one. Not good odds.

Probably Vince would make four against her. Because of Vince she was alive, but she wouldn't trust him any more than she would trust a rattlesnake under her bed covers.

Already one entertainment hostess was saying that Dawn Keighly was known to take drugs, though the only pharmaceutical she took was aspirin. She didn't even drink more than an occasional glass of wine or a beer. Her mother had been addicted to drugs and alcohol, and that wasn't anything she wanted to emulate.

She wanted to contact the police, but quite a few top cops were also in the high ranks of Nirvana Now. They were given a lot of perks by Grant, and she didn't trust the justice system to believe her over them. Grant and Jarret—and even Sunny—would have said she was accusing them for the publicity. Or Grant might even have accused her of wanting to control Sunny. He would say—with a show of great sadness—that she was mentally unstable.

And if she said that Grant or Jarret was drugging Sunny, the same thing would happen.

If there were some way she could convince Sunny to leave Jarret...

That wasn't possible. Sunny could sometimes be the sweetest person in the world.

And she could much more often be the stubbornest.

Sunny would not believe that her Prince Charming meant her harm. She could not believe that his wonderful father who adored her had done her wrong. And without her belief, no one would believe her.

Her best option had been to disappear.

"Coffee?" The cheery voice brought her back to the present. She pulled herself together. Her hands shook but she kept her voice steady as she said yes.

Telling herself not to think about Sunny, Raine glanced around the truck stop diner. Though it was midafternoon, about a dozen booths were occupied. The seats looked clean, and there was a giant-sized TV on the wall, a news segment showing on it. Except for the two couples across the aisle, the other diners looked like they were truckers. By this third day of her flight from southern California, she could recognize truckers from the other travelers.

A tune started in her mind.

Driving, driving, driving, driving, driving...

Driving away from hurt and pain and stabs in the heart...

"Is that a song?" the waitress asked.

Raine froze, her fingers that had been tapping the tabletop becoming still. "Just a tune I heard on a kids' show."

"Sounds real good to me. Sometimes those kids' songs are better than the ones for adults." The waitress poured coffee into a cup, then plucked the plasticized menu from behind the napkin holder and handed it to Raine. "I'll be back in a jiffy," she said, then scurried away in her black skirt with matching apron and tennis shoes.

Raine glanced out the window. It was misting out, gray and cold, reminding her of her new name, which she'd chosen because it wasn't too dissimilar from Dawn. The name suited her. So much of her life had felt like a cold, driving, and unforgiving rain.

Maybe that's how Sunny had felt, despite her name that promised happiness. Maybe that's why she'd chosen Nirvana over her sister.

Could Raine blame her for that?

The answer came quickly. When Sunny was agreeing that she could be killed so Sunny would get control of her songs, then, yes, she could blame her. Hell, yes.

Unless Sunny really had been drugged. Raine frowned. That thickness in Sunny's voice, the slurring, still bothered her.

The cheery waitress returned, and Raine shut off her thoughts and ordered a bowl of tomato soup. Something warm and comforting.

Across from her and one booth up, two middle-aged couples were talking enthusiastically about a vacation place where the husband wanted to stay for the winter. Tired of her own thoughts, she leaned forward.

"Door County is a paradise in spring and summer," the woman said in a loud voice, "but it's practically dead in winter. Unless you like to ice fish, snowmobile, or sit around in bars, there's nothing to do."

"They have crafts," the pudgy man next to her said. "The women get together and do stuff."

The woman gave him a look that should have singed the brown-and-gray hairs off of his sagging jawline. "*You're* the one who wants to go there. *You* go and do stuff."

"I like Door County." His voice was loud with defensiveness. "I like Trouble Bay. And I like it that it's not a tourist trap in winter. It's in Wisconsin, not as many mountains as Colorado for the rabid skiers, but there's nothing wrong with ice fishing."

"If you like that kind of thing." The wife sniffed. "The owner of the dress shop in Trouble Bay told me that her store closes after Labor Day, and she flies to Florida. She said the population shrinks from twenty thousand to less than one thousand. This time of year, almost all the stores are closed."

"I know towns like that," the male across the table from them said. "So small that if a stranger walks into town, everyone knows about it by sundown."

Raine sucked in her breath. If what they said was true, she wouldn't have to be vigilant twenty-four hours a day in a place like that. She wouldn't jerk out of sleep in a strange bed every night, trying to remember where she was and why she was there.

Taking an instant to remember a powerful man wanted to kill her.

The waitress came with Raine's coffee and took her order. As soon as she left, Raine took her new cell phone out of her purse and typed in Door County and Trouble Bay. A peninsula in the northeastern corner of Wisconsin popped up on the small screen.

She skimmed the glowing descriptions of Door County as a vacation mecca, going back further to a darker time. In the eighteenth century, it had been known to Frenchmen as Death's Door territory.

Death's Door. A chill sliced through her, and she sucked in her breath and forced herself to keep reading. A narrow strait separated the peninsula from Washington Island, and apparently navigation had been tricky back in the day, hence the scary nickname.

Her lips twisted. Working in the music business, she was used to tricky.

Her sister's marriage had made it trickier.

Raine shut off those thoughts and found Trouble Bay, seeing that the Lake Michigan waters formed a bay around the Door County peninsula that led to Green Bay in the next county over.

The waitress came with her soup and crackers and a glass of water, warning her the soup was fresh from the pot and was hot.

She told the waitress that was fine. She felt frozen inside, and right now hot suited her.

As soon as the waitress left, a familiar voice brought her gaze up to the large TV that hung on the wall. Her breath sucked in, she stared at a couple who could have easily posed as the plastic figures on top of a wedding cake.

The woman newscaster talked quickly, but with the chatter from the tables near her, all Raine could catch were a few words from the TV: *Sunny. New husband. Nirvana Now.*

If Raine hadn't been so angry and so scared—and so hurt—she might have cried.

The picture switched to one of Sunny and Dawn. Sunny, the bright and sparkling sister. Dawn, the pale sister with dark eye makeup and thick hair that reached halfway down her back.

Raine allowed herself to relax, so happy for her recent haircut. The short, curly hair with wispy bangs emphasized her cheekbones and made her face look elfin. And it didn't hurt that her eyes behind the black-rimmed glasses were a blue-green and gold color combination instead of the bright blue from the contacts she had formerly worn.

Not only would no one recognize her, she liked this perky look.

The images on the screen switched back to Sunny and Jarret—the golden couple, though Jarret had light brown hair and eyes to match.

Sunny matched him, too, with her white-blond hair, sky-blue eyes, pouty lips, and a face shaped like a 1950s Barbie Doll.

Raine's throat closed. It hurt to look at Sunny. It hurt to think of her betrayal.

She forced herself to look away. She forced herself to finish her soup and drink her coffee, though she'd lost her appetite. When the waitress walked by, Raine stopped her and asked for takeout coffee. She had a long drive ahead of her.

Sunny knew she hated cold weather, the reason Raine had driven to Colorado. But as she'd driven the last few miles, she'd felt like this was the wrong decision. Colorado attracted ski-loving celebrities who might recognize her as Sunny's sister, despite her haircut. Seeing through makeup and new hairdos was part of their profession. She should have thought of that before.

If she drove to a small town in Wisconsin, she wouldn't have to worry about running into anyone she knew.

The waitress came with the takeout coffee. Raine paid her, telling her to keep the change. As she hurried out of the diner to Howie's brown sedan, she shook inside. Maybe it wasn't true that people's insides tied up in knots, but it felt that way to her.

Sunny had the fairy-tale life she'd always wanted. She was married to the prince. Her father-in-law was the king.

But Raine knew there were no real fairy tales. Jarret Wellington was no prince. And his father was no king. They were just real people.

Real *greedy* people.

People who would do anything for adulation and money. Lots of money.

Even murder.

But Raine wasn't going to let them kill her. She was going to *live*.

Three

TODD DIDN'T TAKE it personally when the black Labrador retriever kept shying away from him. He was human, after all, and the dog was clearly an intelligent animal who knew that humans broke promises, hearts, and bones.

Humans killed.

But he and the dog had been together in this alley seven days already, with him sleeping behind the dumpster in the big box that he'd found a few weeks ago, wrapped in the sleeping bag he'd bought with his own money. He'd put layers of Styrofoam beneath him, and he'd set up a makeshift shelter out of corrugated cardboard.

January was gone. February was a frigid bitch. Todd didn't know how the dog had made it through the frozen nights before he'd gotten here. There was a garage for trucks a half mile away that was open all night. Maybe a dog-loving mechanic had let him sneak in and sleep in the break room at night. Or maybe he'd found a way into a shed or a garage.

Todd knew about finding warmth in strange places: public libraries, laundromats, big chain bookstores, toilets in big-box stores, and a few other odd places.

He preferred this place, in the narrow alleyway that no one but him, the dog, and a couple truck drivers seemed to have discovered. The aroma from the Italian restaurants had drawn him here, and he didn't want to leave.

Neither did the dog. Todd was feeding the dog every day,

and each night, he'd offered the dog the choice to sleep with him.

So far, the dog had run away.

This night, though, it was colder, with snow pelting down. The box was sturdy, and Todd was sure it would make it through the night okay... But he wasn't sure about the dog.

He opened up one side of the box. The dog stood in the small place between the dumpster and the brick wall of the building, so skinny and undernourished it was able to squeeze in. The dog trembled, either from fear or from the cold, and he watched Todd with eyes that were yellow in the eerie night light.

Not yellow like crazy or hungry or evil.

Yellow like fearful and sick. Yellow like not eating enough.

Todd wondered if his eyes looked yellow, too. He hadn't looked in the mirror for probably a couple months. Even when he used a bathroom at a gas station, he avoided looking in the mirror at the man with the too-long hair and beard and wearing too many layers of clothes.

He and the dog both showed the signs of homelessness. The dog's ribs and knee bones stuck out, and it looked like a dog skeleton covered with a dull black coat.

A dog that wouldn't make it through this freezing-cold night.

The thought was like a punch to Todd's chest.

A freezing wind slapped him in his face, the only part of him exposed to the air.

"Come here," he said, and somewhere he heard a scuttling sound. Another animal. Maybe even a mouse or rat, but Todd couldn't worry that any of these animals would hurt him. It was the cruelty of humans that worried him. That same cruelty kept the dog from coming closer to him.

"Come here," he repeated, in case the dog didn't hear his raspy voice, ruined by his screams in Afghanistan.

Still, the dog didn't come.

Todd pushed back from the opening, and he cried. Not for himself. For the dog. He cried until he fell asleep. And then he dreamed that the dog was looking at his face, sniffing him. Sniffing down his sleeping bag.

He knew he was dreaming, but how peculiar that the images in his mind were of the dog, and not of his usual nightmares of people dying and screaming.

How peculiar that he felt a body lying next to him. Sharing his warmth. How peculiar that he put his hand on the body, and he felt short, cold hairs...

FOR A FEW seconds, as Sunny entered her father-in-law's sunlit office that looked more like a fancy sitting room with its pale gray leather, the marble tables, and, most of all, the ocean view, she had a feeling of unreality. As if none of this were real. As if it were all a dream. As if it were still her and Dawn against the world. The two of them trying to survive— her with her sparkling personality and her voice that critics said sounded like an angel's, and Dawn with her songwriting skills and her music.

Grant stood and called her name, his hands out, dignified and handsome with his thick white hair and still-virile-looking body. Approval glinted in his eyes, and she felt a frisson of uneasiness. She could hear Dawn's husky voice in her ear. *His first wife died in an accident. Then his second wife died in another accident. I don't like those odds.*

The dreamlike quality, as if she'd tumbled down into a crystal bowl, splintered.

Another man stood from the other corner of the room. Her brother-in-law, Vince. Half brother-in-law, she supposed, since his mother was the second wife. With his blackish hair and his darker complexion, about five inches shorter than Jarret, Vince took after his mother's Italian side and looked nothing like Sunny's tall, handsome husband.

Just as Dawn looked so different from her, with her ash-blond hair and her average height while Sunny was taller with bigger breasts and longer legs. So many fans told her she looked like a movie star.

When Dawn overheard them, she would always snicker.

The memory made Sunny straighten her spine.

Then her spine relaxed, and she blinked away heated tears.

She missed Dawn. Missed Dawn so much that it hurt her chest, and she put her hand to her head. It felt stuffed, her brain fuzzy. Not like herself. She hadn't felt like herself for weeks now.

She wanted Dawn. Dawn would take care of her. Dawn always took care of her.

"How's my favorite daughter-in-law?" Grant Wellington strode toward her, his arms held out.

Uneasiness shivered through her again. Then Grant took her hands in his, and his pale eyes stared into hers. She felt his approval, like the sun's warmth settling on her. As if he were the father she had never had. The father who loved her and would always be there for her.

That was better. She should trust him, shouldn't she? He was her husband's father.

"I'm wonderful." She smiled at him, because that's what she always did. Smiled so people would like her. "Everything is wonderful."

"Ah, young love." Grant's eyes sparkled.

Jarret put his arm around her shoulders and hugged her to his side. "True love," he murmured.

She looked up into his smiling face, and something shifted in her, as if she were standing on a cloud now, looking down at the mere mortals.

Jarret loved her. He worshiped her. He'd promised to take care of her.

"I'm worried about your sister." Grant put his arm around her, and Jarret released her while Grant drew her gently to a velveteen, sea-green settee.

He was like the father she'd always wanted. Loving. Approving. Admiring. Why did people say such bad things about him? Not all people but some people. And they said it in whispers.

Shouldn't that have told Dawn something? Told her that the others were jealous?

After all, he was helping people walk the path to God and Nirvana Now. Nirvana was the same thing as heaven. *Bliss.* The place where pain didn't exist. Where people didn't swear or sweat or say bad things about you.

Wasn't that what everyone wanted?

Except the evil ones.

She knew about the evil ones. So did Dawn.

"You're frowning." Grant rubbed his finger on the skin between her eyebrows.

She immediately forced her facial muscles to relax. She was only twenty-seven, though she told everyone that she was twenty-four.

After all, three years were nothing—except in her business.

She took in a deep breath. "Has anyone found Dawn yet?"

"There have been sightings, and we're looking for her. But so far, nothing. Jarret and I thought you might put out a plea to her to come back to you?"

"We've talked about her on TV already."

"Not at all of the places," Grant said. "Just a few."

"She might be in trouble," Jarret said. "You want to save her, don't you?"

"Save Dawn." Sunny shuddered. Why did she feel so weak? "Yes, I need to save her. I'll do this."

She gazed up at Grant, who was watching her with approval. Then she turned to Jarret, who looked at her with so much love that she felt transcendent.

Her eyelids lowered, she turned her head slightly toward Vince.

His mouth was twisted. His eyes narrowed.

She stiffened. It was wrong to feel this way, but right this second, she hated him. Really, really hated him.

She wished there were some way he would disappear, too.

☂

"I'D LOVE TO let you sell my paintings," Jenny Schwartz, Chuck's old girlfriend, said, "but the art mart will be making our stuff look cheap."

Chuck stood in the kitchen instead of her studio attic, but he knew what her work looked like. He'd even posed for one of the paintings when he was in his early twenties. Nude. She'd giggled all the way through it.

But now she just smiled and shook her head.

"Would I cheat you?" he asked.

She frowned. "Of course not."

"Then what do you have to lose? You're a great artist, but you don't sell all your paintings." He put up his hands. "None of you do."

"The thing is, we've all agreed that this isn't a good idea." Still frowning, she scratched the back of her neck. "You know I'd do just about anything for you, Chuck. I don't want to hurt your feelings. But no one's done this before, and it's not like you're an entrepreneur."

He stared at her as she made a sad face.

"You're not mad at me, are you?" she asked in a baby-girl voice.

"No, honey. I'm not mad." He turned.

"Where are you going? Can't you stay?"

He didn't answer. He just kept walking. Finally getting that it wasn't just a few crazy people who didn't believe in him.

It was the whole damn town.

Four

TODD. THE MAN'S name was Todd. Dog sat by the man's feet and lay down his head on his paws. Still wary but he could run fast if he had to. Faster than the man. So he closed his eyes, because the weariness lay heavily on him. The sadness.

Some days, before the human had come to the alley, Dog had thought that maybe he could fall to sleep and never wake up. He was so cold and so alone and so sad. Grieving for his family that had thrown him away.

But now the man had come every night. Every day he would leave, and every day Dog would think that he wouldn't return.

Todd had come back today again. And, again, he'd fed Dog. It was a cold night, colder than the other nights, the cold sliding through Dog's skin and muscles and bones.

Dog inched up to the man's side. All the way up to the top of his shoulder. Dog could hear the thump of the man's heart and his fast breaths.

There was a space between them, and Dog could feel the man's warmth through the sleeping bag and the covers.

Slowly, hardly daring to breathe, he pushed up closer to Todd's face, Dog's body just touching the covers wrapped around Todd, as if Todd were a baby.

Dog didn't want Todd to wake up. Didn't want Todd to push him away. The old family never let him sleep with them but Todd had patted the space next to him, saying, *"Come here, Dog. Come here."*

What if he'd really meant it?

What if he'd really wanted Dog to lie next to him?

Slowly, slowly, Dog lowered his head and closed his eyes.

Todd's hand settled on Dog's back.

Dog waited, shaking in his worry and nervousness. But nothing happened. Todd didn't move or talk. His breathing was the same as before. He must be touching Dog in his sleep.

"I'm glad you're here," Todd said, his voice slurred like he was more asleep than awake. Then his breaths slowed with sleep, his hand on Dog's head sliding off to the side, so Dog's head was between Todd's chest and his hand.

As if Todd were embracing him.

Dog waited for what seemed to be a long time. When Todd still didn't move, Dog pushed up close to Todd. Just for tonight. Just for now.

☂

CHUCK'S EYES OPENED, and he stared up at the high ceiling. Snow pelted like small stones against the windows, and dim light seeped through the shades. He guessed it was late in the morning, but time didn't matter to him. He didn't want to roll out of bed, and there was no reason he had to. No guests this time of year for the bed-and-breakfast. No wife and kids like most other thirty-one-year-old men he knew.

He didn't want to do anything. The room was as cold as his mood. Worse, as cold as his heart.

It was a bad day. A day he didn't want to face. At least no one was here to witness his self-pity. He was the only person in the eight-bedroom house. Four suites on the second floor, two upstairs, and two on the first floor—one for his mother, and he had the smaller one.

Normally the emptiness wouldn't have bothered him,

but for weeks now he hadn't been his normal self, the easygoing guy who took life as it came, always with a smile. Never hurting anyone, but always out for fun and a good time.

Those days were done. He'd finally gotten some ambition—his brilliant idea—only to find out that no one cared. No one believed in him.

He wasn't sure when the change had happened. Maybe after the July Fourth shootout.

And then the shootout in the B and B on Christmas Day. The day that Trouble Bay, located in the Door County vacation haven of Wisconsin and one of the lowest-crime areas in the state, had turned into a Wild West town.

And now his formerly uptight mother was living with her professor/screenwriter boyfriend in Madison, leaving Chuck in charge of the bed-and-breakfast.

At least she'd trusted him. Maybe that's what had given him the idea that he was the kind of guy that people could count on. Maybe—

The front doorbell rang with a sonorous, important tone.

He rolled out of bed. Pulled on his jeans. Grabbed a sweatshirt, jerking it down over his head as he strode to the front of the big house, the wooden floor cold under his bare soles. He didn't have time to stop and put on his socks. No one but paying guests came in the front door, and in February, they didn't have a lot of those. The B and B was still his living. At least for now.

Reaching the front door, he glanced through the small window. This was something he wouldn't have done a year ago, but after the two recent murders, most of the town residents were locking their doors at night, and even he was a little more cautious, squinting at the woman on the front porch.

She stood alone, her eyes cast down. A stranger wearing a black knit cap and a puffy jacket. Her shoulders were hunched against the cold, as if she were trying to fold herself in two. Something about her looked lost. Forlorn. In her nondescript clothes and her thinness, she reminded him of a waif from a fairy tale.

He opened the door, and her eyelids opened wide, her head up. She stared at him, her lips slightly parted.

"Hey," he said.

She didn't answer.

He smiled, falling back into old habits. Putting on his charm like other men put on their socks—which his cold feet told him he still wasn't wearing. Not that he thought every woman fell for him. But he liked women, and for the most part, the feeling was mutual.

Perhaps not this woman. When his mother had told him that the bed-and-breakfast was his, she had made him promise that he wouldn't sleep with any of the guests. She wouldn't have to worry about this woman. She emanated melancholy. Everyone in town knew he liked women who flirted and danced and made him laugh. Good-time girls for a good-time guy.

Yes, everyone knew that leopards didn't change their spots, and good-time guys weren't to be trusted.

His bare feet were getting colder, and his thoughts were growing ugly. He gestured her inside. "Come on in. It's warmer in here than out there."

She blinked and shook her head. "I'm sorry, I'm..."

"You're letting in the cold air. Do you want to stay here? Or are you selling something?"

"Um..." Her eyes were big behind a pair of black-rimmed glasses, and he stood there with the door open, the frigid air and a few snowflakes floating in.

She reminded him of a wary fawn, afraid of being caught. Afraid of being wounded. Afraid of death.

The tightness of his shoulder muscles relaxed. Okay, he'd had a lousy week. He didn't have to make her uncomfortable. "If you'd rather go someplace else, I can recommend a couple of places."

She blinked and shook her head, then stood straighter. "No. I'd like a room. I'm not sure how long. I—"

"Are we going to talk about this while you stand outside in the cold?"

"Umm." She looked at the car on the street. A brown sedan was parked on the curb in front. The kind of color that no one looked twice at. Some might call it boring.

Some might call *her* boring.

They would be mistaken. He could see this woman wasn't dull in any way, despite her puffy jacket, her knit hat that squashed down her hair, and her makeup-free face. Around here, there were a lot of makeup-free faces, and there was nothing wrong with that. But he could feel her wariness. Giving him invisible signals that he needed to be careful with her.

"I guess..." She stepped forward, like a nervous fawn during hunting season. He stepped back, letting her in.

He closed the door behind her, and she waited for him to lead the way through the living room to the kitchen. Once in the kitchen, he excused himself to get his socks and shoes on. Her right eyebrow lifted, but he strode away, not explaining.

He had his own reasons for his wariness but his reasons were new. He had the feeling hers was old stuff. That her wariness was embedded in her skin and her heart and her DNA.

In a couple moments, he headed back, his socks and shoes on. She was gazing around the kitchen with its brightness and bigness. The other rooms in the house were classic, but except for the rustic maple dining table, the kitchen appliances were bright and modern. Top grade.

The guest-book tablet was on the counter, and he clicked onto the registration page.

"Your name?" he asked, his fingers on the keyboard.

"Raine with an e. Last name Copperfield."

He typed slowly, paying attention to each key. "I'll need a credit card or—"

"Cash," she said. "How much do I have to pay in advance?"

"How long are you staying?"

"At least a week."

He gave her the options of the bedrooms on the second floor, and the suites with the whirlpool on the third floor. She hesitated before choosing the second floor.

He glanced up, seeing the closed face; her expression was pensive, her thin eyebrows pulled inward. The bones of her face looked small. Delicate. Ethereal. With her dark blond curls, she made him think of a fairy or an elf. He felt her reluctance. Or maybe it was stronger than that. More like trepidation.

He wasn't Mr. Sensitive, but even he could see something was off here.

"How much do I owe you?" she asked.

"Is someone after you?" he asked bluntly. "Is someone trying to hurt you?"

Her chin jutted out, and it wasn't the chin of a fragile creature. It was the chin of a fighter. A survivor. A woman who wouldn't back down.

A sizzle slashed through him.

"I don't know you," she said, her voice firm, "and my problems have nothing to do with you."

He shook his head slightly. Something had happened to him. He wasn't sure what it was, but it had felt momentous.

Later, he would try to figure it out and make sense of it. Right now, she was glaring at him, and he had to reply.

"When you're in my place, you're under my protection."

"Are you kidding?" Her eyebrows rose.

"I mean every word."

She sighed, the frown between her eyebrows smoothing, her shoulders slumping. "I'll pay for the week in advance." Her voice sounded tired. The tone of someone who'd traveled too far and just wanted to stay in one place. "How much?"

He told her the amount, reminding himself that she was no maiden hiding from a dragon, and he sure the hell wasn't any knight. Reminding himself of her stubborn chin. That chin belonged to a woman who could take care of herself.

She turned to the side to forage inside her purse, her head down. Below the shorts curls, the back of her neck was exposed. Long and narrow and vulnerable.

Then she raised her head and put money on the table. He printed out the receipt.

"Can I park my car in the parking lot?" she asked.

"You can park in the garage." He enjoyed looking at her face with the delicate bone structure. Except for that chin, she had a heart-shaped ballerina face, with sad, pale eyes behind her glasses. "There's room for another car. My mother's usually in charge of the place, but she's in Madison with her boyfriend for the winter."

"You don't mind?"

"I like him. He makes my mom laugh."

"You're lucky then. Your mom, too. My mother... Well, never mind." She half turned toward the living room that led to the front of the house. "I'll move my car."

"I'll open the garage door."

She left for the front door as he grabbed his jacket, then headed out the back door with the garage door opener. He waited while she pulled in. As she parked her car, he glanced behind the street and saw a curtain twitch in the flat above the diner.

He turned his back. No doubt he'd be getting a phone call from at least one of his neighbors sometime today, but he had the feeling that Raine wouldn't want to be talked about.

Too late for that. If she didn't want to be talked about, she should have stopped off at Sturgeon Bay, the biggest city in Door County. In winter in Trouble Bay, the second biggest entertainment was watching Packers games at the bar. The first was gossip.

The trunk popped open, and he stepped to the back to push the trunk up all the way while she hopped out of the driver's seat and strode to the back of the old sedan.

"I can carry my own luggage," she said.

"You could but you don't have to." He reached inside for two large suitcases. There was a guitar case inside, too. He stepped back. "You sing?"

She leaned forward, took out the guitar case. Shivering, she said, "Not very well."

"Let's get you inside, into the warmth." He pulled the trunk lid down, then gestured for her to go first. She hurried ahead of him, holding her guitar case and going on ahead of him as he closed the garage door.

Once inside, he took the lead up the staircase to the second floor. She chose the room in the back of the house with the extra window in the kitchenette. Tall trees, leafless until summer, blocked the view from the smaller houses behind the B and B.

"You need help?" He set down the suitcases but remained inside the doorway.

"I'm fine. Are you this helpful to all your guests?"

"Yes. And don't worry. I can read your *no flirting* signals."

She looked startled.

"This time of year is different from the other three seasons," he continued, making his voice matter-of-fact. "Most of the dining places are closed until April. During the day, the café across the street is open until two. After that, there's just the bar with pub food. Of course, your breakfast will be served here. There are some restaurants that are open year-round not too far from here. I can give you a list."

"Where's the pub?"

"A few blocks down. I can take you there later."

"Not necessary. I'll find it by myself." She turned her back to him in dismissal.

He remained where he was. "Usually I leave the front door open for guests until after ten, but since it's just the two of us, I'll just leave the back door open."

"That's okay with me. Is there a grocery in town?"

"A small one. At the end of town on the left. It has the basics. I'll leave my phone number for you."

"Do you have a card with the inn's phone number?"

"Not the business number. My personal number."

She stood still for a moment, then bent to take clothes out of the suitcase, her exposed neck slender and vulnerable. "It's not necessary. I'll be okay."

"I'll leave it anyway." He frowned. "You have a pen?"

She sighed, then straightened, picked up her cell phone, and handed it to him. "Just put it in."

"Under Chuck," he said.

"Chuck." She looked straight into his eyes, hers a pale blue that reminded him of the dawn light, when the world turned mysterious. And her lips pressed together, the corners pulled up slightly, holding back a smile.

Something warmed inside him for the first time today. He was getting to her.

He smiled at her, staring straight into her eyes.

She stepped back, the hint of a smile shutting down, her facial muscles tightening.

He stepped back, too. He'd have to be as dense as the frozen waters of the bay to not realize this wasn't a good day for her.

That made two of them.

"See you later," he said. And he left for his one last try at his own good day.

Only he already had a bad feeling about it...

Five

TODD HAD PICKED up the letter with the law firm return address at the post office the same time he'd gone for his hard-won disability check. The check wasn't a lot of money, but he gave most of it to other veterans. So many needed the money more than he did. Giving them money made him feel better. It kept some of the darkness from falling down on him. From wrapping around him. From suffocating him.

But today was different. Today he had to take care of the dog.

He bought food at the grocery store. Not dog food but people food. Real meat from the deli. It cost too much, but Todd wanted to do it just this one time.

He wanted the dog to love him.

He still had the letter zipped up in his jacket pocket. He'd read it when he got back to the alley. His parents weren't alive. His Dad had died of a heart attack when he was a teen. His mother had died in an auto accident his first year in the Marines. He had no siblings, and the friends he'd had before he'd joined up had no doubt forgotten him.

There was no hurry to read the letter. It was probably junk mail.

☂

RAINE FORCED HERSELF not to look up Dawn Keighly online. Or Sunny Wellington, her sister's married name, though most people still knew her as Sunny Keighly, the singer.

Not songwriter. Not even one word of the songs that Sunny recorded had been written by her. Not one guitar string had been plucked by her.

Thinking about it, Raine's head grew hot, and she imagined a cartoon image of herself with smoke coming out of the top of her head.

She snorted, a flat, humorless note. She should be unpacking, she should be worrying about what to do next, but a gnawing need in her chest was growing wider and longer and stronger. Without any commands from her mind, her hands reached for the guitar case, pulling out the guitar, as if it were calling to her. *Play me. I've been lonely. I've missed you.*

She cradled the acoustic Martin in her arms. It was like cradling a baby, as if it were a living thing. And wasn't it in some ways alive? Made out of layers of wood to withstand changes in temperature for the traveling musician. From hot and humid to a frozen hell. Taking her through eight years of traveling with Sunny.

She had three guitars at her L.A. condo, but this was her favorite. Her baby.

Her fingers strummed, and words formed in her mind. As if she'd turned on a switch, she sang them, starting soft and uncertain, then changing to low and sure.

You weren't crazy, mad, demented.
Not that I knew or suspected.
I was always there for you
I thought you'd be there for me, too.
But someone offered you a golden ring,
A ring attached to blood-stained strings.

Her fingers slashed against the strings, the clashing sounds discordant notes in her head. Her hand dropped to her side. Her shoulders sagged, the music vibrating in the air. Her heart vibrated with it.

She set down the guitar on the dresser, the words and

notes dimming. As usual, panic grew inside her. She needed to write the notes down. Needed to do it *now*. Even if the lyrics made her want to throw up. Want to cry. Want to shove her clothes back in the suitcase and run again.

She grabbed her purse from the bed, dug into it, and pulled out a small pad of paper and a pen. Plopping onto the bed, she jotted down the notes and the words. Changing things, hearing the voice and the music in her mind. Adding a verse. Finding a bridge. Adding another verse. And another.

By this time it was a mess, but she couldn't stop. She imagined spatter painters worked this same way. Just going and going until the moment came when they just...

Stopped.

Like now.

Her hand drooped. Her fingers opened. The notebook fell out of her hand onto the rug under the bed. The pen rolled after it.

She felt like a wet noodle, as if her spine had lost its backbone. No surprise. She'd been using her stiff backbone for too many years. Since she was a teenager, and she and Sunny knew that they had to take care of themselves because no one was taking care of them.

Her shoes were still on, and it took her two tries to get the right shoe off, then one to get the left off. Fatigue overcame her. It took all her energy to wiggle under the sheet and the covers.

As she closed her eyes, she felt something next to her. Her guitar. She'd left it on the bed. Other women slept with their lovers. She slept with a guitar.

She sighed. She could finally relax. No one would look for her here. Not now. Not yet. For this moment in time, she was safe.

But, oh, God, for how long?

Six

THE SKY WAS darkening when Dog smelled Todd. He didn't want to depend on another human, but he couldn't help the way he felt. Happy. Excited. Todd was back! Todd was coming back to him!

Along with Todd's smell came the smell of meat that was different from the meat that came from the dumpster. Dog wanted to run to him, but fear and uncertainty held him back. He stayed in the alley, and with every step Todd took closer, his tail wagged faster.

Then Todd was in the alley. "I've got something for you!" He took huge strides down the alley.

Dog knew that tone with Todd's voice higher than usual. It meant a chew toy or food or a—

It was food! It was! Dog smelled it, his mouth watering. He quivered with excitement.

Nearing Dog, Todd reached inside a bag and whipped out a long piece of meat. Unable to stop himself, Dog jumped up and snapped just as Todd pulled the meat back.

"Hang on." His hand flat, Todd crouched down and held out the meat to Dog.

Dog clamped his teeth around the meat, then danced away, putting the meat on the ground so he could chew it as he kept an eye on Todd, in case he tried to take it back. Eating quickly because Todd was human, and Dog knew that humans couldn't be trusted.

When he was done, Todd bent and held out his hand that

still smelled like meat. Dog couldn't resist licking Todd's palm. He licked it again and again and again, even when he knew the meat was long gone. Todd laughed, the sound bright like the sun in the sky, his hand on the jacket over his belly, his upper body bending forward, with tears leaking out of his eyes. Dog stopped licking and knocked his head against Todd's knee. Letting Todd know that he liked him.

More than *like*, he *loved* Todd.

He hadn't wanted to feel this way, but it had happened anyway, like the sun shining in the morning. He was Dog, and he understood that he was made to love.

Todd held him close for a long moment, breathing hard, then he sat down on his cardboard and sad, weeping noises came from his throat. Two rivulets of water flowed down his cheeks.

Dog whimpered, waiting as Todd's sobs quieted.

"It's been so long since someone cared," Todd whispered. Then he reached into his pocket and held up an envelope. "And I got mail." He squinted at the envelope. "It's from a lawyer in Sturgeon Bay. That's near Trouble Bay. Where my aunt lives. I hope she's okay."

He tore open the envelope. Dog waited, his tail wagging.

Todd stared down at the paper for a long time. Then he slowly raised his head and stared into Dog's face. "We have a house. My aunt died last month. A heart attack. The lawyer has her will, and she says that I inherited a house. You know what that means?"

Dog stared at Todd, not understanding what Todd said. He couldn't tell if it was something bad or something good. All Dog knew for sure was that it was getting cold out. That he wanted to crawl into the box with Todd. That he wanted to sleep at Todd's side and share his warmth. Listen to Todd breathe in and out. Listen to his beating heart.

"It means you and I will have a home." Todd's hands shook, and Dog stretched his neck out and licked the backs of his hands.

With a sob, Todd kissed Dog's forehead. "I don't know if I

can do this," he whispered hoarsely. "I don't know if I can live in a house like normal people."

Don't worry. Dog nuzzled his head against Todd's chin. *I'll protect you. I'll make sure no one hurts you.*

☂

SUNNY, HER FATHER-IN-LAW, Grant, and her husband, Jarret, sat on the patio of Grant's Beverly Hills home, sunlight sparkling on the pool waters. It was in the mid-seventies, and Sunny wore shorts because she knew that Grant liked looking at her legs. She had great-looking legs, as did Dawn. But hers were longer, and Dawn didn't have her breasts or her ass.

One thing that Sunny had learned early on about performing when they'd started in country bars was that men liked curves. Dawn had never seemed to mind that she was the star and Dawn was the guitar player. She'd even joked to Sunny that she was the mutt of the family, and Sunny was the golden retriever.

She sniffed. It hurt to think about Dawn. Dawn had always been there for her.

Until now.

A footstep made her turn her head. Her brother-in-law. Despite the cloudless sky and the sunlight, she felt cold. Vince was different from her husband. Darker. Shorter. Wiry instead of tall and lanky. His mother had been Grant's second wife. A mistake, Jarret had told her, then he'd frowned and his lips had pressed together.

He hadn't said anything more, and Sunny hadn't asked. But she didn't like the way Vince looked at her...as if she were just a body to him. As if she weren't special. It reminded her of the way she'd felt before she and Dawn had crept out of their house when she was eighteen. When she'd been...

Oh no, she didn't want to think about that. Oh, no, oh, no, oh, no.

"What's the matter, honey?" Jarret's hand was warm on her shoulder, but she still shuddered. "What is it?"

She looked from him to Grant to...no, not Vince. He would watch her as if he knew what she was thinking, and she couldn't have that.

No one knew. No one but Dawn. And Dawn would never tell. She'd promised, and Dawn always kept her promise.

"Dawn," she got out.

"Don't worry," Jarret said. "We'll find her."

She looked at him, needing more reassurance, but he was turning to Grant. "Isn't that right, Dad?"

Grant leaned over in his chair toward her. "You know you're my favorite daughter-in-law, don't you?"

She tried to smile but she couldn't seem to make it work. She was his only daughter-in-law, and when Grant said that, she was supposed to giggle and tell him that he was her favorite father-in-law back. But right now, she couldn't force a giggle out of her throat.

"You're worrying about your sister," he said. "We'll find her. We'll take care of her for you."

She shivered again. She loved Dawn. They were sisters. There for each other when no one else had been. When she was ten and Dawn was eight, a man her mother knew had come into their room and crawled into her bed. She had whimpered, but Dawn had screamed and screamed and screamed, until the neighbor in the next apartment pounded against the wall and said he was calling the police.

That's when the man had gone away.

Dawn's voice had changed that night. Broken. So when she spoke now, it was husky, and she couldn't sing. Instead, she wrote the songs and the music, and Sunny sang them. The songs that had made her a singing star. The songs that had brought her to Jarret's attention.

To this marriage.

But now Dawn refused to share her songs. Sunny put her hand on her forehead, because it felt funny. Her brain felt funny, too, but she could hear Jarret's and Grant's voices in her head: *Dawn could write other songs for other singers. Your singing made the songs popular, not the other way around. Dawn was being selfish.*

She looked up at Vince, sending him her most helpless look. "You'll find her, won't you?"

"I'll try."

The steely look in his eyes gave her shivers. She almost felt bad for Dawn.

"Where would she be?" Grant asked, his pale eyes shining as if he were in touch with some heavenly source.

A memory stirred in Sunny's fuzzy brain. During his services in the light-filled church, sunlight streamed in through the vaulted skylight to surround him like a halo. The first time Dawn had seen it, she'd leaned over and whispered, "That's so awesome. You need to find out how he does that. You can do it for your next show."

It had taken all Sunny's willpower to keep from bursting out laughing.

Now, the memory made tears warm her eyes. "I don't know where she would be."

"Any usual hangouts?" Jarret asked.

She shook her head. "We asked all her friends. We looked at all the places she should be, and we can't find her anywhere."

"That's the problem," Vince said, and he had one of those baritone voices that, as much as Sunny distrusted him, rolled through her like warm honey. "We shouldn't look where she should be. We should look where she shouldn't be."

"That doesn't even make sense," Jarret said.

Vince stood. Though he was shorter and leaner than Jarret, Sunny had seen him working out, and he had muscles where all the muscles should be, giving her what her mother used to call *Oh, my God* moments while waving a purse or a book in front of her face, as if she were so hot she had to fan herself.

Not that it meant anything to Sunny. She had Jarret.

Grant's oldest son and the next leader of Nirvana Now. She wasn't dumb enough to trade him for his younger brother, who would only be second-in-command.

"Where are you off to?" Grant asked as Vince turned away.

Not looking back, Vince said, "To find her."

Sunny's heart beat fast. If anyone found Dawn, it would be him.

Oh my, oh my, oh my.

Seven

"YOU INHERITED A house. Wow." The Veteran's Administration counselor, a dark-complected woman in her late thirties, had the kind of hour-glass figure that Todd used to like before Afghanistan. "I'm sorry for your loss."

He nodded. He'd met his aunt only a few times but he recalled liking her, a blunt-speaking woman who had sent him a hundred dollars when he'd joined the Marines but said in her note that he should've gone to college instead.

"Do you need help with the legalities?" the woman asked.

He shook his head. His brain was still working but his nerves were shot. Though he was better than he used to be, people made him nervous.

He trusted no one.

Dogs were different. He trusted dogs.

"I have my ID." He was a Marine. A *former* Marine. *Semper fidelis* and all that bullshit.

His hands curled tightly in his lap. Being in this office made him nervous.

"The house is in Door County," the woman asked. "Do you have a ride? A car?"

He shook his head.

"A taxi would be expensive. I can see if there's any public transportation—"

"My dog," he said. "I have a black lab."

Her left eyebrow rose. "Those are bigger dogs. You might need some kind of a carrier or portable kennel—"

43

"I can't put him in a kennel. It would be like being in jail."

"It's for the dog's own safety," she said.

"I'll walk to Sturgeon Bay with the dog first."

Her forehead crinkled. "I'm not sure, but that's probably close to two hundred miles. We vacationed in Door County a few years ago. It took us over two and a half hours by car. And we took I-43. It will take you a few days to walk there."

"We can hitchhike. People still do it."

She sighed, then bent forward over her desk. "Look. I like you. I shouldn't do this, but my brother manages the truck stop in South Milwaukee. I can ask him if he can find you a ride."

He nodded, his lips pressed together because this was the kind of thing people said they would do but they never did.

She picked up the phone. "I'll call him right now."

As she dialed, tears warmed his eyes, and he blinked hard to stop them from falling down his face. He wasn't used to people going out of their way to help him.

It was the dog. He knew it. Ever since he'd befriended the dog, his life had begun to change.

☂

"HEY." CHUCK STOOD inside the resort owned by his friend and former boss—a relative through marriage somehow. His mother would know, but she had better things to do in Madison right now, and it wasn't important to Chuck. All he knew was that if the former Marine's mother's car hadn't broken down outside of town, it wouldn't have led to his mother marrying Duke, the owner of the resort, and now August was in charge.

Chuck had never felt envious. He wished August and his pretty wife nothing but happiness. Chuck had always been content just living his life every day. Fishing in summer and winter. Playing pool and having a few drinks in the local bar at night. Flirting with the women, whether they were fifty or twenty.

And in summer, there were pretty girls, and then, as he grew older, women to flirt with. They didn't have to be beautiful or perfect. He liked women, period. They smiled and made him laugh. And sometimes they were intimate, and that was good. Sometimes they didn't want to, and that was also good.

It was all good.

Until now, at the age of thirty-one, it had suddenly happened. The Great Idea. And with that great idea, he saw great possibilities. Suddenly contentment and hanging around with his friends and flirting with women wasn't enough. Suddenly he wanted *more*.

"Hey, Chuck," August said. He was darker than Chuck; his eyes were a piercing brown. "What's up?"

"I'm here for a business discussion." He stood straight, though August must have known why he was here. News in a small town like Trouble Bay traveled faster than eagles flew.

"Let's talk in my office." August turned.

His steps firm, Chuck followed August into the office he'd been in often when he'd worked here during the tourist season when he was younger. Mostly smiling at the tourists and making them feel happy as he signed them in, sometimes helping them with their luggage and giving them advice on places to go. Flirting with the girls and the women. Easy and fun and light.

But now, as he stepped into the room, his heart felt heavy in his chest. August sat behind the sturdy cherrywood desk that an ancestor of Duke's had purchased many years ago. It looked right in this room, and so did August with his serious expression.

"You know what I'm going to say." Chuck sat on the other side of the desk, leaning forward. "Gossip here travels faster than lightning. You know that I bought Ed Gamet's farm."

August nodded. "You're putting up some kind of art warehouse."

Chuck curled his hands at his sides. "No one seems to believe in me but I'm not ready to give up. I want to make this happen. I'm committed to this. If not from the artists here, then from somewhere else. From Sturgeon Bay, if I have to. Hell, artists from Green Bay. And if you don't want to help, someday you're going to look back on this and say that not backing me was the dumbest move you've made."

The serious expression on August's face lightened, and he held his hands up, warding off his words. "Whoa. You're going too fast, soldier."

"Soldier?" Chuck raised his eyebrows.

"Today you're a soldier." He nodded his chin at Chuck. "The first time I've seen you fight for anything."

Chuck sat back. August looked like he might be receptive. *Might* was only five letters but it was a big word. Almost as big as the four-letter word that came with it. *Hope.*

"I know that in the past I was the guy who backed away when things got rough," Chuck said.

"Considering where you came from," August said, "that was bound to happen. Either take the calm way or the angry way. You took the better turn."

Chuck frowned. He knew what August was referring to. Not his mom. No one said anything bad about her, except that she might be too perfect. Too upright, and too uptight. Only recently, in the last year, had she lightened up. But August was talking about his father, who'd been a womanizer, a gambler, and a drinker before he'd been murdered when Chuck was a kid. Probably by a jealous husband.

"Not many people would say that to my face," Chuck said.

"Blame it on Ellie." The corners of August's mouth curved up. "You know how she is. A whirling tornado. She's rubbing off on me."

Chuck laughed. "You're stupefied by love."

"Stupefied?" August leaned forward with a wide grin. "That's a word I never thought you'd say."

"I dated a college girl about eight or nine summers ago." Chuck felt lighter now. Not as dark as when he'd woken up this morning and hadn't wanted to roll out of bed. Maybe the unexpected guest with the sad eyes was good luck. "She was from Illinois, and that was her favorite word. She said it meant being made stupid by something astonishing."

August laughed, creases in his cheeks.

Chuck grinned. It was coming back to him. Not the girl but his thoughts that someday he'd like to meet a girl who would stupefy him. Make him stupid with love.

It hadn't happened yet, and by now he was pretty sure it never would happen. After all, the love bug hadn't bitten him yet, though it had nipped at him plenty of times. He just wasn't the guy who felt emotions deeply and strongly, and that was okay with him.

"I'll tell that to Ellie," August said. "She's going to love it."

His grin straightened, and so did Chuck's. The atmosphere in the room darkened, the guy humor gone, back to business.

The tension returned to Chuck's shoulders, and he looked at August straight in his brown eyes. "What will it take to convince you that I'm serious about this? That I've got a great idea, and the town will profit from it?"

"Keep talking."

Chuck leaned forward. It was either freeze or dive in, and he'd always been the guy who dived first. Usually out of recklessness and stupidity. So far, he'd been lucky. He hadn't hit his head on any rocks yet.

"For the last few winters now," he said, "when it's slow in town, I've been watching those makeover shows on TV."

"You're a handy guy," August began, and Chuck raised his right hand to stop him.

"Handy doesn't mean I'm creative. I can fix things and put stuff together, but I've always admired people who do it all. Either from scratch, or they take something old and make it look better or different and unique. These people have an imagination that I'm missing. I see what it is. They see what it could be."

"You've got something there. Trouble Bay has a wealth of spectacular artists."

"And woodworkers and glassmakers and specialty builders. And more that I can't even think of." Chuck sat back, settling into storytelling mode. "Two weeks ago, I ran into Greta Harmon at the grocery store. She's a few years older than me. I'm not sure how well you know her. Her family moved to Green Bay before you were around, but they used to come a few times a year to visit Ed Gamet, Greta's uncle, usually in summer. Greta's family always stayed over at the B and B, because Ed's house didn't have any air conditioning."

"I heard Ed was in a nursing home in Green Bay," August said.

"Dementia." Chuck grimaced.

"That's tough."

"Yeah. Greta's mom was Ed's only sister. There was just the two of them. Ed married and—"

"I remember his wife," August said. "They would come over and eat. I think she died before I left for the Marines. An aneurysm."

Chuck nodded. "They never had kids, and Greta and her mom are the only relatives left. Greta mentioned that they're putting Ed's farm up for sale for a bargain price. It's on the highway, not the lake road, so they won't get the big tourist money. And this time of year, no one's buying anything."

"True," August said, "but—"

"I know what you're going to say. Once tourist season is here, they'll get more money, even if it's not a lake road."

"It's probably a five-minute drive to the lake," August said. "You could walk there or ride a bike."

"Yeah, but the thing is, none of it's going to make a

damn difference to the family or Ed. They come from a long-lived family. Ed's mind is shot, and his legs are bad, but Greta said that according to the doctor, his heart's okay, and so are all his vital organs. He'll probably live for years, and all the money will go to the nursing home. When his money is gone, Medicaid will pay for the rest."

"Until he's gone, too," August said.

The thought saddened Chuck, and he didn't reply immediately. Across from him, August scowled, and they sat in silence for a moment.

"At least Greta and her mom will be visiting him," Chuck said. "Making sure he's getting taken care of."

"That's good." August nodded.

Chuck didn't reply right away. He wondered who would be taking care of him when he was old. Would he be the guy who never got married? Who never fell in love? Always the good-time guy even as an old, old man?

He sat straight, pushing those thoughts away. "So I told Greta that I'd buy it."

"You're not a farmer," August said. "Even if you were, to make money now, you need more land than Ed owned. Even to make a half-decent living. Times have changed since Ed's family lived at the farm."

"That goes back to what I was talking about before," Chuck said slowly. "My idea of the Trouble Bay Art Mart for the tourist season. To start with, I could put up a big pole building and maybe two or three smaller ones. One of the smaller ones might be a craft mart. The third one could be for food. Maybe, when the townspeople get the stick out of their butts, we could even have a Trouble Bay Flea Mart in the open grounds."

"Diversify," August said, his forehead creased.

Chuck nodded, because *Diversify* sounded better than *We'll have room for another building, so what the hell.* "In the art mart, we can have places for different artists to put their stuff. Some of it will be okay outside, too. New stuff or old items made new again, better than ever. We can promote it as unique décor for homes. We could have jewelry or artwork. Lithographs. Paintings. Wearable art. Anything that works."

"Sounds ambitious."

Chuck held up his hands, his fingers forming quote marks. "We can say 'Come for fun, go home with one-of-a-kind finds.'"

August chuckled.

Chuck dropped his hands. "That's just an idea, but you know what I mean. I waited until the deal is done, and now I need to involve the others, and..." He stopped himself from slumping in the chair.

"It's money you want," August said, as if it were a fact.

"It's not money. Not so much, anyway." He frowned. "I pretty much emptied out my savings for the down payment. I owe monthly payments with interest, yeah, but I can just about handle it. I could wait for summer, then sell the property to someone who would want to build houses or condos or put up stores. I'd probably make a big profit. But that's not what I want."

He stopped a minute, his throat dry, then grabbed his coffee and took a couple swallows. He set it back on the table next to him, then looked at August, who watched him with a blank expression.

"Trouble Bay is *my* town. My home. I thought this was something that everyone would be interested in. Right now, people have to come to the artists' studios or houses to see their work. Some of them get into different galleries or shops. And the tourists go to the wineries and the restaurants. They go on the tours and to the shops. But for the most part, the artists aren't selling as much as they could. I could show their work at the art mart, and the artists don't even have to be there. I could hire college students, and it will be jobs for them, too."

"You want it to be more of a cooperative?" August asked. "Maybe that's the problem. Artists' egos."

Chuck looked straight into August's eyes. "It's not egos. I

could see it in their faces as they talked to me. It's me. They don't think I can pull it off."

August's gaze dropped, and Chuck knew then that August had heard the talk. More than he'd let on. Chuck knew then that, like the artists he'd talked to, August didn't trust him.

"I'll talk to Elle," August said, "but I don't know if I'm the right person to help."

A cold knot tightened in Chuck's belly. No, he didn't want August's advice. He didn't want his help. He wanted August, who was so successful and smart and responsible, to say that he believed in him.

And he hadn't.

"That's okay. I understand." He got to his feet. If the town didn't believe in him, there wasn't much he could do. Trust couldn't be bought; it was earned. And the only earning he'd done was to be around when someone wanted to have a good time.

The blame wasn't theirs, it was his.

He nodded at August, then turned and strode out of the office. When he was halfway across the reception area, he admitted that he did damn well blame the townsfolk, the artists, and even August. He'd always believed in them. But they didn't believe in him.

He wondered if maybe they were right...

"Wait!"

Chuck turned. August stepped toward him, stopping a couple feet from Chuck.

"This could be a great thing for the town," August said. "Or it could be a flop. But it has a lot of possibilities. If the townspeople don't want to be a part of it, don't give up so damn fast. You mentioned putting out feelers to the other towns." He made a sweeping gesture toward the south. "You'll get takers. You know you will."

"Yeah, but these are my friends here." The thought that friends didn't believe in him left a lump in his chest.

"The first lesson of business," August said, "is that when it comes to money, no one's a friend."

Chuck shoved his hands into his pockets. This wasn't true for him. If a friend asked him for support, asked him to believe in them, he'd say yes without hesitating.

"There's something I learned in the Marines, though I didn't appreciate it then." August half smiled but his eyes remained serious. "Some people are leaders, and most people are followers."

Chuck listened. He'd always thought he was neither. That he went his own merry way.

"So, when you make progress," August went on, "be sure to tell everyone. When you sign someone on, make sure the whole town knows. Mention it at the bar or the diner. Let them know you're talking to other artists or crafters or whatever. Once that happens, you won't have to worry about them coming to you. You'll just have to worry about all of them coming at the same time."

Chuck straightened his spine. August did believe in him, after all.

He wanted to say something smart, but his words stuck in his throat. Instead, he tugged August to his chest and pounded his back, not able to speak for a moment. Stepping back, he nodded several times, then turned away and walked out.

Later he would thank August, but some things were better said with a couple thumps on a back.

Eight

"GLAD TO HELP a fellow vet." The burly rig driver in the truck stop parking lot near the Milwaukee airport was about eight inches taller than Todd's five nine, and Todd guessed he was a good eighty pounds heavier. Normally the trucker would've made Todd anxious, but he had a friendly grin, and his chest and arms were open, the classic signals of hospitality.

"Thanks." Todd glanced down at the dog at his side. He'd bought a leash and a collar this morning, and then had worried that the dog wouldn't like them. After all, he wouldn't want a collar around his neck. But the dog hadn't twisted away or growled or barked at him. He must have been someone's pet at one time.

Todd wondered what had happened.

The trucker said he could drop him off halfway between Green Bay and Sturgeon Bay. Todd nodded. He and the dog could walk the rest of the way. He appreciated this much help in one day. First was one of the guys from the shelter. Todd had gone over there yesterday to let them know he had to leave, and to apologize for not giving them money this month.

He'd thought they'd be aggravated, but instead the social worker had offered to drive him and the dog to the truck stop. When she'd dropped him off, she'd hugged him. And yesterday the Veterans Administration counselor and her brother had helped to hook him up with this ride.

Now the trucker was bending down to pet the dog and tell him what a good-looking boy he was. The trucker stood. "What's his name?"

Todd felt panicked. The driver would think it would be odd that he didn't know his dog's name. He might think he stole the dog. He might think the dog wasn't his.

Swallowing, Todd's gaze darted to the side, and he saw the name BAXTER on a parked truck. He turned back to the trucker. "Baxter. His name is Baxter."

"Baxter." The trucker grinned at the dog. "He looks like a Baxter. Needs to put some meat on him."

Todd's heart was slamming in his chest, but he nodded. "I'm working on it."

"You can use some meat on you, too."

Todd shrugged. "I'm okay." As long as he didn't think too much, he would be just fine. After all, dogs didn't think much. It worked for dogs, and maybe it would work for him.

☂

"SHE'S GONE. LIKE air." Grant Wellington's brows contracted, and he scowled.

Vince sat back in his father's over-decorated office, one leg crossed over the other as his father raved the way he'd never do if anyone could hear him besides his sons, the two people he trusted most. In fact, the only two people his father trusted.

Fool.

Vince kept his expression emotionless. He'd been doing this since he was seven, after the unlikely accident that killed his mother.

He wiped those thoughts from his mind, the way he'd learned to do long ago in front of his father. His brother, too, who was always quick to tattle on him. After all these years, Vince could hardly remember his heiress mother, who had fallen down two flights of stairs and broke her neck.

He just remembered how much his mother had loved him. How beautiful she was. How much he'd loved her.

Funny how accidents happened to his father's wives, except his third wife, Talia, a former model and actress—usually playing the other woman—who had died of cancer two years ago.

The fact that his father had known she'd had cancer when they'd married had brought him a ton of good publicity. So had the photos of him holding Talia's hand and gazing lovingly into her eyes. Telling her that she was going to Nirvana, where he'd meet her when God was ready to take him.

"Vince!" Grant's voice was harsh.

"I have leads," Vince said.

"What leads?" Jarret, in the chair to his left, scowled.

Vince smiled. His older brother hated it that he was smarter than him. Vince switched his gaze to his father, ignoring his brother and his giant ego. "I'm off to follow one of the leads."

"Where?" Grant asked.

"Wherever it takes me, Father."

Grant's face turned red. It wasn't a good look on him.

Vince stood. He knew how far he could go before his father exploded. "I have a few ideas. If they work out, I'll let you know." As he walked away, he felt the frustration building up behind him.

"I want you to tell me everything you find out," his father called out in his *I'm not pleased* voice.

Vince opened the door and didn't reply. His father used words like a boxer used fists. The only way to handle him was to get out of the ring and not engage in the fight.

Or to fawn over him, the way Jarret, Grant's mini-me, was doing now so Grant wouldn't take his anger out on him.

The door closed behind Vince, and he strode down the hall, the lush carpet muting his footsteps. Someone was running up the stairs, doing this for exercise. It had to be

Sunny, the princess to the prince. Or, as one entertainment show called Sunny and Jarret, "The Golden Couple."

Too bad the tabloids didn't know that beneath the golden princess's perfect breasts beat a treacherous heart. And wasn't she moving slower than usual?

Sunny turned onto the hallway. Seeing him, her eyes widened, her steps faltered, and she came to a stop, her blond hair in curls over her shoulders, her blue eyes wide.

"Vincent," she said. "I'm glad to see you before you leave."

He stopped about four feet away from her, wiping all expression from his face.

"I'm worried about Dawn."

He didn't say anything. Waiting to see what else she would say.

"Isn't there anything you can tell me?" she asked, her voice thickened.

"Is there anything *you* can tell *me*?"

She took a step back and shook her head, looking confused.

He raised his eyebrows. "Drinking already?"

"I don't drink." Her eyes flashed with anger. "And you already know everything I know."

"I'm not sure that I do. I think you have a few things that you're not telling me."

"I don't know what you mean by that." Her voice trembled. "I love my sister. I wasn't asking anything unreasonable of her."

"Of course not." Something twisted was building up inside him, constricting his chest and his lungs. "If you have any more questions, ask your husband." He strode past her, then headed down the staircase, aware of her gaze on him. Aware of her frustration and her anger.

Aware he shouldn't have said anything to her. Aware she might complain to his father and brother. He hadn't said anything incriminating, and they might not believe her. But right now she was the golden girl, and for a long time, he'd been the dark horse.

They might remember that sometimes the dark horse won the race.

🌂

SEVENTEEN MINUTES LATER, he was in a booth at a café, where he opened up a cell phone that wasn't connected to his name or his family or Nirvana Now.

Think like a woman on the run.

He wasn't on the run. He was on the hunt.

As his phone lit up, he thought that he might be like the leopard that hunted alone.

The corners of his lips lifted slightly.

In the short time he'd known Dawn—*observed* her, the way he observed everyone—she hadn't said much, but he'd noted the one person she trusted. Her business manager. The reason his phone right now was connected to her manager's computer.

Skimming through Howie Stein's emails took longer than he liked. Stein was one of the best in his field, known for putting his clients' interests first, and for his loyalty and honesty. What Stein didn't know was that his housekeeper's techie son didn't share his integrity. He could be bribed.

A lot of the names were familiar, but Vince still glanced through them, in case Dawn or her manager thought it smart to use another client's name. There were also names Vince didn't recognize, some of them most likely made up: Harvard, TJ, Delta, Raine, Mary Lincoln, Whistler...

She could have been any of them.

But no mention had been made of Sunny or Grant or Jarret. Or him.

He leaned back, his eyes closed. Then he sucked in a breath, opened his eyes, turned off his phone, drank his coffee, finished the avocado and tuna sandwich, left a hefty tip, and got up to leave.

Fifteen minutes later, as he was speeding on the freeway,

it hit him that there was a connection in one of the names. *Raine.* Not only was it an uncommon name, it was the opposite of Sunny.

He kept his eyes and attention on the traffic, but his mind was spewing out ideas. Nothing had stood out about the messages from this person called Raine. Whoever she was had written a song. Since Howie managed songwriters and musicians, that wasn't unusual.

Raine had said she was staying at a nice place, and there was a hot guy... She had ended that with a smiley face.

Reading it, he'd smirked. He'd even chuckled softly. The only smile and chuckle he'd had while skimming the emails. Probably the reason the name had stuck in his mind.

He shouldn't get excited about this Raine. It was unlikely that she and Dawn were the same person. Dawn wasn't the type to joke about a hot guy. She'd been the quiet one, staying in the background, letting Sunny bask in the spotlight.

His father had thought it would be easy to convince Dawn to give him the song rights. That she would be a pushover.

Vince hadn't been so certain. He'd noted her stiff spine, and it had occurred to him that she was a smart woman and perhaps she was quiet because she didn't like her new brother-in-law or her sister's new father-in-law. Or himself. Every time Vince had caught her eyes, her nostrils had pinched together.

Still, he didn't know a songwriter by the name of Raine. One who knew Howie well enough to send him casual messages. Wouldn't a newer songwriter be more cautious and polite? More businesslike?

Though songwriters weren't exactly the average businessperson.

He would check to see if anyone with the name of Raine was involved with the music industry or had signed up with Howie's management company.

Amazing the things one could find out on the Internet.

In any case, he would keep checking the messages. He'd wanted to tap Howie's cell phone, but the housekeeper's son had told him that Howie's phone had been hacked before by a rival, and they had their phones checked often. The most the son could do was hook him up to Howie's computer so that his hookup looked legitimate.

An odd phrasing, Vince thought, but a lot of things looked legitimate. Like Vince's father, his brother, and his brother's wife.

Dawn, the little he'd known of her, had seemed legitimate. Real.

And this Raine, who made a smiley face next to her comment about a hot guy, seemed legitimate.

It wouldn't hurt to have the housekeeper's son track down Raine's IP address and pinpoint her location.

The phone on the car's Bluetooth rang. His father. He frowned. Time to pretend again that he was the loyal son.

"Come back to Nirvana," his father ordered in his rich Shakespearean actor voice, minus the English accent. "Come to my office. We need you. There's been a sighting of Dawn."

Nine

FEAR HAD A smell, and Todd stunk of fear. Dog whined for him, but the other man didn't seem to notice, doing most of the talking. After a while, the driver pulled off the big road with all the fast cars and onto a smaller road with slower cars. The truck pulled onto the side of the road, making loud noises as it stopped. Todd jumped out, tugging Dog down with him.

As Dog peed on the snow, the truck pulled away. Dog looked up at Todd. Were they going for a walk?

Or was Todd going to throw him away like his other human had done? Would he take off his collar, get back in the truck, and just drive away?

Dog started to shake, and Todd squatted down and hugged him tightly, like he never wanted to let him go. Dog put his chin on Todd's shoulder.

You're my human now. Don't throw me away.

Todd straightened, and they headed back to the truck. Dog was happy to scramble back up the steps.

Todd was keeping him! He wasn't throwing him away!

☂

IN THE TINY sitting room, Raine sat on the gray chair and placed her laptop on the folding snack table in front of her. The sun from the window shone onto her laptop as she typed in her real name. A long list of headlines popped up about Sunny Keighly's triple-Grammy-winning songwriter sister, Dawn Keighly. Besides their last names, the headlines had one word in common: *Missing*.

She snorted. Sunny would be happy that her name was first. Raine clicked on the first headline. A thin, pink-haired woman wearing too much makeup stood in front of a mic, looking out at the audience with wide eyes.

Raine groaned as she remembered their first time at the Grammys. She had been up for three songwriting awards. Sunny had talked her into the pink hair, the raccoon-eye makeup, and the silvery dress that made her look like a 1920s flapper.

Considering her size-B bust, she'd appreciated the dress more than the hair and the makeup, though her hair was too long for the era.

She didn't have to look in the mirror to know that she looked nothing like her three-years-younger self who had given the worst—and the most quoted—speech of the night. She clicked on the video from E! cable channel, activating the sound. Might as well hear the worst.

"Oh, my God, oh, my God, oh, my God." Her voice kept cracking. *"I was so sure I wouldn't win."* The audience laughed and clapped, and then she'd stumbled over more words, thanking the musicians, her manager, and only at the end did she remember to thank Sunny. Not because she hadn't thought of Sunny, but just because she'd wanted to make sure she gave credit to the musicians striving to make a living.

Raine winced as she babbled like an idiot.

Why was E! showing the whole thing, anyway? Why not just her picture?

"And most of all, thank you to Sunny, my beautiful and talented sister, for singing my songs so wonderfully."

The camera shot to Sunny, who was standing and clapping and beaming. So happy for her.

The video disappeared, and the host and hostess of the show, both of them thin and witty, appeared.

Her finger shaking, Raine pressed a key, and the picture blanked out, the sound shutting off but not her mind.

Her thank you. Sunny's smile right after she'd said "my songs."

That had to be evidence.

She needed to tell Howie. Though he wasn't her lawyer, he was managing her money. She trusted him. If anything happened to her, she didn't want Nirvana Now to get the money. She'd already signed a will leaving everything she had to a military foundation. If Grant Wellington wanted to take the foundation to court, it would make him look bad. She'd be dead, but he wouldn't be able to touch the money.

Grant still might go after her songs, but her Grammy speech might be proof that Sunny didn't have any part of writing the songs.

Her laptop darkened, falling into sleep. As these and other thoughts swirled through her mind, she leaned forward to turn on the laptop again.

Someone knocked on the door.

She raised her head, becoming still. Not answering.

"Raine?"

She recognized Chuck's voice, a tenor, strong with a nice rasp to it. Her breath puffed out. Her heart beating fast, she called out that she would be right there. She was dressed in yoga pants, a Louis Armstrong sweatshirt, and thick socks. Nothing matched, but she was warm, and that's all she cared about. Not that she'd ever worried about matching. That had been Sunny's thing.

Some days, she wouldn't dress until late afternoon. Sunny had hated it.

You'll never get anywhere dressing like that.

And her reply these last three years. *Really? I'm the triple Grammy winner.*

She was smiling when she opened the door. Chuck stood in the hallway, smiling crookedly.

A hum whispered through her. Her heart thumped.

He was yummy-looking in a rakish way. His smile reached his eyes, saying, *I like you. I'm happy to see you.*

Oh, no! Oh, no, no, no. Oh, *never*.

Her brother-in-law, Jarret, with his light brown hair, was handsome, too, but in a smooth way. He smiled, too, but his eyes never lit up. His eyes never smiled.

And the breakfast Chuck had made this morning had been delicious. So not only was Chuck good-looking, he could cook.

What more could a woman want?

Good in bed.

Yes, definitely that, too.

But looking into his eyes and seeing a little fire in the blue depths, she swallowed and thought, *Oh, no. I don't need this.*

She might *want* this, but she didn't need it.

Sex was so inconvenient.

"I'm going to Sturgeon Bay," he said. "I wondered if you needed anything."

"Warm clothes." Apparently all the cute shops she'd seen online in Colorado when she'd researched Trouble Bay had been closed until the weather warmed and the tourists swarmed.

She stared at him, making a mental note to put that rhyme in a song. It was cheesy. But she liked cheese. That made her a cheesy girl.

He cleared his throat.

"Um." She cringed inwardly. She was so much better with song lyrics than talking to hot-looking guys.

"I was thinking of food," he said. "Or, you know, toilet items. Not clothes. If I learned one thing about women, it's that they don't like the clothes I buy."

"Too sexy?" she asked.

He laughed.

"That's okay. I'm fine for now." She put her hand on the door, ready to shut it. "I can drive myself. Enjoy your day."

"Wait." He slapped his hand on the door, holding it open. "I've got to talk to a couple people, but I can drop you off on a street where there are a few shops, then meet you at a café."

"I don't like to inconvenience you."

"No inconvenience. How fast will you be ready?"

She glanced down at her yoga pants. They would have to go. Too thin for the weather. This wasn't southern California, and she didn't want to stand out. Maybe she should do something with her face...or maybe not. The public pictures and videos of her on the Internet had been from events where she had full makeup on. She had long hair and was dressed for fashion instead of comfort.

"Ten minutes," she said.

He nodded and left.

She turned, and for the first time in months, she felt a flutter in her belly. An excitement.

She got ready quickly, brushing her teeth and putting on moisturizer with sunscreen, then her leather boots that she'd bought in Colorado because they looked like biker boots. Another piece of her disguise, because no one had ever seen Dawn Keighly wearing biker boots, though they were pretty cool.

She was reinventing herself, and she liked her new name and her new look.

As she hurried out of her suite, she remembered she had planned to email Howie about her acceptance speech at the Grammys and Sunny's smiling reaction. Then she glanced at the clock on the wall and decided later would do.

She had a date. Okay, not a date, but that flutter was back in her belly. Not that she thought Chuck had any interest in her her. And certainly at this stage of her life, when she was worried about staying alive, she shouldn't hook up with anyone. She was lonely, and she needed to stomp down on her libido. Stomp down hard.

What she really needed was winter clothes. Chuck was

good-looking, but she didn't need a man, no matter how hunky he looked. She just needed warm clothes.

And maybe she needed a hero.

Better yet, she needed to turn into her own heroine.

Ten

"THIS IS WHERE I leave you," the trucker said. "You going to be okay?"

"I'm fine," Todd said, though he wasn't fine. He might never be fine again. But the trucker had his own job, and he'd done enough for him. He'd stayed with Baxter at the truck stop while Todd had used the bathroom inside. After that the trucker had gone inside for lunch. Ten minutes later, he'd come back out with a bacon lettuce tomato sandwich for Todd and a hamburger for Baxter. When Todd had tried to give him a twenty, he wouldn't take it.

There were good people in this world. Real good.

Too bad they hadn't run the war that, officially, wasn't even a war.

He started to shake, and something licked his hand. Baxter.

His shakes calmed. The war was gone. He had a dog to take care of now. In Afghanistan, he'd had to be strong for his fellow Marines. Now he had to be strong for his dog.

Todd dropped onto the side of the road. "We'll be okay," he said, and he was surprised that it sounded like he meant it.

☂

IT DIDN'T TAKE Chuck long to drive to Sturgeon Bay, Door County's county seat. "Are you shopping for anything special?" Raine asked as the car entered the city.

"Talent," he said.

She stiffened.

"Artistic talent," he added, and out of the corner of his eye, he noticed her body relaxing. "I bought some farmland," he continued. "A few acres."

"I wouldn't have taken you for the farming type," she said in her husky, slightly broken voice.

He wanted to ask her what type she thought he was, but that would be a prelude to flirting, which would be a prelude to something more. Slowing for an icy patch, he reminded himself that guests were hands-off. His mother's top rules, and no woman was exempt from the rule. Not even one with short curly hair, a stubborn chin, and the sexiest voice he'd ever heard.

"It was a farm," he said, "but I'm not a farmer, and it's too small to make a decent profit now."

"So why buy it?" she asked.

"We have a lot of talented artists and craftspeople in Trouble Bay who can do just about anything. Right now, some of them have their works in different Door County shops or galleries. Most have their houses open to tourists during the tourist season. They advertise in the local magazines and newspapers and even Internet ads."

"Doesn't sound like the best way to sell a product."

He glanced over at her. "That's what I thought. I had an idea that I could put up one or two big buildings to showcase their works during the tourist season."

"If they sell anything, you'd get a percentage," she said.

"That's the idea."

"Or you could charge by the square foot."

"I don't know how that would be fair to artists who do the bigger stuff." Feeling her stare on him, he took a quick glance at her, seeing the frown on her forehead.

He turned back to watch the city traffic, heading to the

shopping area. So now she knew what he was like. Not the most ruthless businessman on the planet.

The same thought everyone else in Trouble Bay had about him.

"I like that idea," she said. "And you're right about the square footage. Just because something is smaller, it doesn't mean that it's worth less. Or that bigger is worth more. So what's the problem?"

His surprise at her approval stopped him from answering. He turned down a street lined with small shops, and he pulled up in front of the first boutique. As she unhooked her seat belt, he twisted toward her.

"How do you know there's a problem?" he asked, because it was either ask her or lean over and kiss her.

"It was the way you talked. As if you were trying to convince me." She frowned slightly. "Or convince yourself."

"I'll have to work on that."

Her forehead smoothed. "We all have to work on that."

"You, too?"

"Everyone I know. Most of us fake it."

"Not in Trouble Bay. Most of us have known each other forever. We know too much about each other to fake anything. Warts and all."

"That sounds a little scary."

"Not scary. I wouldn't want to hide my feelings all the time. That would scare me."

She smiled, but it was a twisted, sad smile. "That's the reason we have music and songs. They say the things we don't want to admit that we feel."

He sat back. This was getting too serious, too solemn, and he didn't do serious or solemn. That was something else everyone in town knew about him. "I'll be back in an hour. We can meet in the café at the end of the street. I'll buy you lunch. If you don't like the clothes, I can drive you to Walmart."

"See," she said, opening the car door, the freezing air swooshing in as she looked behind her, "we're going on with our lives, and there's no problem after all."

Without volition or intent, words spurted out of his mouth. "Me," he said. "I'm the problem."

Her eyes widening, she scooted back into the passenger seat, closed the door, and faced him. "Do you have a criminal record?"

He shook his head.

"Do you drink? Do drugs?"

"No drugs. I drink sometimes but not to excess."

"You sound like a reasonable man." Her blue-green eyes behind the black-framed glasses stared into his. "You look like a reasonable man. And you talk like a reasonable man. So, once again, what's the problem?"

He grimaced. He'd rather strip naked than talk about this. "It's nothing."

"Really?" she asked. "*Really?*"

"You're one of those."

She raised an eyebrow.

"You don't stop until you get the right answer." He swiped his gloved hand over his hair. "Okay, here it is. I'm not a businessman or an entrepreneur. I've never had an idea like this before. No one in Trouble Bay has had an idea like this."

"There's not a time lock for ideas," she said. "It can happen when you're ninety. It can happen when you're nine. Look at Isaac Newton. If the apple hadn't fallen on his head, he might never had thought of the theory of gravity."

He stared at her, unable to speak, as she nodded firmly.

It felt as if someone had socked him in his stomach.

"And when he first told people his theory," she continued, "I'm guessing a lot of people didn't believe him."

He still stared at her. Her expression was calm. Her eyes behind the black-rimmed glasses seemed large, though her glasses might have a magnifying effect.

"They probably mocked him," she continued. "Scorned him. I bet it took a lot of people a lot of time to agree that Isaac was right."

He stared at her, not saying anything.

"You just have to keep asking until you find the right people." She cracked the door open once again and slipped out of the car. On the sidewalk, she twisted around and nodded at him. "I'll see you in an hour."

The door clunked shut, and he watched her hurry to the store door, bundled in her knitted scarf and a knitted hat, plus that puffy jacket.

Reaching the shop door, she pulled it open and stepped into it. Only then did he pull away from the curb, heading to the home of a sculptor a half mile away. As he drove, he kept thinking of the advice that August and now Raine had given him.

He needed to fight for what he believed in. That might be easy if he were fighting for someone else. But he was fighting for himself.

He gripped the steering wheel tightly. Did that mean he didn't believe in himself? Or maybe he didn't want this enough?

He was the kind of guy who liked things that came easy, and this wasn't going to be easy.

Should he say the hell with it and sell the land to someone else?

Probably he'd end up selling it to a developer who would put up condos with a pool in the back.

Nothing wrong with that, and he'd make money on it. Not a lot, but he wouldn't come out a loser.

But it wasn't as good as his idea. It wouldn't be as good for the town of Trouble Bay.

He frowned and turned into the street of the sculptor.

How much did he want this?

Eleven

THE LAWYER MADE an appointment for Todd the next afternoon. Todd put away his cell phone, angry at himself. He'd forgotten how the rest of the world worked. The functioning world. They made appointments. They planned ahead. They had more to do than think about eating and sleeping and survival.

He looked down at Baxter, not dwelling on his stupidity. If he dwelled on all the things he'd done wrong, he would be even more useless than he already was.

"It's too cold to find shelter outside," he said.

Baxter tilted his head, as if he understood him. Well, why not? Who said dogs were dumber than humans?

"We'll have to get a room." A sinking, helpless feeling overwhelmed him, combined with a sense of panic that made him cold and then hot and then sick.

He looked around but no one popped up to help him. No genie, no magic leprechaun. No miracle happening for him.

He needed to help himself. Somehow. He needed to use his brain. He didn't just have himself to worry about now; he had Baxter.

RAINE ENTERED THE restaurant across the street, and it felt as if she'd stepped back into the 1950s. The walls were paneled with light oak wood, the tabletops were a darker maple, and there were gingham ruffles on the windows.

Four tables were already full, ten faces turning her way. Her heartbeat quickened.

Then she realized they didn't recognize her. Though Sturgeon Bay was the county seat of Door County, it was a small-sized city, especially compared to L.A. This time of year, they probably saw mostly the same faces, and new ones were scrutinized.

She would be more anonymous in a bigger city. Maybe Green Bay. Or even Milwaukee or Madison. Or Chicago or Minneapolis.

The list of cities grew in her mind, and so did the panic. Perhaps she should—

"Are you meeting someone?" the waitress asked, a long-faced, tall woman with a few wrinkles about her mouth and eyes and a friendly smile. When Raine agreed that she was waiting for someone, the waitress sat her at a table for four.

Raine took a chair that faced the door, then set her bags on the chair next to her and ordered coffee. As the waitress scurried away, she took deep breaths and opened the menu. Her panic eased. Right now she was warm, with new clothes. And her hot host—she smiled at the alliteration—had driven her here and was driving her back.

Why not enjoy the moment?

Before it got worse.

The waitress returned with the coffee. Raine set the breakfast and lunch menu down, deciding to go with the squash soup. Unless she took up cross country skiing, she didn't think she'd get much exercise in Trouble Bay. An extra twenty pounds would change the way she looked, but she preferred to rely on her short haircut and glasses.

Vanity could kill a person, she thought, a private joke that made her feel more like crying than laughing.

Then the door opened. Sunlight streamed in, and a sun god strode in.

That's what it felt like for about five long seconds, even

though the golden-haired sun god was Chuck, a man going through a life crisis of his own.

But for those seconds, he looked like he should be the hero in a cowboy movie. Or the rebel space pilot ready to fight scaly-skinned aliens. Or the pirate hero, despite his blond hair. There was just something about his sculpted face and the firm way he walked, his eyes on her.

He reached her table, and she looked up at him, their gazes locking. She should say something, but her words were caught in a time warp. She was tired, sad, and lonely. And needy. Too needy.

And he was the only one she'd talked to all day. She'd given him advice, and he'd been nice enough to drive her here.

He hadn't made any passes at her. Hadn't flirted. But that warm, honey-coated tug was undeniable. Like electricity running from him to her. She'd felt it. She suspected he'd felt it. They'd both nicely ignored it.

If they ignored it long enough, maybe it would go away.

"Chuck!" The other waitress, a curvy redhead about the same age as Chuck, stopped and put her hand on his arm, her nails a bright blue with green stripes. He turned, and she smiled up at him. "I haven't seen you for a while."

"I've been busy. How's the baby?"

"The *baby* is four years old." She rolled her eyes, then looked behind him at Raine. "*Men.*"

"Men," Raine said, though she always got those same comments from mothers. She was just as bad at remembering ages of children. She was much better at remembering lyrics and music.

"You're not from around here, are you?" the waitress asked.

"Just visiting. I'm from Colorado."

She kept her gaze on the waitress, but out of the corner of her eye, she saw Chuck stiffen. She swore at herself, remembering that she'd put a California address on her sign-in. Santa Cruz, not Los Angeles. As if that made a big difference. But Howie's car had California license plates.

"Tell Russ I said hi," Chuck said. "Great to see you."

The waitress said something back to him, then turned to tell Raine her name, clearly fishing for Raine's name.

Raine smiled and nodded, but her voice seemed stuck in her throat.

"Raine," Chuck said. "Her name is Raine."

The waitress's forehead furrowed, and Raine pulled herself together. This was not the time to fall apart.

"Nice meeting you," she said, her voice croaking more than usual.

"You should have chicken soup," the waitress said. "It will be good for your sore throat."

Before Raine could answer, the waitress was telling Chuck he should give her hubby a call, then she swished away.

Raine held on to her menu, thankful it wasn't shaking in her unsteady hands. She needed to be on her guard at all times, to act calm and confident, and to give a good reason why she'd come to Door County and Trouble Bay. Maybe make up relatives who had visited in the summer, and she was here to write a book or something.

She held back a groan. She hated this. Hated the need for it.

Chuck sat across from her and picked up his menu. Their waitress came with coffee, not asking him, saying she hadn't seen him for a while. Asking how his mother was.

Raine tried to remember what this conversation would be like in Los Angeles. Usually, if a waitress recognized her, the waitress would say she was a singer, and Raine would put on her polite face and wish her well. But mostly no one knew her. Most of them only knew Sunny, which suited Raine.

"Ready to order?" the waitress asked.

Raine looked up at the smiling, long-faced woman who didn't know who she was. All the woman expected from her was an order, a tip, and perhaps some decency and politeness.

"A bowl of chicken dumpling soup," she said. Next time—if there were a next time—she would have the squash soup.

"I'll have chicken dumpling, too," Chuck said. "Add a turkey and avocado sandwich."

"Healthy," Raine said, and the waitress chuckled.

He smiled crookedly, and she was once again struck by his good looks. She'd thought she was immune to good-looking men. The same way someone who worked in a chocolate factory might be immune to chocolate—though it was harder to imagine an immunity to chocolate than to men.

After all, she knew men. She liked men. She'd thought she'd loved a couple through the years, only to realize that one was cheating and the other one had too many problems he wasn't willing to fix. Some guys always had problems.

This one had problems, though she suspected he normally avoided them. She wished she could avoid hers, but hers were life-or-death problems. And Chuck was her host, not a man she was dating. She was staying for only a short while.

That left one intelligent conclusion.

She needed to stock up on chocolate.

☂

DEB SET THEIR food in front of them, and Chuck thanked her. Two men walked in. One he'd seen around at a few local bars, and they nodded a greeting before Deb hurried away. Chuck was picking up his sandwich when Raine asked, "So, how'd it go?"

He took a big bite of the sandwich and chewed, watching her. Not ready to answer right away. She spooned soup into her mouth, and her eyes half-closed in a *yum* expression.

"Good," he said, still holding the sandwich.

She swallowed. "What does *good* mean? Is the sculptor in? Or is the sculptor out?"

"Jamie's putting up two pieces."

"Is that good or bad?"

"What do you think?"

"I think you're evading the question. If he sculpted something like Michelangelo's *David*, then it's amazing. If he sculpted a duck this size..." She held up her hands about five inches apart. "Not so amazing. Which is it?"

"Somewhere in between."

"I see what you mean. Your friend Jamie's like one of those people who only put their toe into the water. He's not a jumper."

"A toe dipper. Yeah, that's Jamie." He smiled, but he could see by her frown that she didn't believe his smile. He turned back to his food, away from her gaze that seemed to know what he thought.

He wasn't surprised. He'd never been good at pretending.

When he looked up, she was slipping her spoon into the soup, her head down.

They both were silent for a few minutes, and he could could hear the waitresses talking to the customers. He recognized a woman in the corner, though he didn't recall her name. Linda, Laura, L something. Then she shifted, and he saw she was pregnant, a soccer-ball-sized pregnancy now. He thought maybe four or five months.

He wanted a family someday. He wanted a wife and one or two children. Maybe a dog or two.

But first he wanted to fall in love. Deeply in love. He was waiting for love to hit him the way a bat hit a fast hardball. With a slam that knocked it out of the field.

"You should have musicians," Raine said.

"Huh?" He raised his head.

"A small band or even just a singer with a guitar or another instrument. And refreshments."

He stared at her.

"To attract tourists." She frowned. "What's the matter?"

"You're reminding me of my mother."

"Seriously?" Her eyebrows rose.

His lips flattened. Was he nuts to compare her to his mother? He knew women better than that.

He grabbed his sandwich, raised it to his mouth, and took a big bite. Sometimes it was better to keep his mouth full of food instead of words.

"Music attracts people," she said. "You wouldn't need a band. Maybe a guitar player and singer who would play for minimum wage and tips. An outdoor venue is different from your bed-and-breakfast. You're used to people coming to you. You advertise at a few places and give good service and food. Get good reviews. You know you have a great product, and only seven rooms to fill. It's limited. But you're stepping into a whole different area now."

"I've had other jobs."

She dipped her spoon into the chicken soup. There was silence for a few moments while they ate.

Voices drifted from the other tables, but he didn't listen. Too busy looking at her when he was sure she wasn't looking at him, then looking away when her gaze shifted to him.

This was reminding him of seventh grade all over again, when he'd discovered the wonder of girls. He stopped a groan, remembering that he'd nearly flunked seventh grade.

Finishing the Reuben, he wiped his mouth with a napkin, then leaned over his plate. "I've been a bartender, and I worked the front desk of a resort. A few construction jobs, too, but I'm good with people. I've always been good with people."

She swallowed the chicken soup, then dropped her spoon in the bowl and pushed it slightly away. "I believe you. But remember the Pied Piper story? The way all the people followed him? People are more likely to come to the tent when there's music and food."

"I'd have to get a license or permits."

She raised her eyebrows.

He sighed. This was how she reminded him of his mother. That look. As if she expected him to do what she said. Like a dog hearing a whistle that meant *Come home, boy. Come home now.* And the dog would stop whatever he was doing and run home as fast as he could.

"You don't have to do anything now," she said. "But think about it. You have a great idea, and you should believe in it. Then tell everyone you're going to do it."

"And that will make the townspeople follow me like the children followed the piper?"

"First," she said, her words clipped, a line across her forehead, "you don't need the townspeople. They aren't your buyers."

He leaned forward, giving her his attention.

"And they aren't your sellers, unless they're the artists. You already have a sculptor—"

"On a very limited basis."

She raised her eyebrows. "The basis isn't anything you have to share with the others. He's agreed to put two of his works up, and that's all they need to know."

Something was happening inside him. Bubbling up his chest. He recognized it. Happiness. Laughter. *Joy.*

And more. Attraction. But the pull had happened the minute he'd seen her, though he'd only seen a different side of her then. Closed in. Hiding. Scared.

This confident woman telling him what to do...this must be the real Raine, opening up and showing herself to him like a flower unfolding its petals.

He'd wanted to comfort her. He'd wanted to help her. He'd—

He shut off his thoughts. Later. She was giving him business advice. He didn't need to take every piece of advice, but he realized he'd be a fool not to listen.

"What other artists are you talking to?" she asked.

He scrambled to think. "A guy I know finds old stuff in the winter, fixes it, and resells it. His wife helps him, too. In summer he works on the docks."

"What to you mean by *old stuff?*"

"Old farm equipment or dairy equipment. Or even old kids' wagons. Things like that."

"Sounds interesting."

"His wife does stuff, too."

"What kind of—" She shook her head and grinned. "Never mind. If you think it's good, then you should ask them."

"They aren't real artists."

"What do *you* think? Do you like what they do?"

"I do."

She raised her eyebrows, not saying anything more. Letting him come to his own conclusion.

He sucked in his breath. What was he afraid of? That he wasn't the smartest guy in the room?

Hell, he knew that.

He'd always been a follower and never a leader. But he'd never wanted to lead before. He'd never wanted to do anything like *this*. He'd never had that sense that this was his apple falling on his head. His painting on the chapel ceiling. Something he could do. Maybe something he *needed* to do.

Now he did. Things changed. People changed. People grew. And even if the doubts still fluttered inside his belly, so what?

Doing something different was scary. Making him wish that he could move back to the time before he'd started this. Before he'd bought the farm.

But not before she'd walked into the B and B and asked for a room.

That part he didn't want to change.

He exhaled. He couldn't turn back time. He was committed to making the art mart work. "Music sounds good to me."

She beamed at him, and it was like the sun coming out in one big burst.

He wanted to kiss her.

He wanted to leap over the table. Grab her, and kiss her like she was his Reuben, his corned beef and sauerkraut. And he was her Swiss cheese and rye bread.

"Ready to leave?" he asked, because of course he wasn't going to kiss her like that. Of course he wasn't going to leap over the table.

He'd had his Reuben sandwich already.

Later tonight, he would eat something else.

And later, in a week or two, she would leave Trouble Bay and probably never come back.

She picked up her purse.

"I'm paying," he said.

"No, I—"

"I'm paying," he said more firmly, and he put two bills on the table, looking her in the eye.

Her clothes didn't look expensive and her car was old, but she'd paid him in cash. He had the feeling that this money was nothing to her.

She was a mystery. An enigma. A woman on the run. He didn't have to be a genius to figure that out.

And, he...he was a man who was either about to lose a lot...

Or gain a lot.

Only time would tell. It scared the hell out of him, but he was going ahead with it anyway.

Twelve

THE TRUCK STOP was busy. Todd looked around the parked cars and trucks and the ones coming in and out and a couple gassing up. In the perimeter, he spotted a woman in a blue jacket with a trucker's hat walking a grayish, small-sized dog. He headed toward her.

He had the feeling it all depended on the dog, but the squat dog of dubious parentage immediately lunged to stick its nose in Baxter's butt.

"Apparently dogs know something that humans don't," the woman said. She looked to be in her fifties, with a roundish face and kind eyes. "Wouldn't it be nice if we could tell if humans are worthy of our respect by smelling their butts?"

"It would," he said. "Especially on voting days."

She laughed so hard that she bent over, her arm pressed against her stomach.

Watching her, he felt...odd. Pleased. He couldn't remember the last time he'd made someone laugh like that. It reminded him that he used to like to laugh.

The thought of it—that it was something more that had been lost to him, as well as his hope for a family and normality—made tears sting his eyes. He blinked them away as she dug a tissue out of her jacket pocket and wiped away her tears of mirth.

"I'm going to run in and get something." Every word felt forced, but he had to do this for Baxter. And maybe for himself. "A friend dropped me and Baxter off. Do you mind holding Baxter for a few minutes?"

She beamed. "You go along. The dogs and I will be in the black Jeep." She pointed by the car near the front. "We'll wait for you there."

He thanked her and hurried away to book a room in the rest area. Within five minutes, he returned to the Jeep and thanked her. Then he and Baxter headed for the small trucker rooms. No one spotted them walking in, so he was lucky again. The room was tiny, but it was cheap and it was warm. Certainly better than sleeping outside. Though it was early afternoon, talking to so many people had drained his energy.

He plopped down on the bed, and Baxter crouched on the floor, making a whimpering sound. Todd patted the mattress next to him. The bed was narrow, but it was roomier than the cardboard box he'd been living in.

"Come here, Bax," he said. "Come here."

Baxter jumped on the bed and flopped down next to him, pressing against his side, on top of the covers. Only then did Todd close his eyes and drift off, wondering what tomorrow would bring.

VINCE GLANCED AROUND him in the coffee shop. He wore jeans, a long-sleeved Lakers shirt, purple basketball shoes, and an Angels cap pulled low over his forehead. Not many people would connect him to Nirvana Now. People saw what they expected to see.

He had his phone in front of him, but he kept looking up. It had been a hell of a week, with a couple hundred sightings of Dawn reported to them, along with photos. He knew right away that nearly all of them weren't her. He'd traveled to check out three. Two were in their teens. One was a fifteen-year-old girl in a Texas town staying with her father while her mother was on her honeymoon. Another was a foster child in St. Paul, Minnesota, with long blond hair and blue-gray eyes, who wanted out of a bad placement. For her, he'd ended up staying another day to talk to the Minnesota Department of Human Services.

The third was a Scottish tourist, a mom with her two sons and her husband. They all thought the mix-up was the funniest thing.

Not a good week.

He'd flown back to Jarret's scowls, Sunny's peculiar sleepiness, and his father's anger that none of the three were Dawn.

As always, he kept his calm while they complained and blamed him.

They had their agenda. He had his—and it wasn't the same as theirs.

"Get the girl," his father had said. "I don't care what the fuck you do, but find her and bring her to me."

Vince had snapped around and marched out of there.

Grant had probably thought that Vince was rushing to obey his orders.

In a way, he was.

But not the way his father wanted...

The coffee shop door swooshed opened. Vince looked up. A tall, lanky, white-blond college-age male stood in the doorway, glancing around, his expression furtive.

Vince stood. Idiot. He might as well wear a guilty sign hanging on his neck.

Spotting Vince, the man headed toward him, walking fast, as if he were in a foot race. Vince kept a cringe off his face. Imbeciles abounded in every part of life.

"Sit down," he said.

Axel's glance shot to the counter. Vince stifled the words he wanted to say, pulled out his wallet, found a ten, and handed it to Axel. "Here. Get yourself something to drink."

He took a seat. The last time they'd met here, he'd paid for Axel's coffee, too. At the end of their meeting, he'd given Axel five bills, all of them hundreds.

After Axel had insisted on meeting with Vince in person today instead of passing information over the phone, Vince had put extra bills in his wallet.

He sat down to wait for Axel. This wasn't any sleazier than a lot of other things he'd done for Nirvana Now. For his father. But it wouldn't go on much longer. Vince had waited a long time, but Dawn's disappearance was the turning point.

Putting on his inscrutable expression, he checked his cell phone. He skimmed the frantic texts from Jarret, who was reporting another Dawn sighting. Sunny was claiming that it wasn't Dawn, but Jarret wanted him to check it out.

He texted back to Jarret that he should to listen to his wife.

Another text dinged before he could put it in his pocket. He glanced down. Jarret. Insisting that he look up the new lead.

Instead of texting Jarret back, Vince texted to Sunny: *Vince here. Jarret wants me to check up on the new Dawn sighting, but if you say it's not your sister, then it's not your sister. Will you tell him to stop wasting my time?*

Grinning, he put his phone away. Jarret may look like the man ready to take charge, but in reality, he was a chicken hiding from a starving dog in the hen house. Any little thing made him quiver with fear.

That's what happened when your mother died unexpectedly. When you knew your father was a manipulative bastard.

When you knew he probably killed your mother.

Either you became scared.

Or you became vengeful.

Axel sat across from him, bending forward, a tall man trying to look small as he gulped down his coffee. Vince shut down his thoughts about Sunny and Jarret as if he were closing a door, and he concentrated on Axel.

Finally, Axel set down the cup and nervously looked Vince in the eyes.

"What do you know?" Vince asked.

"There were only two messages from this Raine." Axel's voice was jumpy. "One was from an IP in Colorado. The other was in Wisconsin. Could be either. I can't tell you the exact location, but I can narrow it down to—"

Vince shook his head. "No." His voice was short. He'd hoped both calls had originated from the same place. And only two calls? If that's all there was, this Raine, whoever she might be, could be traveling on to another place already.

"You want me to keep checking to see if she's emailing Howie?"

"I'll check myself."

"Oh, yeah." Axel looked down at his hands, then up, then down again. He was tapping the tabletop nervously. "About that, I can't leave the connection on forever. Howie probably won't notice that another phone is connected, but it's possible that he might. I don't like that it might happen."

Vince looked at him. "I'm willing to take a chance."

Axel's gaze slipped up to him, then down again. "My mom... She'll know it's me. Howie's a nice guy. A good boss. I can't get her fired."

Vince didn't reply, his gaze steady.

Axel's Adam's apple wobbled, and his fingers tapped on the cup. "Howie's wife... She knows I had a problem. You know..."

Around them there was a hum of voices, but Vince still didn't reply. It wasn't necessary. The first time he'd talked to Axel on the phone, he'd known Axel was an addict. He'd known before Axel had finished his first sentence.

"I can't let her find out," Axel whispered in a hoarse voice. "My mom's done so much..."

Vince looked away. This was uncomfortable.

"I promise I'll check every day, but I gotta take the connection off." His voice was pleading. "Just, please... Don't do this. I promise I'll check. Every day."

Vince sighed and brought his gaze back to Axel. "This

Raine might not be the one I'm looking for. It might be someone else."

"I know who you're looking for," Axel said, his voice rising. "The missing songwriter. I know what to look for. And if I have to, I can copy all the messages and send them to you. I'll give you the Colorado and Wisconsin locations. That's the easiest thing I can do. If there are more emails, I'll give you those. But I just can't let my mom be fired."

Some of the diners were turning to stare at them. Vince shrunk down an inch into the seat. "Okay, I'll trust that you'll keep your word. I have no intention of making you do anything that will cost your mother her position. And I don't want anyone to know what you're doing."

Without any warning, Axel started crying. Vince froze in his seat and closed his eyes. Maybe he should fly to Colorado or Wisconsin. Anything to get away from his father and brother and all the other crazy people.

Maybe he'd even get lucky and find Dawn.

Thirteen

THE SUN WAS waning when Todd bundled up and took Baxter outside to the snowy edge of the parking lot. In his duffel bag, he had food for Baxter and himself, plus a small plastic water bowl for Bax. After Baxter finished doing what they'd come out to do, they headed back to the rest area, where they ran into a redheaded trucker with a laughing woman who smelled like she'd bathed in perfume.

The trucker and the woman headed into the room next to Todd's. The trucker winked at Todd. "You don't say nothing," he said, glancing down at Baxter, "and I won't say nothing."

Todd nodded. He'd seen a lot worse in life than a man sneaking a woman into a room. If this had been before Afghanistan, more than a dozen years ago, he might've been the one doing the sneaking.

The thought didn't make him angry anymore. Just a little sad. In their room, he plopped back down on the bed, but there soon came feminine cries from the next room and a man's grunts. He was pretty sure the woman's cries were fake, but who was he to judge? Just a guy who'd been sleeping in a cardboard box the night before.

He petted Baxter's head and wondered if he'd ever be with a woman again. He didn't know if it would ever happen, if he would ever be normal, though for a long time he'd wondered if normal was a myth.

At least he had Baxter now. At least he wasn't alone.

RAINE COULDN'T SLEEP. She was in a cold place with a cold heart, and she knew that on the floor below her, Chuck slept.

Or did he? Was he awake like her? Was he lonely?

Did he ache for the touch of a woman? For *her* touch?

No, of course not. He had friends. Female as well as male. If he slept alone, it was by choice.

The moonlight slipped through the edges of the shade, and she remembered times like this when she was young, and she used to hear her mother and whatever man she was with at the time laughing—or sometimes crying. Or other times screaming at each other.

Or sometimes there was just silence. Just her and Sunny alone in the house.

If Sunny was awake, Raine would make up songs for them to sing, and their voices would keep away the monsters.

When Sunny was asleep, Raine would sometimes open her eyes, hoping to see Peter Pan slipping through the window.

Of course, she knew the answer was no. But there was always the chance that maybe, just maybe, he was real and she could fly off with him to Neverland.

She would open her eyes slowly, hardly daring to breathe, and then...nothing. No Peter Pan. No Tinkerbell. No Lost Boys.

Just two little lost girls.

She rolled out of bed, her hand over her mouth. Why these memories now? Why?

Sunny wasn't having them. Peter Pan had never been the guy Sunny had hoped for. She had always hoped for Prince Charming. And she'd gotten him, too, though Jarret's charm had seemed superficial to Raine from day one.

Raine clicked on the light, giving up on sleep. She was wearing flannel pajama bottoms, and she slipped a sweatshirt over her long-sleeved cotton top, then stuck her feet into fuzzy, warm slip-ons. Only then did she pick up the guitar.

It was like holding a lover. The only lover she could ever trust.

"Hey, darling," she whispered, "let's make some sweet music, okay?"

She strummed, closing her eyes, listening to the vibration in the air. The sound was her breath. Her heartbeat.

Her words came slowly, but they came from her heart.

I don't know what's wrong with people.
I don't know where the meanness comes from
People think it makes them look smart
If their put-downs make others look dumb.
But they don't know, they don't know, they don't know
That meanness bounces back and shrivels the soul

IN THE HALLWAY, heading out of the bathroom, Chuck heard tuneful singing, the voice husky yet pure, and the guitar strings strumming. *Raine.* Her singing voice suited her name. A soft rain.

He couldn't make out the words of the song, but he felt the emotion. The poignancy. It twisted inside of his belly. It grabbed his heart.

And then it stopped suddenly.

His breath that he hadn't realized he'd been holding whooshed out. His shoulders sagged as he turned into his room.

Even with just the guitar music and no words, he could tell it was a love song. It filled him with a forgotten yearning. He wanted to be in love, but he was wary of love. Though he was still a child when his father was murdered, he remembered the fights and the tears.

And sometimes the silence when his father didn't come home at night.

People who'd known his father said that Chuck looked like both his parents, but his personality was like his father's.

Maybe they were right. He didn't know. But he wanted them to be wrong. He'd vowed not to marry until he was so madly in love he couldn't stand to be away from her every night.

So far, that had never happened. He was beginning to despair that it ever would.

The strums of a guitar began again. Raine's voice sang softly, the words too low for him to hear, but her voice and the music still touched his heart. Still pulled at his soul. As he listened, he could hear the rasp in the voice. Then louder. And louder again, sounding like a cry.

It *was* a cry. And another. And another.

He fought an urge to rush up the stairway, burst into her suite, then hold her in his arms and rock her.

Yeah, right. She'd kick him out of her room, and tomorrow she would be gone.

He stayed where he was, but he couldn't stop the way he felt, as if his heart was beating harder. And the yearning inside him ached more than ever.

It wasn't sexual. The sound from upstairs was like a mewl of a kitten. A whimper of a puppy. A cry of a baby.

Sounds that he responded to. That made him want to pick up the kitten, the puppy, the baby...

The woman.

He stood still. Thinking. He had an idea...

STUPID. STUPID. STUPID. Tears never solved anything. Raine had learned that at a young age. But sometimes trying to stop tears was like trying to stop the rain.

She sat on the edge of the bed, rocking back and forth,

stifling her tears so no one would hear.

Like her mother. Or her mother's boyfriend of the night.

She hadn't thought about it for the last ten or more years. She'd thought her mother's neglect hadn't affected her anymore. That she'd gotten over it. But she'd been lying to herself. The memories and the wounds were still hot spots in the back of her mind. The little girl she'd been curled up in bed, her covers pulled tightly over her head, thinking, *I can't cry. She'll yell and call me a baby. She'll yell at both of us.*

When she'd cried, so had Sunny. They would hold each other sometimes, until they fell asleep.

Always together.

Until a man had strode into Sunny's life and charmed her with his phony smile and his false words. And her sister, so strong and confident—yet so needy—couldn't see that instead of the golden prince, he was a *false* prince. A serpent in disguise. And his father was the ugly giant who'd brought evil to the kingdom.

And like a fairy tale gone bad, the two princesses became enemies.

Hot tears slid down her cheeks.

Stupid. Stupid. Stupid.

Someone knocked on her door.

She inhaled on a sob, then froze, staring at the door.

"Raine."

She cupped her hand over her mouth. Chuck. Had he heard her sing? Or cry?

If he was going to ask her what was wrong—

"There's a Star Wars movie on in twenty minutes. Or a Jennifer Lawrence movie. That one started already. Want to watch either of them with me?"

She stood but didn't answer, still staring at the door, as if she could see through it.

"I'm making popcorn," he said.

More tears spurted from her eyes, and she scrunched her face, pulling them back. "Okay," she said. Her voice was thick with tears, but it was usually husky. Maybe he wouldn't notice. Maybe he hadn't heard her sobbing.

"You like butter with your popcorn?" he asked.

"Yes."

"See you downstairs."

She stood still, listening to his footsteps clomp down the steps.

She exhaled, her shoulders relaxed. She started to turn.

Then his footsteps stopped when he must have only run down about seven steps. She stopped too, and listened to his footsteps clomp back up the steps. Listened to him stop on the second-story hallway.

"You don't have to worry about me trying anything," he called. "I'm not attracted to you."

A laugh blurted out of her, and in her head, the word *liar* popped up. To hold the word back, she slapped her hand over her mouth.

Instead of crying now, she wanted to laugh wildly. Maybe laugh until she cried.

Because it was ludicrously funny to think that he wasn't attracted to her. He wasn't attracted to her the way she wasn't attracted to him.

That didn't mean she was going to act on it. It just meant that she wanted to.

"No worries," she called, and her voice was up and down like a teenaged boy going through puberty.

"If you're wearing pajamas, don't bother changing," he said. "I'll wear mine, too."

She put her hands over her mouth to stop her laughter again. She was a mess. A big mess.

If she went downstairs, it might be a big mistake. A bigger mess.

But her life was already a giant mess. What was one more? After all, she didn't have to stay here. She could just pack up and leave.

Fourteen

TODD WAS SWEATING, small cries coming out of his mouth, when a whimper woke him, a tongue licking his chin.

He opened his eyes and realized hot tears were tracking down his face. He shook his head, shaking away the images of troops dying in the desert he had come to hate. Exploding. His best friend gone. Dead.

It had seemed so real as he'd relived that nightmare day.

He'd seen it, he'd smelled it. He was sweating, just like he'd done that day. He was wishing it had been him instead of Donnie.

Baxter whimpered, crying for him. Todd turned and held Baxter, tears dripping down his face onto Baxter's short-furred neck.

RAINE WAS WARM, and someone was holding her. Sheltering her. In her mind, a man and woman were kissing, but it wasn't her, though they looked familiar. A loud male voice was talking enthusiastically about a self-propelled vacuum cleaner.

She was asleep; she knew that much. But her sleep was thinning with every breath. And she was feeling so warm and wonderful, with an arm around her back, that she fought against waking up.

If only that voice would shut up.

But it didn't, and she started to feel too warm now. She noticed her neck was cramped.

She groaned and pulled away from the arms, looking into half-lidded, sky-blue eyes.

Chuck's eyes.

He smiled. "'Morning, sleepyhead."

She groaned again, immediately knowing she was wearing her pajamas, and they'd fallen asleep on the couch with the TV on, which was now apparently trying to sell the viewers a new and powerful and lightweight vacuum cleaner.

She vaguely remembered him pulling her to him and sighing. Both of them sighing.

It felt like a mistake now, but halfway through the Star Wars movie it had felt right. As if it were natural to be held by him. Inevitable.

Then she'd fallen asleep.

She leaned back. The dim early morning sunlight peeped through the curtains. Cool air hit her face and her neck, and she'd much rather be snuggled against his neck again. Skin touching skin. But she gazed into his bright eyes and stayed inches away from him.

"Nothing happened," he said, his voice sounding like he'd swallowed a fistful of gravel.

"I know."

He grinned crookedly. "Too bad."

She laughed. When she was with him, her laughter came so easily. So naturally. As if her life wasn't messed up, and she wasn't fearful that people wanted to kill her.

"I need to shower," she said, and then grimaced and hoped he wouldn't take it as an invitation to share her shower. Or her bed.

He put his nose to her shoulder and sniffed. "You smell good to me."

Her heart beat faster. This had been a bad idea, though it felt so good. She shimmied her butt away from him, then pushed off the couch. "The infomercial is annoying."

"Yeah, I know." He reached for the remote. In a second, the sound turned off, the screen turning black. He looked at the clock on the wall. "It's barely six. You going back to bed?"

"I don't know." She stretched her neck. Though she'd slept sitting up for about six hours, she felt good. Deliciously good. "What about you?"

He stood and smiled. A slow, warm smile.

She punched his upper right arm. He laughed.

"We're flirting," she said. "We have to stop this."

"I know." He curved his hand and fingers over the side of her face. "But I don't want to."

With a sigh, she put her hands on his ribs, and she could feel the warmth of his skin through the thin T-shirt. She pushed away from him, then her hands dropped to her sides. "That's how life is. Doing things we don't want. Eating vegetables instead of chocolate bars. Not sleeping with the host."

"I don't sleep with paying guests."

"I bet you've flirted with many."

He stared at her, and his eyes darkened, his pupils dilating. "I'm not flirting with you."

"My life is complicated." Her voice cracked, and she swallowed.

"Then boil it down. You're running from someone, aren't you? Tell me who it is, and I can watch out for him."

"This isn't the Old West."

He stared at her.

"Okay, okay." Her eyes were heating, tears not far away. "You're right. I am running from someone."

"There, that wasn't hard. Now, what's his name? Who is he?"

She shook her head. "I can't tell you. If I do, you might be in danger." The thought made her hot, then cold, then sick. She pushed him away, strode to the stairs, then ran up them. Reaching her suite, she closed and locked the door.

She felt sick. Not just sick at heart but sick to her stomach. She raced to the bathroom, then bent over the toilet and began to puke.

CHUCK STOOD IN the hall outside the suite, listening to her puke. The door was locked, and instead of knocking again, he turned away, then clambered downstairs, heading into the kitchen, where he grabbed the extra set of keys for all the rooms.

A moment later, he stood outside her suite again, breathing too fast and listening to the toilet flush.

Once again, he called her name. She still didn't answer. He turned the key in the lock and stepped inside. The bathroom door was open, and he strode toward it. She was sitting on the floor next to the toilet, her face flushed, her head bent between her knees.

"I'm calling the doctor." He started to turn.

"No." Her voice broke.

He continued to walk away.

"Please," she whispered. "*Please.*"

He slowed, then turned back to her and knelt by her side.

"It's the flu," she said. "I think it's the simple flu."

"What do you want me to do?"

"Go away."

"I can't do that. I can't let you do this alone."

Her eyes teared up. She started to say something, then surged up on her knees, leaned over the toilet, and puked again, a brownish liquid coming out of her mouth.

He pushed up to his feet, flushed the toilet, then he knelt and grasped her upper arms. He'd often said that the one thing he would never do was work in a hospital because he couldn't stand taking care of people when they were throwing up. Yet here he was, wanting to take care of her.

She leaned over the toilet again.

He straightened and headed into the bedroom and opened the closet door. Seconds later, he returned to the bathroom and wrapped the extra blanket they kept in the closet around her.

"Don't worry," he said, "I'm taking care of you now. You're not alone."

She sobbed, and this time she didn't tell him to go away.

Progress, he thought, as he held her lightly, because some women just couldn't be held too tight.

Fifteen

THE SUN WAS bright. The air was biting. Todd and Baxter headed out toward Sturgeon Bay. Todd thought it'd take about three or hours by foot. He wasn't supposed to be at the lawyer's until three this afternoon, and they should be there in plenty of time. He had a backpack and carried a large duffel bag. He was ready for anything.

Next to him, Baxter panted happily. He was ready for anything, too, but he was looking at it with joy today. So different from the dog Todd had first met.

So different from him. The only way he looked at anything new was with trepidation.

RAINE'S HEAD POUNDED. Her skin felt hot. Her eyes didn't want to open, her lashes stuck together until she forced them apart. She knew right away she was alone. Good, she told herself. Good. But she knew she was lying. She rolled over, and that sick feeling was still inside her throat. Her hand touched the sheet, and it was warm.

A toilet flush came from her bathroom.

Chuck was here. He'd stayed with her to make sure she was all right.

Immediately, she relaxed, the sick feeling easing, her mind sharpening. She hadn't closed the shades last night. Sunlight was filling the bedroom, and she guessed it was midmorning. She turned her head. If the clock on the dresser was right, it was a quarter to ten.

The bathroom door opened, and Chuck stepped out, blond stubble on his cheeks and chin, his blue eyes bright. He wore last night's sweats, and they looked good on him. On him, anything looked good.

It struck her for the first time that he had a similar coloring and height to her brother-in-law. Chuck's hair was lighter, but the big difference was that Chuck made his own mistakes and fumbled with his own problems.

He didn't have his father smooth over his life like her brother-in-law.

And when she'd needed him, he'd been there for her.

She doubted that Sunny could say the same thing about Jarret, the prince-in-training. The prince under the thumb of the wicked king.

A song hummed in her head.

"You okay?"

Nodding hurt her head, and she winced.

"Breakfast?"

She evaluated herself. "I just want to sleep."

"You should see a doctor."

"That's not necessary. My stomach has settled down. I'll be better when I wake up."

He stared at her, not saying anything for a moment, then he took a step back. "What about water? Or tea?"

"Maybe water and an aspirin."

"Anything else?"

"I think it's either something I ate or the flu. You shouldn't have slept with me. If it's the flu, you probably have it, too."

"You're that type of woman." His voice lowered. "The kind who takes the responsibility for everyone else's problems."

She made a face. "It's a bad habit I need to break. But don't sleep with me until I'm healthy again."

He laughed, and her eyes snapped open wide. "I mean—"

"Hey. Don't ruin the moment." He grinned at her.

She couldn't stop the smile on her face. She should probably be thinking about Sunny. Every time one of them had been sick, the other seemed to be sick, too. They'd been weird that way since childhood. But that had been when they were together most of the time.

There was no reason for Sunny to be sick now. It had been a week since she'd seen Sunny. But Chuck, now...

"You should take an aspirin, too," she said.

His grin widened.

"And call one of your artist friends."

He laughed. "If you're nagging me, you must be feeling better."

She watched him head out of the room, his head high, a spring to his step. She felt hot and cold and stuffy...and she missed her sister, the missing a constant ache in her chest...

Yet she was smiling.

All because of a man. Stupid, stupid, stupid.

☂

THE DOOR TO the bedroom suite Sunny shared with Jarret clicked open. She closed her eyes, pretending to sleep, though her heart was pounding like a wild rock band drummer was in control of each heartbeat. She forced herself to breathe softly as she sent a silent message. *Go away, go away, go away.*

"Honey?"

Her stomach roiled. This was not good. She wanted to puke on him. Puke all over him.

It made her wonder about Dawn, as so many things made her wonder about Dawn.

Was Dawn puking, too? They always got sick at the same time. Of course, her condition wasn't something that Dawn would catch, and it was silly to think of it. But she missed Dawn. Being with Jarret had seemed so wonderful, so like her dreams when she was little. He was the handsome prince from her dreams who swooped down and saved her from the world.

But in her dreams, Dawn had always been there for her. Her maid of honor, or whatever princesses named their best friends and their best sisters.

That was over, she reminded herself, feeling the fuzziness in her brain. Dawn had left her. Betrayed her.

Dawn was jealous of her. That's what Jarret and Grant told her. All these years she'd been the one in the spotlight, except for the times when Dawn had won a songwriting award.

But like Jarret and Grant said, it was *her* singing that made the songs so good. *Her* dancing. *Her* pretty smile. The way *her* fans loved her.

If it weren't for Dawn's image all over the TV now that she was missing, hardly anyone would know that she was alive.

If she was alive.

The thought that Dawn might not be alive made her stomach turn over, and she slapped her hand over her mouth.

"Honey." Jarret knelt, his face level with hers, a frown on his forehead. "We're having a baby! That's wonderful news!"

The thought passed through her mind that someone from the doctor's office must have called specifically to tell him.

Something like that would make Dawn mad. She would be angry that they told him without her permission, even if Jarret was the baby's father.

Grant probably knew, too. If someone from the doctor's office had called Jarret, no doubt they had called Grant, too.

Dawn would tell her to go to a doctor who respected her privacy. She would even call the doctor's office and tell them that she could report them for telling people without her permission.

For the most part, Dawn was quiet. But if she thought

someone was taking advantage of Sunny, she turned into a snarling bulldog.

Not Sunny, though. Sunny wasn't going to get mad about it.

"Sunny—"

Sunny turned, then leaned over the bed and threw up on him.

For one second, it felt gloriously wonderful—and then Jarret swore and bounded up, wiping vomit off of his face. "What the fuck did you do?" His mouth twisted with anger. "What the fuck is wrong with you?"

Sunny stared at him, her hand against her left breast, feeling the pounding of her heart.

The last time someone looked at her like that, the next instant she'd been slammed against the wall so hard that her breath had puffed out of her lungs. Then he'd ripped her clothes off.

And then—

Dawn had slammed a baseball bat on his head.

"Fucking bitch," Jarret said, his voice harsh and his face turning a purplish red.

"Get out." Her voice shook. She wished she had a bat right now. She wished she were as brave as her sister. "Get the hell out of my bedroom."

He stilled, staring down at her, three frown lines on his forehead, and she could practically hear him thinking that perhaps he'd made a mistake.

Perhaps he'd shown his true self to her too soon. Shown her that he wasn't Prince Charming after all, because she'd just seen the truth about him.

Instead of a prince, he was the devil.

Sixteen

IN A PANELED office above a women's clothing store in downtown Sturgeon Bay, Attorney H. Ankton, a tall woman with short, red-orange hair, shook Todd's hand firmly. Without a pause, she bent down to pet Baxter, then told him to sit, looking from the dog to Todd. Both of them immediately sat, Todd on a chair in front of the large desk, and Baxter on the faded Oriental rug. The attorney seated herself behind a large maple desk and gave him her sympathies on the death of his aunt.

Todd thanked her. He'd liked his mother's much older half sister, though he'd only seen her about a dozen times during his childhood. A former teacher, his aunt used to send him books for Christmas and his birthday. When he was a teenager, she'd sent money instead of books. Usually twenty dollars, and he'd liked the money as much as he'd liked the books.

"Call me Helen," the attorney said. "Sarah and I were in a book club together for many years. We were friends."

"Helen." He repeated her name, imprinting it in his brain, because that's something people did. Normal people, anyway. And pretending to be a normal person was making his underarms sweat.

"Your aunt was a wise woman," Helen said.

Todd nodded, and that was the first of his many nods as he learned that his aunt had left a trust for him, and Helen was the executor. Helen said Sarah hadn't left a lot of money, but there would be enough to repair the roof, pay the bills and taxes, and a modest amount left over.

"Roof repairs." He stared at her, tension creeping through him.

Helen told him the roof should be okay until spring, and he nodded again, wondering how much she knew about roofs. She went on to say that it was a small house, and his aunt had sent the bulk of her money to a breast cancer foundation. Though she'd died of a heart attack, his aunt had had breast cancer many years before.

Todd nodded again, though he hadn't known that about his aunt Sarah. In addition to his PTSD, he now had a family history of cancer and heart problems. And he had a roof to fix.

Life had gotten better, perhaps. He wasn't certain about that. But he definitely knew that life was getting more complicated.

Helen continued to speak, and he continued to nod until her voice became a buzz in his ears. At one point he had to wait for her to use the bathroom. When she came back, she began talking again, and he was sweating more. Then he started shivering. He tensed his muscles and slowed his breaths so she wouldn't see that he was at the start of an anxiety attack. He needed to pretend he was calm. Needed to do this for Baxter. Baxter needed a home.

Maybe he needed one, too. Someplace safe. Someplace warm. Someplace with walls to keep out the weather and the bad guys.

He could live in his aunt's house, just him and Baxter. Even without his aunt's money, he thought he could pay for the expenses with his disability compensation. Even the roof. He could—

The silence stopped his thoughts, and he looked up. Helen was watching him, and there was sadness in her face. "Are you okay?"

He nodded.

"It's a lot to take in."

"I've got it," he said. "What do I need to sign?"

It took about ten minutes to sign all the papers—mostly because of Helen's explanations for each one that he pretended to understand. He put Helen's card in his backpack, though he already had her phone number, and an envelope with official documents that he no longer remembered what they were. The deed, and some other things. He excused himself to use the bathroom, and when he came back, he saw the dog lapping water from a white bowl on the carpet.

"I thought Baxter might be thirsty," Helen said. "I gave him half a ham sandwich. I hope you don't mind."

His underarms grew hot again. "Baxter and I have only been together a short time. He's a stray, and was even skinnier than this when he found me."

"I'm not accusing you of anything." Helen stood. "Thank you for helping him. Thank you for fighting for the country."

He turned his head away from her, unable to speak. He wasn't good with people. When he spent too much time with other people, he unraveled like a badly knitted sweater.

What if she realized he was unstable? What if she went to the courts and said he shouldn't have the house? Or, worse, if she said he shouldn't keep Baxter?

As for fighting for the country, the part that terrified him was that he was angry about what had happened. Angry because someone higher up the Marine food chain had decided to cut down the number of guards at their outpost. Angry that some of his friends had died in an attack a week after the guards had been removed.

Swallowing, he reminded himself that nothing he could do would change the past. Reminded himself that he had Baxter. Reminded himself to breathe.

"Thank you for your help," he said. The words came out stilted, but they were the words a normal person would say. It had been a long time since he was normal, but he remembered the expected behaviors and the words.

"Do you need a ride?" Her expression was doubtful. "I can call a taxi for you."

"I'm fine." He backed away. It was nearly five now. He and Baxter would be just fine.

He felt Helen's concern and kept himself from yelling that he didn't need sympathy. Instead, he hurried out of the office and down the stairs. Once outside in the open air, he breathed deeper, the tightness on the back of his neck easing.

"We're going to be okay," he whispered to Baxter. "We're going to be just fine."

They started walking. He wasn't sure how long it would take, but a sleeping bag was rolled up tightly in his duffel bag, and they would be okay.

☂

VINCE SAT IN his father's Beverly Hills home office, an impressive room that left Vince unimpressed. He knew the man behind the glamour, and the picture he always saw was ugly and twisted and false.

He wore his T-shirt that said I LOVE ROCK & ROLL, and his father scowled, then forced his mouth into a smile that was obviously false. But so much about his father was false that Vince would only be shocked if Grant said he was doing something true.

"You called?" Vince asked.

His father's eyebrows arched, though his forehead only moved slightly. "I have important news to share."

News he couldn't share on the phone? Or email?

Vince nodded. He'd been packing to catch a plane tomorrow morning. There had been no more emails to Howie Stein from the mysterious Raine in Wisconsin, and he was getting antsy. His mind wasn't telling him to go. His gut was.

"You're going to be an uncle," his father said.

Vince stood still for a few seconds before speaking,

choosing his words carefully. "I'm surprised. Sunny and Jarret had said they were planning to wait a few years before having a baby. I thought Sunny had booked concerts for this summer."

"Mistakes happen." Grant's eyes glittered. "She was on the pill, but everyone knows that contraception doesn't always work."

Vince felt like a big fist had socked him in the belly. Socked him hard. With the intent to hurt. He stared at his father. He wouldn't doubt that his father had been behind changing Sunny's pills with placebos. Perhaps he'd bribed Sunny's gynecologist to change the prescription. Or her pharmacist.

"Congratulations," he said coolly. "You're going to be a grandfather."

"The next leader of Nirvana Now," he said, his voice booming.

"The *next* leader? Does Jarret know this?"

His father blinked, and his face tightened, his complexion darkening. "There's no need to tell him. He'll find out in due time."

Vince stared at him, keeping his expression neutral, not saying anything.

"You didn't expect that *you* would be the leader," Grant said, an edge of disparagement in his voice, his eyes glittering again.

He's on something.

The thought was another punch in Vince's belly. He'd suspected before that his father had a Napoleon complex. But those eyes...

"No." He didn't elaborate. He'd always known he was second, and he'd never cared. He had his own agenda, and it wasn't leading the church. "Are you still seeing the doctor?"

Grant scowled.

"The anti-aging specialist from India?" Vince asked.

"Enough." Grant slammed his fist on the solid maple table next to him, and it rattled. "My brain power is faster and sharper than it has ever been. My mind has expanded." His eyes narrowed, and his voice lowered to a hoarse whisper. "I have the skin of a baby."

"Sure you do." Vince kept his eyes on his father. As if he were a venomous snake who might strike any second. With his father, that might be true. "What do you want me to do?" he asked, changing the subject, because if he didn't, his father would hold his anger at him in his mind, and it would grow and grow and grow... And the result would be ugly. For him, not his father.

"Find the sister." Grant's voice shook with his fury. "I want the songs. I expected them, and I'm going to get them."

"The child might be female." Vince stood.

Grant's face reddened. "A girl will do. I'll teach her how to rule."

Rule? Did he think he was a king?

Yes, he answered himself. *Yes, he did.*

He needed to find out if one more thing he'd suspected was true.

"Why Jarret's baby? Why not have one of your own?"

Grant stared at him, and his red complexion turned a purplish hue, like a ripe turnip. He stood. "Get out." His voice roared, and he pointed at the doorway to the hall, his finger and hand shaking. "Get the hell out before I kill you."

Vince strode out, glad that his father didn't have a gun. Glad that he'd already decided to get the hell out of California. No matter if Wisconsin was snow-covered and had Jack Frost nipping hard at noses, he was eager to go there.

By the time he returned, his father might have forgotten that the last time he'd seen Vince he'd wanted to kill him.

And Vince had learned something about his father. He'd heard the rumors, and now he knew his father couldn't have children anymore.

At least one good thing had happened in the world.

SUNNY FELT HOT and then cold in the library adjacent to the hallway, the one that hardly anyone used. It was lined with bookcases that were crammed with books. She knew that when her father-in-law was young, his family had been poor, and he'd spent a lot of time in the public library.

He was proud of his poverty. Proud that he'd surmounted it, and now he had his own massive libraries. One in the Beverly Hills mansion. Another in this even bigger mansion in the Nirvana Now compound that was located in the hills an hour or so away from L.A. Grant had insisted they stay there until the paparazzi found someone else to stalk.

Sunny frowned, not wanting to think about Dawn's disappearance. Too afraid, too angry, too guilty, and too scared. But everything she did came back to Dawn. Even this place. When she'd told Dawn about the library story, to convince her that Grant was a good guy, Dawn had said, "So now he has a library he doesn't use? Wouldn't it be better to give money to inner-city libraries?"

Sunny had glared at her. Dawn had given money to two L.A. inner-city schools for their music departments, so Sunny just told her that she was acting holier than thou. She'd known that Dawn's comment was a dig at her for not matching her. For not donating anything.

It was easy for Dawn to give away money. She didn't need to pay for clothes and musicians and transport and hotel rooms and roadies and everything else that went along with singing and looking good.

But every time she passed the library, she thought of Dawn. And waiting in the library was worse, because all she could think of was Dawn, and she fidgeted from one foot to the other.

Footsteps came down the marble stairs, and she scuttled to the library doorway, watching the flowing stairway. Grant and Jarret almost always took the elevator, but Vince took the steps.

As soon as he reached the first floor, she stepped out and called his name.

He turned. There was no surprise on his lean face. No expression at all. Just coldness.

"Congratulations on your pregnancy," he said as she hurried to him.

Her face flushed. So he knew already.

Anger flushed through her.

"I don't want anyone to know about this until *I* tell them."

"That's something you should tell your husband and father-in-law."

She frowned.

"Is that all?" His left eyebrow rose, and he half turned. "I have to—"

"Wait! I..." She stopped and gulped and gave the hallway a sweeping glance to make sure no one saw her talking to him. She looked back up at him. "Do you have any news from Dawn?"

He stood still, all emotion wiped from his face. "No," he said finally.

"Do you have any idea where she is?"

Again his answer was slow. "No."

He started to turn, and she grabbed his sleeve.

"Wait!"

He looked at her fingers gripping his shirt, both his eyebrows twitched up. She glared at him and kept her hold on his shirt. She wasn't going to let him faze her. She'd sung on street corners when she was a teen. She'd sung in motorcycle bars.

And long before that, she and Dawn had hidden in closets from one of her mother's boyfriends. Clinging to each other and shaking, their hearts beating fast.

They'd survived. They'd triumphed.

They. Not she. All that time she'd never been alone.

"If you see her, will you tell her..." She stopped and stared into his eyes that now were sharp with interest, as if he wanted to hear what she was going to say and had just been pretending to be bored.

She swallowed and let go of his sleeve, her arm dropping to her side. "Tell her I miss her."

"What about the songs?" he asked. "You want me to tell her anything about that?"

She stared at him, and she started to shake.

The rumble of the elevator coming down stopped her from replying. She glanced at the bronze-colored doors. It had to be Jarret or Grant. She didn't want to see either of them now. She twisted around, then ran back into the library.

There was nothing else she could tell Dawn. If she said anything, it would be a lie, and Dawn would know. Dawn *always* knew. The reason she hated Dawn now as much as she still loved her.

Seventeen

TODD ORDERED TWO meatloaf dinners and one coffee to go. After that, he bundled up, then he and Baxter started their journey.

He vaguely remembered walking along the lake road behind Sturgeon Bay with his parents, his mother raving about the scenery, and his father saying that the back roads were longer, but she was right. It was pretty. Bay Shore Drive, the road was called. All these years later, Todd thought about taking Highway 42. It would be shorter. And it was cold outside. Very cold. But if he'd taken the shorter, faster, and more comfortable road, he would have had a different life. A better life. A regular job, and maybe even a wife and kids.

"Guess I never learn," he said to Baxter. "You ready to take the back road?"

Baxter barked, and Todd laughed, the tension easing. They were two fools together, him and the dog.

☂

OLIVE DREYER HAD pink and white hair that reached her shoulders. She was thin and barely five feet tall, with smile creases around her eyes and her cheeks. She opened the door for Chuck, and her eyes squeezed, as if imagining him in a picture frame.

"Chuck." Her voice was deep for someone so thin and

small. "You're letting in the cold air. Come in."

He stepped inside and she stepped back. Olive lived on a small piece of land with one of the best lake views in Door County—though many places in Door County had the best views.

"Coffee or tea or hot chocolate?" She gave him an elfish grin. "Or rum?"

He laughed. It was just past eleven in the morning. "I'll take rum another time. I just stopped by to tell you about my new project."

"I know all about it already."

"In that case," he said, "you may as well pour the rum."

She crackled with laughter and slapped her knees. "Take your jacket off, go sit in the studio, and I'll get the rum. You tell me about the project and the new guest you took to Sturgeon Bay yesterday, and I'll tell you about the paintings."

He groaned. "You want to hear about Raine?"

"Raine? I heard she had an odd name. I haven't seen her, but I like odd names and odd people."

"I would never have guessed." Though Olive reminded him of an elf, she was one of the most popular artists in Wisconsin. She painted like a fairy with a wand, as if adding magic to every painting she did.

She cracked up again. When she stopped laughing, she said, "Your mother told me that she made you promise not to sleep with any of the guests."

"That's right, I did."

"You know that promises are made to be broken." She winked at him.

"Can we get back to my idea to showcase the talent?"

She made a face. "Do we really have to? I wish you wouldn't. If you really want to do this, you should talk to lesser-known artists. Some of the artists who aren't as popular as me. I'm doing just fine here."

"In that case," he said, hearing the stiffness in his voice, "I should get going. Let's save the rum for another time."

"If that's the way you want it, Chuck." She tilted her head. "You were always so cute. It probably wouldn't be hard for you to find a smart girl to help you with the B and B. Not hard at all."

He finally got away from her. He hadn't even mentioned the artist he'd signed up in Sturgeon Bay, but he'd decided he didn't need to impress anyone. The townspeople were supposed to be his friends. His shoulders slumped.

If the people he'd known his whole life didn't believe in him, who would?

Raine. She believed in him. But if Raine knew him better, would she feel the same way?

He sat in his car for a minute before he started it—only because he knew Olive was watching him out of her window. Hell, she probably had a friend on the phone already and was saying *Now he asked me to be part of his thing. I felt sorry for him. You know how much I like him. But I just can't lend my paintings to something like that. He calls it an art mart, but it's really like a flea market for artists. I wouldn't stoop to that. Any artist who agrees must be desperate.*

She was right about one thing. He was desperate.

He wanted to head back to his house, but he'd told Raine he would do this, and he wasn't breaking his word to her.

☂

RAINE DRANK THE elderberry tea that Chuck had left for her, saying his mother swore it was good for the flu, and he knew from a couple of his own unfortunate experiences that his mother was right. She had laughed weakly and said she hoped he wouldn't have another unfortunate experience after sleeping with her all night.

"That's not the kind of sleepover that's going to give me flu germs," he'd said with a grin, and she'd laughed again.

Even when she was sick, he made her feel happy. At the

same time, he made her sad. This was such bad timing to like a man so much.

After he'd left, she'd eaten the toast he'd left on the tray on her bedside table, taking one small bite at a time and swallowing slowly.

Shortly after noon, she dragged a quilt down the stairs, then wrapped it around her and turned on the TV in the front room. She watched a team of government agents, and they were all beautiful, even the men, one who Sunny had dated until she'd caught him sleeping with a fan.

Sunny always did have bad taste in men.

One day Raine would like to see imperfect people on these TV shows who weren't just there for comic relief while the beautiful ones got all the hefty roles.

She switched the channel and settled down to a show about people in Alaska looking for houses. Watching the show made her wrap the quilt more tightly around her. She should make more tea, but she was so tired. At least she wasn't crying, feeling sorry for herself. But even if she felt a little self-pity, all she had to do was think of Chuck.

She hardly knew him, but he made her feel like he cared. He wasn't perfect, she could tell that. He wasn't going to set the world on fire, and that was okay. She didn't want a fire starter. She wanted...someone to love her.

This need was new. Unlike her. Part of her alienation from her sister. Part of her weakness from the flu, and the need to have someone take care of her.

Or maybe it was part of the human need to love and be loved.

Of course, Chuck didn't love her.

Of course, she didn't love him.

They hardly knew each other. But something about him made her feel he would have her back. He wasn't a pack leader, like some of her mother's former boyfriends, who also fit in the *mean son of a bitch* category. Nor a man like Grant Wellington, who wanted to be God. Or the Devil. Nor was he a wannabe leader like Jarret.

It hurt like a fist in Raine's belly to know that Sunny had turned on her, but she understood her sister's need to believe that a man would love her and take care of her and make sure everything would be all right for the rest of her life.

That didn't mean that she forgave Sunny. This was what life with their mother and her always-changing boyfriends had done to Sunny. She was warped, and because of that, she'd turned on Raine.

Well, screw her, screw her husband, screw her greedy father-in-law who wanted to be God, and screw every man she knew.

She clicked off the TV, then turned her face into a pillow and told herself that later she would be strong, but for now she would just sob herself to sleep.

Eighteen

TODD GLANCED UP at the sky. Darkness was coming swiftly. He and Baxter had stopped about every twenty minutes or so, whenever Todd found a place to sit that would block the cold wind. He would take the thermos of water and a shallow bowl out of his backpack and pour water for Baxter to lap up. If he ran out of water, he planned to find clean-looking snow and put that in the bowl and hope it would melt.

Todd spotted a house ahead that looked closed up. Vacant for the winter. All wood and glass. Very likely the house of a summer resident. He steered Baxter toward it, then headed around the back to the patio. The door was locked, and he didn't try to open it. It might have an alarm. But the wind was blowing toward the east, and there were some snow-free areas on the all-weather planks.

"It's not going to be comfortable," he said to Baxter. "But this is going to be our home for the night."

Baxter looked at him with love in his eyes. Todd bent to hug Baxter's neck, the side of his head against Baxter's head.

"It's going to get better. I promise you that it will." A variation of an old kid's vow popped into his mind. Todd didn't know where it came from, but his voice was low and intense as he said, "I promise or I hope to die."

CHUCK TOSSED HIS keys on the kitchen table and sat down heavily on the chair nearest the back entrance. He put his elbows on the table and lowered his head into his hands, another day of defeat dragging him down.

Outside, the sun had darkened. He didn't move. He didn't know what time it was, nor did he care what time it was. He just wanted to sit and not talk to anyone in town again, nor have anyone talk to him.

"Hey." The voice was soft and feminine.

He didn't look up.

A hand settled on his right shoulder. A slight hand. Raine. He wanted her to go away. Because of her, he'd talked to one artist after another. If not for her, he would've given up. Said, *The hell with it. The hell with them.* But after her pep talk this morning, how could he have given up so easily?

Instead he'd talked to seven local artists. The most humiliating day of his life.

His eyes were closed, but he closed them even more tightly. He wasn't ready to talk. To admit that the people he'd known his whole life and he'd thought were his friends didn't believe in him.

If he stayed here with his head down, she would go away. She would know he was defeated. Defeated people needed to suffer alone.

But she didn't go away. And she didn't talk, her hand still on his shoulder. She just stayed silently behind him.

Slowly, the tension eased out of him. He sucked his breath all the way down his lungs, then let it out in a long exhale. He recalled that she'd been sick this morning.

He peered up. Her eyebrows were contracted in concern. Her eyes were steady on his.

"How are you feeling?" he asked.

"Awful."

"You shouldn't be standing here."

"Come into the living room."

"I had a bad day."

She stared at him. "I threw up twice this morning."

"No one in town trusts me to be successful, so that means I win. In fact, I win for a lifetime, not just for the day."

"Have you talked to everyone in town?"

"Of course not. I talked to a few before this, too. Probably another half dozen."

"In that case, you haven't talked to everyone in town, so you can't definitely know that. Besides, *I* trust you. *I* believe in you."

He turned his head away. He just wanted her to go away. "Then you're the only one. Your being sick can't top that."

She sighed, her hand slipping off his shoulder. He felt her behind him for a few long moments before she spoke, so softly her voice was close to a whisper. "I wish you were right."

He whipped his head around in time to see her heading out of the kitchen.

SHE HAD WANTED so badly to tell him the truth. Probably because he was the only one who cared for her, though that was just a delusion. He was her host. Nothing more. In reality, they hardly knew each other.

She needed to leave this place before she started to believe it for real.

She trod upstairs to pack, every step an effort, as if she'd just finished a marathon. She was past the puking part, but her body felt like one big ache. She'd slept all day, and she just wanted to fall into the bed and sleep some more. Her brain was as sluggish as her body, otherwise she wouldn't have said anything to him.

Stupid, stupid, stupid.

Footsteps strode after her. She tried to speed up, but she

was like a car with only one speed, and that was slower than a turtle.

When the arm curved around her waist, she was three steps away from the top, and her legs were shaking. Her whole body was shaking.

"What's wrong?" he asked. "I told you my problems. You can tell me yours."

She shook her head. "I'm tired. Just let me go. Just let me sleep. That's all that I need."

There was a sigh in her ear. He loosened his hold and lowered his arm around her ribs, stepping up next to her. When they reached the hallway, he scooped her up, and she squeaked, like she was Scarlet O'Hara and he was Rhett Butler.

She would much rather be a kick-ass heroine, saving him from the evil villain instead of him saving her. But that wasn't going to happen right now when she felt like a used washcloth. If she saw a bug on the floor, she wouldn't be able to vanquish it, much less a villain.

For this one time, she allowed her head to lean against the sweatshirt covering his chest. There was muscle under it, and she closed her eyes. For the second day in a row, she was using his strength. For the second day, it felt as if someone would make sure nothing bad happened to her. As if someone cared for her.

Though she knew all of that was bullshit, and the only one she could count on was herself, for this one night she would allow herself to believe that everything was going to be okay. That as long as this man was holding her, she would be safe and impervious to harm.

In her room, he lowered her to the unmade bed with the covers already pushed to the side. He pulled them over her just as a fit of the shivers struck her and she clamped her teeth together to keep them from chattering.

"You okay?" He gazed down at her, his expression worried.

She nodded fiercely, hunching her shoulders against the chills.

"No, you're not."

"I'll be okay..." Her teeth chattered, and she couldn't finish the sentence. "Just so...cold."

There were a few seconds of silence. Then he crawled next to her in the bed, pulled the cover over him, and spooned against her side, his warmth transferring to her.

"Better?" he murmured.

Tears heated her eyes as she nodded.

How had this happened? She was supposed to help him. She wanted to know how his day went. After all, she was the strong one.

At least, she had been the strong one for Sunny. But now Sunny leaned on her husband. The golden prince. It was fool's gold, but Sunny only saw the glitter.

She shook her head back and forth, not because of the cold but because she wanted to stop these thoughts. Her body was sick but that would heal. Her heart was different. She wasn't sure if her sick heart would ever heal.

Chuck put his arm around her. She sighed and burrowed into him.

A ridge pressed into her hip, growing thicker and longer. She closed her eyes, telling herself it didn't mean anything. It was a normal reaction of his male body to her female body, but for a few seconds, she let herself believe that someone cared about her. That someone wanted her.

Then, with a sigh, she wiggled her bottom slightly away from him.

"Did it bother you?" he asked.

"I know it's just biology—" she began.

His crack of laughter stopped her.

"Biology is pretty damn good." Laughter lingered in his voice. "Don't worry, I won't do anything. You're sick, and even if you weren't, I promised my mother I wouldn't, umm..."

"I know what *umm* means," she said.

He pressed against her again, and this time the ridge was gone. Most of it, anyway.

She sighed. He laughed again, then so did she.

It had been nice. Maybe it had been nice for him, too.

And she wasn't shivering anymore. A man's hard-on had cured her. She held back another laugh, and they lay like that for a while, his breathing and hers taking on the same in-and-out rhythm that made her once again think of sex, though she was not in any way horny. Instead she just felt safe and warm and cared for.

Did Sunny feel the same way when Jarret held her like this? If so, Dawn almost couldn't blame her.

Well, yes, she did. But at least she understood. That didn't mean she forgave her, it just meant she knew her sister was weak and needy, and wanted so badly to love that she would...

Steal from her sister.

That she would know Raine's life was in danger and not care.

That she would metaphorically stab her sister in her back and kick her to the curb.

That—

"You're tensing up again," Chuck murmured. "Go to sleep."

She closed her eyes and forced herself to breathe evenly. To relax. Even though she knew it wasn't going to make a difference. Even though it felt so good to have him cuddled up against her. So good that she felt herself falling, as if in a dream, with his warm body against her, and his warm breath on the side of her face, and his strong arm holding her to him. Giving her the feeling that everything was going to be all right.

Of course, that wasn't true. Everything was far from all right. But just this once, she would put it aside. Just this once, she would allow herself to drift off and listen to the beating of her heart in time with the beating of his. Just this once, she would tell herself that everything was going to be fine—and she would believe it.

Just for this once—right now—she would close her eyes, and when she woke up, ready to face reality, she would deal with...

Everything.

Nineteen

TODD HAD WOKEN up to sunlight and a barking dog. It had been dark last night when they'd come to this house with no lights on. Todd had taken the chance that it was someone's summer home, and he guessed he'd been right. Thanks to his exhaustion and the empty house blocking the wind, he'd slept well, despite the below-zero weather.

Squinting his eyes against the bright sun, he saw Baxter at the end of the back porch, his legs stiff and his head up, barking at something Todd couldn't see. A deer, perhaps, or a turkey. Or maybe an animal bigger and meaner, more skilled at killing and eating.

Todd was glad that he'd tied the end of the leash to the railing.

As he thought that, it occurred to him how much he'd changed in a short time.

That's what caring did. That's what responsibility did.

He got up. Todd didn't want Baxter to use the porch as a toilet.

Leave no footsteps. Since he'd started his hellish journey after he'd been released from the hospital, that had been his mantra. And one more. *Do no harm.*

"Come on, Bax." He unwound the end of the leash from the porch railing. "Elimination first, and then food and water. After that, our feet have some walking to do. Today we're going to our new home."

VINCE HAD ONLY planned on reading Howie's email from the mysterious Raine, but he still skimmed the beginning of Howie's other emails. The first sentence from Elena made him sit straight in the café and then check the IP address.

The same Beverly Hills IP that Grant and his father and, sometimes, himself used.

He started to read...

Howie, I know you're in touch with D somehow. Don't worry, I haven't said a word about it to anyone. In fact, I told you-know-who that you and D weren't close anymore. I've been so afraid. Every day since D left, I've been more and more afraid. You've probably heard that I'm pregnant. The news has been leaked, without my consent. I'm not happy with my father-in-law. I'm not happy with J, who seems to be ruled by his father.

And I'm real suspicious about a few things. I'm not sure if I should tell you, but I want you to tell D. I'm scared lately. Real scared. Please send this to D. Please send it right away.

Tell D I miss her. I miss her every day. I don't want a husband who is ruled by his father. I know they think I'm stupid, and maybe for a while love did make me open the stupid door. But now it's my eyes that are open, and my stupid is closing.

I'm afraid to say anything more. I feel like a prisoner here. I'm sending this message from the cell phone of the cleaning lady while she cleans the house. I'm paying her a lot of money not to say anything. I'm sorry I acted the way I did. Please tell D that I won't do it again. Please tell her that I need her. It wasn't the real me who agreed to those things they wanted to do to her. I think I was drugged. I think I still am, but not as much as before because they don't want to hurt the baby.

Things aren't right here. I don't trust anyone. I'm flushing the pills the doctor prescribed down the toilet.

Love you and miss you.
S

No name at the end. Just the initial.

There was no reply, and so far Howie hadn't forwarded the email. Neither had he deleted it.

Howie might have called Dawn. He probably had her number.

Things were happening. Moving on.

Vince needed to start moving on, too.

He stared out of his sliding ceiling-to-floor glass doors in his condo that led to his patio where he could see the ocean view. Today, the sun had shone all day, and it was in the low seventies. Paradise.

He looked up the northeastern edge of Wisconsin, the source of the IP address. Twenty-five degrees, and that was during the daytime. At night it should reach thirteen degrees.

Tomorrow, snow was predicted.

He walked to the glass patio doors, staring at the sky for a long time.

He'd been raised in a house of insanity. Of make-believe. Maybe another man could make believe that black was white and his life was okay but not him.

That knowledge left him floundering in a gray world, and he was tired of gray.

It was time to stop thinking. To stop plotting. Time to start *doing*.

Twenty

THE AIR SMELLED crisp. When Todd and Baxter had stopped last night, Todd had been glad to drop the backpack and duffel bag. Today, he felt strong and he walked with energy, as if he were eighteen again, nearly twenty-three years ago, when he'd first joined the Marines. Everything smelled clean. Through the tree branches, he caught glimpses of the frozen lake and white-blue sky. So beautiful that he stopped to take a big breath of air, letting it fill his lungs.

He glanced over at Baxter, whose eyes were bright and his doggy smile matched the way Todd felt inside.

They started walking again. He wanted to believe this was a wonderland, but he wasn't ready to go to that happy place yet.

Nothing was that good. Where people lived, so did hatred and meanness.

And sometimes murder.

☂

"I'M MUCH BETTER," Raine said at the kitchen table.

Chuck smirked, and she wanted to throw the perfect soft-boiled egg at him. She knew she was grumpy today, like an old man who complained about everything. Chuck was right, and she should have stayed upstairs. But she hated lying in bed another morning with the energy sapped out of her. When she'd plodded down the stairway this morning, gripping the railing tightly, she could swear she heard her bones creaking.

It was the aftereffects of flu. The body healing itself, and it was healing too slowly for her. She should feel happy that she'd had only one awful day. But she'd had too many awful days in her life, and she was only happy now for the good ones.

"You ready to go ice fishing?" he asked. "Or snowmobiling?"

She glared at him. Those were two activities she'd never thought of doing, though if she felt more energetic, she might try them.

"Or quilting," he said. "Some of the women in town get together and make quilts. Another group knits and crochets. We have a few men in that class." He glanced at the tea in front of her that was cooling by the minute. "Drink your tea. The ginger and cinnamon in it are good for flu and cold."

"How do you know that?"

"My mother."

"Is she a doctor?"

"No, but Google ginger and cinnamon and flu, and see what you can find. At least it won't cost you an arm and baby-making ovaries. By the way, my mother also says that when I'm grouchy, it means I'm on the mend."

"*Baby-making* ovaries?"

He shrugged, his eyes laughing at her.

"And your mother would say I'm grouchy?"

"Nah, but she might say you're bitchy."

"Seriously?"

"I'm never serious." His smile flattened, and two vertical lines indented between his eyebrows. "Just ask anyone in town. They'll tell you I'm the good-time guy."

"Where I come from, people are always telling other people what they are. But in reality, they know nothing."

"What kind of a place do you come from?"

"A place where looks are everything. A place where gossip is king."

"We don't have the looks judging—though I suspect that might be different in the schools."

"Everyone is judged by looks to an extent." She thought of her sister and the man she'd married, both of them as pretty as could be. She shuddered. She thought of all the men her mother had hooked up with. She shuddered harder.

"Need a blanket?"

She shook her head, then took another sip of the tea, imagining it flowing through her, healing her and revving up her sluggish brain cells, calling, *Wake up, cells! Wake up! Get your brain matter up and running.*

She took another sip of the odd-tasting brew and thought of the health benefits of chocolate. She wondered if he had any hot chocolate instead of tea.

"What does your mother say about your art mart idea?" she asked.

He stilled.

"You didn't tell her?" She raised her eyebrows.

"No reason to tell her."

"Is she in touch with any of your neighbors? Don't you think someone has told her?"

He shrugged. "She's probably ignoring it until I bring it up."

"Is that what your mother does?"

"Sometimes. What about your mother?"

"She's dead." She put up a hand up. "No sympathy, please. She died a month after my sister and I left home, and it wasn't a surprise. She was a drug addict."

"That must have been tough."

"I had my sister." She lowered her voice to a hoarse whisper. "Or she had me."

"Are you the oldest?"

"She's older. I'm stronger." She narrowed her eyes at him. "And smarter."

"What's she doing now?"

"She's with her husband."

"You sound...angry."

"I don't trust him. On the surface, he looks wonderful, but if you dig a little, you'll see cracks. And every time you look deeper, you'll see the cracks are bigger, too."

"And she knows how you feel," he said. "Is that why you left her? Is that why you ended up here?"

She hesitated, but the words were in her mouth, filling it up, wanting her to open up and tell him. Just like when she was writing a song, the words found the music. And when the songs were done, they needed a voice to sing them. Sunny's voice.

Until now. It had always been her and Sunny, and now... She had no one. Except this man she'd known for such a short time.

Yet he'd been here for her. And she'd been here for him.

In reality, they were just two strangers, but he'd slept with her last night when she was sick, holding her and comforting her. This morning, he'd made her breakfast— which she was paying him to do. But...oh, hell, she had no excuse except that she was human, and she needed to trust someone. She needed to tell someone. This need inside her was as strong as the need to eat and drink. To inhale and exhale.

"I left," she said, her voice steady, but her stomach muscles tensed, "because I was sure someone wanted to kill me. More than one person, actually. I'm pretty sure that it was her husband and father-in-law. Perhaps her brother-in-law, too." She frowned. "I think he has his own agenda."

Chuck's jaw clenched, and he stared at her. Coldly calm now, she picked up the spoon and dug it into the small bowl holding the egg. It had cooled a bit while they were talking, but the yolks spilled out. Perfect. Grabbing the salt shaker, she felt as if there had been a boulder on her shoulders, and now that she'd told him about her problems, the boulder had crumbled into nothingness.

Her hand started to tremble. She looked at it, feeling as if it were a foreign object, not connected to her body, wondering how this was happening.

Her hand shook now. Then it shook harder. The spoon flew out of her fingers, smashing onto the table, bouncing to the floor. "Oooh." She looked down at it on the floor, then up at him. "I'm sorry." Her voice was shaking, too.

She didn't understand it. This was all wrong. It must be from the flu. She wasn't normally a clumsy person. "I don't know what's wrong with me. I just..."

She stopped, her whole body shaking now. She gazed up at him. He stepped in front of her, bending to match her seated height, his arms held out for her. Her mouth gaped open as his arms curved around her back. He drew her against him and up from the chair.

She still shook, and she didn't cry. She wasn't crying. Yet silent tears dripped out of her eyes.

"I'm over it," she said, and her voice sounded funny, too high, and cracking. "I'm okay."

"You'll be okay here," he said, "because I'll make sure no one harms one hair on your head."

Twenty-one

BAXTER SNIFFED THE floors and the furniture. He could smell someone. A woman, though it was faint, as if she had been gone for a while.

Was this home? It was smaller than Baxter's old house, before he was pushed out of the car. But he liked smaller. Smaller made it easier to find Todd. When Todd had opened the door and let Baxter scamper in first, he'd said, "This is our new home."

Baxter knew the word *home*, but not all the other words. His other family, with the dad and the mom and the boy, used to say it often. *We're home, Blackie!* they would call out. *We're home.*

Then they would let him jump on them and lick their faces. At least, the mom and the boy had. Not the dad. Baxter had soon learned that he'd better not jump on the dad.

Was that why the dad had taken him to the city and let him out? Because he'd jumped on the boy and the mom?

Would Todd take him to the city and let him go, too?

He whimpered, and Todd dropped the big bag he'd been carrying and hurried to him.

"What's the matter?" he asked. "Are you hungry? Tired? Hurt?"

Baxter stared up at him, his heart beating fast. *I'm scared you'll leave me. I'm scared you won't want me. I'm scared you'll throw me away.*

RAINE HATED IT that she was crying. So weak and mewling. Though Sunny was the older sister, Raine had been the strong one. She'd had the ideas. She'd written the songs. She'd talked to the bar owners while Sunny stood there with a smile and looked pretty. She was always there to protect Sunny and never worried about herself.

But now someone was protecting her. Holding her with one arm around her back, then sliding his other arm beneath her butt. Lifting her to a carrying position, as if she were a child instead of a woman.

"What are you doing?" She heard the waver in her voice.

"I'm taking you up to bed," he said. "You're still not well. You need to sleep."

She should argue; she should protest. Instead, she leaned her head on his shoulder, like a damsel in distress in an old movie—a *very* old movie—as he carried her out of the kitchen, holding her as if she were breakable.

Later, she would be strong again. Right now she closed her eyes and let herself be comforted and safe in his strong arms.

CHUCK HAD NEVER felt the need to kill a man.

Until now.

He turned into his bedroom and laid her down on the queen-sized bed. Her eyes opened. "What..."

The sad look on her face made him want to hold her again. "This is my bedroom," he said.

She looked at the old-fashioned dresser. Then at the closet that was partially open. He kept the rest of the house neat, but his bedroom, not so much. There was a pair of jeans hanging on the chair in the corner. A sweatshirt on the floor.

He felt like the boy who'd never grown up.

Until today.

He sat on the edge of the bed, and in that moment it became clear to him what he needed to do. With his own life and, more important, with her.

"Don't worry. I'm going to protect you. I won't let anyone hurt you." He leaned toward her and took her hand in his.

"It's not up to you." She looked at him, her eyes sad. "I'm not looking for a hero."

"I'm no hero, but I'm still not letting anyone hurt you. It's a matter of doing what's right." He stared into her eyes. "I *need* to do this. Let me do this for you."

She nodded slightly.

"That's all I want to do," he said.

"All you want?" She swallowed, then whispered, "What if I want more than that?"

He stared at her, and she stared back at him. The whites of her eyes were pink from tears, and so were her eyelids.

"You're a guest. I promised my mother that I wouldn't sleep with"—he stopped, remembering he had slept with her last night—"have sex with any guest."

Not saying a word, she still stared at him.

He should leave it at that. Tuck her in and kiss her cheek...but he was compelled to say more. "And you're not well yet. I don't think you're up to it."

Her stare still didn't waver.

"We could sleep together again. Real sleep. Nothing else." He heard the hesitation in his voice. Not exactly the go-getter kind of guy. Not the alpha guy who won the ladies—though he'd never had a problem with women. Maybe because the women he was attracted to had their own strength and didn't need him to tell them what to do.

But he'd never been with someone who was running from a murderer.

If the tables were turned and it were him someone was trying to kill, he'd be begging her to hold him. To rock him. To never let him go.

"We can sleep together," she said, "for a short while."

He sat on the edge of the bed and took off his shoes. He thought about taking off his jeans, but his self-control could only take so much. So he kept his jeans on and rolled under the covers.

They came together like two teenagers who had been counting the seconds for this moment to happen. That's how it felt to him. She held on to him tightly, and he wrapped his arms around her, his eyes closed, breathing her scent in. Her body was heated, and the salty-woman smell was all hers, no one else.

His hips pressed against her, and he tried to press tighter. Only there was no tighter. There was only him and her.

And she was pressing just as tightly against him.

A small moan came from her mouth.

"This isn't working," he said, but he didn't push away.

"I know." Her whisper sent hot shivers through him.

He thought of telling her that he had to let go. But he didn't.

Maybe if she let go of him first, instead of holding on to him as if he were her lifeline. As if she were drowning, and he was her life jacket...

But he didn't.

He just kept holding her as if he would never let her go. And she held him just as tightly. Just as desperately.

Slowly, her hold loosened. So slowly he could hear the moments tick off on the clock by his bed. So slowly he could see the sky darken. Her breaths changed from quiet and quick to slower and easier. And then sleepier. More shallow. Yet still she clung to him. Yet he still held her.

His eyes closed, and he smelled her, and he thought, *Just for now. Just this. Just for now...*

Twenty-two

A MUTED HOOT jerked Baxter awake. His head lifted from the bed, and he sniffed, smelling the place with walls. A home. The hooting came again from outside the home. A bird or an animal, and it would never get inside.

He still wanted to jump out of bed and bark, warning all the creatures within hearing distance that he lived here now. He was protecting the house, and they'd better stay away. But too many hits with the paper from the dad at his other home stopped him. Instead he remained on the bed next to Todd, his ears up, his body alert. Ready to protect Todd. The hooting finally stopped, and Baxter closed his eyes, his body still tense.

He didn't know if he would ever feel completely safe again.

A hand settled on his side, and he stiffened again.

"What's wrong?" Todd asked. "What's wrong, buddy?"

As Todd's hand remained on his back, Baxter slowly relaxed. Todd had saved him. Todd had taken him to his new home. Todd fed him. Todd let him sleep on his bed.

Baxter would do anything for Todd. Anything.

☂

RAINE WOKE UP feeling as if she were in a cocoon. Feeling happy. Safe. Cared for.

She knew immediately that Chuck was holding her. Her

open mouth was against his chest, and she felt a wet spot on the side of her neck and her chin. Saliva. Her saliva.

Still, she didn't move. It felt too good to be held like this.

There was warmth on her face. Though her face was pressed against his shoulder, she could feel the rays of sunlight on the left side of her face. She guessed it must be midmorning, and they'd slept a few hours.

She felt...glorious. She must have needed that sleep. She must have needed his arms around her, and his body pressed against her.

Chuck's hard body was better than chocolate.

The thought made her giggle.

He sighed and moved slightly away.

Oh, no! She closed her lips, but her mind was saying all the things her voice didn't say.

Kiss me.

Ravish me.

Make me feel good.

Her mind was inappropriate and not so smart today. That's what hormones did to a woman.

She pushed her head slightly away from his, and, sure enough, she felt a string of saliva on her chin. Yuck.

Looking up, she saw his eyes were open. "Sorry about the saliva."

He smiled, and she wanted to melt. Then he lifted his hand, grabbed a tissue from the nightstand, and wiped it off. Embarrassing, though she didn't flinch.

"No problem." He grinned. "I've been around plenty of drooling dogs."

She laughed and reached her free hand up to punch his shoulder, though she was still weak, and it probably felt like a baby's tap.

He moved back from her. "We both needed that nap."

"Sleeping together is becoming a habit with us."

"Some habits aren't good habits."

Some were, she thought. But he was right, because this sleeping together habit would lead to something else, something that he said he'd promised his mother he wouldn't do with the B and B guests. She believed him. He just seemed so...honest.

She sighed, though she was not a fan of sighing. Sighs were for people who yearned, and yearnings were for dreamers who weren't working hard to achieve those dreams. She preferred to do whatever it took to make her dreams come true.

He rolled out of bed and stood, his legs slightly apart. "Feeling better?"

She took stock of herself before nodding.

He smiled, the outer corners of his eyes crinkling.

She frowned. "What is it?"

"You. I like the way you don't answer right away. I like the way you wait to make sure you're telling the truth."

"I can be spontaneous." But even as she said the words, she knew that most of her spontaneity came with her music and her lyrics.

Or when her life was in danger.

She pushed up slightly with her right arm. "But early on in my life, I learned to be careful."

"I know a little what that's like. My dad was killed when I was a kid. Probably by a jealous husband. He was a drinker and he cheated on my mother. He used her."

"I'm sorry," she said.

"Don't feel sorry for me. My mother was strong, and she protected me from the worst of it. I can remember thinking she was too strict, and my father was the fun guy. But you didn't have a responsible parent. You had to be the responsible one. The protector."

She pushed down the cover. If she didn't leave soon, she'd be feeling sorry for herself. "I have to use the bathroom. And after that, we should talk."

"You know what the three scariest words are for a man?" he asked as he helped her out of the bed.

"Your team lost," she said immediately.

He laughed. "Okay, second worst. *We should talk.*"

She reached up and patted his cheek. "Men are so fragile." She walked past him, smiling and happy, even as she knew that Grant and Jarret and especially Vince, the youngest and scariest Wellington, were most likely getting closer by the minute.

Twenty-three

COP. NO, NOT a cop, Todd thought, peering through the peephole in the door. A deputy. Standing on Todd's front porch. The deputy moved to the left, and Todd could see the sheriff's car parked on the street in front of his house.

Baxter was barking loudly, and Todd grabbed Baxter's collar. He wanted to close the door on the deputy and yell at him to go away. But that's not what mentally healthy people did. People who couldn't control their nerves did that. People who expected bad things to happen every day.

And often bad things did happen. Every day.

Todd shushed Baxter, and he finally stopped barking, but Todd could see that the dog's muscles remained tense. Todd opened the storm door a couple inches, the frigid air puffing in.

"Hi, I'm Deputy Pete Masters." The deputy was about six feet tall and rangy. He grinned. "Your lawyer called the department to let me know you're staying here. She said you're a former vet."

"Marine," Todd said.

"Thank you for your service," Masters said.

Todd nodded. Words were easy. The vets Todd saw on the streets and in the homeless shelters didn't need thanks. They needed *help*.

"I live just a few blocks away." Masters jerked his thumb toward the north. "I'm assigned to the town."

"Nice," Todd said. That actually made sense, something that wasn't common with most institutions.

Maybe living in Trouble Bay would be okay.

"You need anything, give me a holler." Masters held out what looked like a business card.

Todd took the card and glanced down at the deputy's name and a phone number. Before he could say anything, Masters was bending to rub Baxter behind his ear.

"Great dog." Masters pulled back. "I'll see you around."

He trod down the sidewalk, his feet crunching on snow, the sound reminding Todd that he needed to shovel his sidewalk.

Todd frowned. This was a strange place. He wasn't sure how he felt about it. All this niceness made him leery. And nervous. If it weren't for Baxter, he might head back to the streets.

☂

GRANT WAITED FOR Vince on the upper patio, leaning on the rail overlooking the ocean. Grant's hair was white and thick, his eyes a darker blue than usual, his skin turning ruddier the last couple years.

Vince was always alert around his father, but in the harsh sunlight he became more alert. Since having two moles removed last year, Grant had avoided direct sunlight. One mole had been on the bridge of his nose. That had been benign but the mole on his left thigh had been diagnosed as melanoma. The doctor had cut it out, and said he was fine now, but for the first time Vince could remember, his father had shown fear. Not today, though. Closer to him now, Vince saw small white particles on his face from what was undoubtedly a high-end sunscreen.

Vince stopped two steps in. Certainly his father hadn't shown fear after Vince's mother had died. In Vince's mind, he saw his father twenty-one years ago, his eyes blazing as he told Vince that his mother had fallen down the stairs and would be watching over him in Nirvana.

In his father's eyes, Vince had seen victory instead of grief.

The mental image stopped Vince, and his father turned. "What's your problem?"

"No problem at all. Aren't we all in a state of nirvana?"

Grant narrowed his eyes. It was clear that he was in one of his brooding moods. When he was like this…

Grant stalked up to him, his mouth set. He lifted his arm. "I don't like the way you talk to me."

There was a second of time when Vince could have stepped aside and avoided the fist. Normally he did. But this time, he let his father's arm swing up into his face, hitting his cheek bone, the smack hard, not holding back. Knocking him to the side so he had to take two sidesteps to keep his balance.

"What the fuck are you doing fucking around, not getting anywhere?" Grant's face was turning redder. "You have all our resources, yet you're doing this all yourself. Not using the normal agencies." His fist came up again.

This time when his father's fist swung at him, Vince put up his arm, stopping it. Instead of stepping back, he stepped forward. "Remember the last time you hit me?"

Grant glared at him.

"I told you if you did that again, I'm walking away."

"And I told you,"—Grant's spittle splattered on Vince's face—"that if you walked, you'd be sorry."

They stared at each other for a long moment. Vince dropped his arm. After a second, so did his father.

"To answer your question," Vince said, "I didn't involve any of the team because I thought you'd want to make sure no one but the family knew what you were planning."

"What *we* were planning," Grant said. "My supporters are loyal to me. They know what would happen if they aren't."

"It's already on the news that's Dawn Keighly is missing. We already have people looking out for her. However,

I'm doing my own research, and I'm keeping what I find out private. Dawn Keighly is a triple-Grammy-winning songwriter. If anything happens to her, and if any of our people even have a whiff of a suspicion that you, Jarret, or I are involved, it will be bound to get out. Someone will tell the press."

"So you do have something." Grant stared into his eyes, as if he could see the truth in his pupils.

Vince stood still, not looking away.

After all these years, he could lie to the devil.

Vince's eyes narrowed as he looked into his father's icy blue eyes. The eyes of the devil.

"I'm not sure," he said.

"Then go find her," Grant ordered. "Be sure."

Vince nodded and stepped back before snapping around to walk away.

It was always a good idea to take a few steps away from his father before turning his back on him.

The second good idea was to walk away swiftly. You never knew if Grant would kick you.

Or hit you on the head with something.

It wasn't until Vince stepped into the elevator that he breathed easily.

In a short time, he would be on a plane, on his way to Wisconsin. On the hunt for his sister-in-law's sister.

And may God help her, because she was going to need all the help she could get.

"YOU DID THIS," Sunny screamed at Jarret. "This was why you were so insistent that I should go to the gynecologist you recommended. The birth control pills she gave me were fake. You set me up, you bastard."

He glanced around, panic on his face. And she felt like someone punched her in her stomach. She hadn't known that for sure. It had been a wild guess.

Now he was looking sick. Good. He was used to being kowtowed to because his daddy was the head of the Nirvana Now Church.

Well, fuck him. She was the one with eleven million Twitter followers, not him. He barely went on Twitter or Pinterest or any of the other sites.

Her followers *loved* her. They *loved* her voice. They *loved* her music.

He didn't love her. He loved who she was. And now she was pregnant, and he was so proud. Not of her, but that he'd knocked her up.

And Grant...he'd hugged Jarret and had said, "We did it! We did it."

Maybe she wasn't the brainiest woman in the world, but as she'd watched them, a chill had gone through her.

Then they'd left to talk about it themselves.

And she'd waited, and she'd waited longer. And now...

Instead of replying to her, he picked up the phone. "Eileen, please make sure that no one comes up to the second floor."

"What the fuck are you doing?" Sunny screamed.

He kept his back to her. "My wife isn't well."

She picked up a glass of water from the side table, and she threw it at him. "Bastard. Will you turn around and *talk* to me?"

"Eileen, tell my father to return home as soon as he can? We have a problem."

She felt cold. Like meat-in-a-freezer cold.

Dawn had warned her about Jarret and his father.

As usual, Dawn was right.

Fuck, fuck, fuck.

She grabbed her cell phone, ran to the bathroom, hearing the footsteps pounding behind her. She slammed the door, and he tried to open it, yelling her name. "Sunny, Sunny, Sunny, you bitch."

The same tone her mother's last boyfriend had used. *"Sunny, Sunny, Sunny, you bitch. Open the fuckin' door."*

144

And then there had been a big bang. A terrible sound.

It's okay, Dawn had called. *It's okay. He won't hurt you again.*

Her hands shaking, Sunny had opened the door, and there was Dawn, smaller and younger. Sixteen years old, skinny and so flat-chested she barely needed the A-cup bra she wore. She was shaking, her face as pale as a ghost. In her right hand, she clung to the handle of a wrought iron frying pan.

Sunny had looked down at their mother's latest boyfriend sprawled on the floor, blood coming out of his head and his ear.

I think we should leave, Dawn had whispered. *He's breathing. But we should leave now.*

They'd taken all the money from his wallet. Their mother had been conked out on the bed, and hadn't woken up while they riffled through her purse. They'd packed clothes, and Dawn had taken her guitar, and in an hour they'd hitched a ride to Memphis.

Ten years later, she was in a similar situation, but this time there was no Dawn around to save her.

She got on her cell phone and called Dawn's number.

It was disconnected.

Her belly churned, and not from the baby. From fear.

Jarret had been quiet for a couple moments, no doubt calling security. She didn't have time to search more.

She had to do *something*. She'd called Howie before, and he hadn't helped at all. She could tell he was angry at her. She didn't blame him, but

Heavy footsteps came. Not in their rooms, but outside. From the stairway.

Then she heard the bedroom door to the hallway open, and Jarret calling out something, the words muffled by the thick bathroom door, but she could hear the urgency in his tone.

Oh, God. Oh, Jesus. Oh, fuck.

It was the security people. He was going to lock her in this place.

She glanced down at the phone and pressed nine-one-one.

Twenty-four

TODD'S SHOUTING WOKE up Baxter. Barking, protecting his human, Baxter jumped off the bed—but no one was in the room. And Todd was still on the bed, one arm hitting the covers.

Baxter's heart was pounding. Todd stopped thrashing but he called out, "*Noooo. No!*"

Whatever was wrong with him was bad. Baxter whimpered, then jumped back up on the bed. He nuzzled his nosed against the side of Todd's face, and Todd stilled, only his harsh breaths making noises now, his chest expanding and then deflating. Baxter whimpered again, asking, *Are you okay? Are you better?*

He nuzzled the side of Todd's face again, letting Todd know he was there. Letting Todd know he would protect him. Letting Todd know he loved him.

Todd had saved his life. Todd had fed him. Todd had given him a home again.

Baxter whimpered once more, and Todd's arms went around his neck. "I love you, Baxter. I love you."

His voice was thick like mud, but Baxter recognized the word *love*. He knew what the word meant. The boy at his old home used to say it to him. It hurt to hear Todd say it, and at the same time, it made him happy.

He licked the side of Todd's face. His way of saying, *I love you, too.*

RAINE'S EYES SQUINTED open to fading sunlight that shone through the lone window in the room. She knew right away she was in Chuck's bed, and that it was comfortable and felt just right. As if she were Goldilocks, and all the other beds had been wrong.

"How do you feel?"

Chuck's voice was like soft butter to her ears. She turned to look at him. He was sitting in a wooden rocking chair in the corner of the room, just watching her.

"How long have I been sleeping?"

"Most of the morning and afternoon."

"I feel...almost human again." She stretched out her legs and noted that the stuffiness in her head was mostly gone.

"Good."

"We never did have that talk."

The corner of his lips tilted upward. "Good. You hungry?"

"I'd like to take a bath first."

His lips tilted higher. "You need help?"

She laughed, remembering that a couple days ago the world seemed like a dark and horrible place, and her life had resembled the song about the only luck the singer had was bad luck.

Now she was on the run, and she'd lost almost everything. It should have been the worst time in her life—and she'd had a lot of worse times—yet she felt...happy. As if those rays of sunshine were playing happy guitar notes inside her heart.

She slid out of bed and stood. Her body was achy, the kind of ache that needed a warm soak. She stretched again and looked to the side, catching Chuck staring at her, his eyes hot.

She was wearing a sweatshirt and loose flannel pajama bottoms.

To be practically drooling over her, he must be imagining what she looked like naked.

She swallowed a laugh.

She wanted to dance but her body was still weak. And if she did dance, she would probably fall.

And she wanted to sing in her croaking voice that would scare him away on the first note.

And she wanted to write a song. A love song.

Stupid, stupid, stupid.

But as she walked down the hallway and then up the stairs to her suite, she heard a song in her head. It said, *"Sometimes the head is stupid, and the body is smart."*

An hour later, she'd changed her pajamas for a sweater and jeans, and she was inside a pub eating a grilled cheese with ham sandwich and fries and thinking that this was the best meal she'd eaten since before her sister married.

A country song came out of the speakers, a woman saying someone was going to miss her. Raine wondered if Sunny missed her, and the thought made her lose her appetite, and she set down the sandwich. She turned to the bar, where Chuck was waiting for the beers he was getting for both of them.

"Chuck said you were sick," a woman said. "Glad you're feeling better now."

She turned. Standing next to their table for two was a fortyish woman on the chunky side with short reddish-brown hair and rosy cheeks.

"You're a skinny thing," the woman said. "Chuck looks smitten."

Raine laughed. In Los Angeles, she was average. Here they probably thought she was anorexic.

"I'm Darlene." The woman grinned. "I used to babysit Chuck. He was a good kid. And cute." The woman sniffed. "I'm glad to see him with a woman again and not trying to get people to sign on for his flea mart stuff."

"Flea mart stuff?" Raine sat straighter. Her skin prickled

but she kept her tone calm. "It's an art mart, and I think it's a great idea."

Darlene gave her a pitying look. "Of course you think it's a great idea. Chuck's single, and he knows how to flirt with the girls. And look at him!" Darlene swept her hand out. "It's hard to resist that face. Even for me, and I changed his diapers."

"What's hard for me to understand," Raine said, her usual husky voice sharp, "is why the people in this town are so set against his idea. I think a lot of tourists would come to the art mart. If I were on vacation here, I would go. He's only charging a low percentage, lower than the galleries, and if it doesn't sell, he gets nothing. And if nothing else, it's exposure for the artist. Maybe someone will want to see the artist's other works. Maybe they'll hire the artist to do something just for them. They'd get all the money for it, and Chuck wouldn't get anything. There's no way an artist would lose money."

"Oh, honey." Darlene sighed and shook her head sympathetically. "You just don't know Chuck like we know him. This is a small town, and we've known him since he was a boy. Chuck isn't an entrepreneur. Chuck is...well, Chuck."

Raine's mouth fell open, and she stared at Darlene.

"We just don't want him taking on something that he can't handle," Darlene went on. "Something that won't be a success. Not for him. We care about Chuck. We don't want him to go bankrupt or do something he'll be sorry for."

There was a noise behind Darlene. Out of the corner of her eyes, she saw Chuck, but she kept her gaze on Darlene.

"I'm guessing you come from a big city," Darlene went on. "Things are different in a small town. We support our friends here."

"Darlene's right," a husky-sized man with a full gray beard said at the next table. "We have each other's backs."

Raine turned to him and saw him nodding smugly.

"And when they turn their backs," Raine asked, "is that when you stick the knife in them?"

The smugness wiped off his face. She pushed her chair back. She hadn't finished the sandwich, but it didn't matter. She'd lost her appetite.

"You're right," she said. "I've come from a big city, and it's a place where I have friends who believe in me and have my back. Maybe not everyone, but in this small town, everyone seems to look at Chuck's past instead of the facts. The facts are that he has a great idea. A *brilliant* idea. It's not that this is a small town, it's that the people in it have small minds."

A noise came from behind Darlene to the left. Twisting slightly, she spotted Chuck, his jaw set, his lips flattened in a line.

She raised her chin and turned back to Darlene and the bearded guy, who still had his mouth open. "I don't see friends supporting friends here. I see friends *judging* friends." She grabbed her coat, then stepped toward Chuck. "I've lost my appetite. Let's get the hell out of here."

He stepped past Darlene, took his jacket off the back of the chair, and turned toward the exit. Raine had noticed the door opening and closing during the last ten minutes or so. This must be the start of the dinner crowd—or bar crowd—especially in the winter when the nights came sooner. The place was already half-full now, and it was still early.

They headed toward the front door. A couple people called out to Chuck, but he didn't turn his head. Didn't acknowledge anyone. He only looked down at her for a moment, putting his hand on her back. Both of them headed toward the exit.

"Chuck!" Darlene called. "Chuck, we didn't mean anything."

Chuck's hand pressed harder against her back. He didn't stop. He didn't look back. He didn't speak.

Neither did she.

Twenty-five

WALKING OUTSIDE, TODD told Baxter about his Marine friends while Baxter trotted alongside him. Todd told Baxter about other things, too, though he knew the dog didn't understand a word. Bombs and explosions and IEDs. About three blocks away from home, his voice rose, and Baxter whimpered.

Todd stopped walking and knelt down and hugged Baxter. "I'm scaring you."

Normally, when he felt like this, it would get worse, and he'd look for a place to hunker down and curl up, his whole body shuddering. But with Baxter, he didn't have the luxury to stop like that. He had to keep going. He had to take care of Baxter.

He stood and forced himself to walk even though he wanted to crawl into a box and curl up in it. Shaking, he put one foot forward, then the other foot forward. Again. And again. And again. After a while, the shudders slowed and then stopped. He breathed easier, his tensed muscles loosening. Everything was all right again. Or as right as it could be when so much was wrong.

Todd imagined that talking to Baxter was like talking to God, because both God and dogs loved unconditionally.

CHUCK DIDN'T SPEAK on the drive back to the B and B. It was a short drive, only a couple blocks, but he'd taken the car because Raine wasn't well. He might have taken it anyway, because the temperature was in the single digits, and he wasn't a fool.

No matter what his so-called friends thought of him.

"Chuck—"

"I don't want to talk about it," he said.

"Okay. I understand. More than you know."

Her voice wobbled a little on the last four words, but he kept his hands on the wheel, staring straight ahead until they got home. He let her out by the back door, then parked the car in the garage. When he got in, she was boiling water on the stove.

"I thought you'd like tea or hot chocolate," she said.

"Or beer."

She shrugged and turned to the stove, standing with her back to him, slender and vulnerable.

He sighed, and it felt as if, along with exhaling his breath, he was letting go of his anger. He stepped up behind her and put his hands on her shoulders, the sweater she wore soft under his palms. He leaned his jaw and cheek against the top of her head.

"I don't want to talk about what happened," he said.

She moved her head slightly, leaning back against him. "Not now...but later you should talk."

He laughed softly, because that was such a woman thing. To put out her need to talk. To let him know it wasn't over.

"I want to sleep with you," he said.

"We have been sleeping together."

He laughed again, and this laugh was more real. The swollen lump of anger mixed with hurt inside him—an ugly, ugly thing—was shrinking a tiny increment with every spurt of laughter. With every moment he held her.

"You're very literal," he said.

The water was boiling, and she reached over to turn off the burner, pulling away from him.

He immediately missed her.

"I like words." The stove off, she twisted in his arms, her face looking up at him about five inches. "I like clearness. I like the truth."

"Even if the truth hurts?"

She didn't answer at first, taking a long look in his eyes, and for a second he felt that she could see through his eyes. See into his mind and his soul and his heart.

"You have eyes like an alien probe," he said.

She laughed. And there was something he hadn't seen on her face before. Total joy.

Looking at her, he felt as if the sun had burst inside him.

He was going to give her the same feeling in bed.

All that had happened at the bar wasn't going away, but for now...for the night...he didn't care.

He moved closer to her, their bodies lightly touching.

"What about your promise not to have sex with the guests?" she asked, her eyes bright and filled with laughter. As if she knew that promises were going to be smashed and burned. *Gloriously* smashed and burned.

He smiled, and inside him his smile was growing and beaming. "That's just for paying guests. I'm giving you your money back."

"I don't—"

He bent his head slightly and his lips angled against her parted lips. Her breath sucked in, a sound between a sigh and a laugh. Then she melted against him, and he pressed against her. Holding her tightly to keep from sinking to the kitchen floor.

Her kiss healed him. Set him on fire. Filled him with want and need. Her arms held him as if she didn't want to let him go. And she moaned as if his kiss and his arms and his body were having the same effect on her.

Setting her on fire.

The kiss lasted moments before he tore his lips from hers. "Let's go to my bedroom."

"My bed is bigger."

"Mine is closer." He kissed her again. She clung to him, and he clung to her, too. As if they were two humans holding each other tightly to keep from drowning.

With a jerk, she pulled away from him. "Now," she said, her voice low. "Now."

Holding hands, they hurried around the corner to his bedroom, their breaths short and fast.

☂

RAINE FELT LIKE liquid. Like warm water. Floating.

She tried to gather all the feelings, all the non-expressions and change them into words and meanings. Words were her livelihood, but lying in bed next to him, the covers pulled over them, her body feeling like chocolate melting in the hot sun, there was only *now*.

How to describe bliss in a lyric? How to describe wonderment? How to describe joining together with a hard male body as ecstasy jolted through you in lightning bursts and made you cry out and cry out and cry out? Telling him that you never wanted to stop.

She closed her eyes. Stopping the search for words.

Next to her, his harsh breaths were slowing, and she smiled slightly. Just for these moments, she would let it go. Just for the moment, she would breathe in and out, and in and out, with her whole body relaxed so she felt—in the loveliest way imaginable—as if she had no bones.

"I've never—" he began, then stopped.

"Me neither," she whispered, not opening her eyes.

He took her hand in his, and she drifted off, thinking that later they could figure it out. Later they would take care of everything. And everyone.

Or maybe they'd just do this again, and nothing else would matter...

Twenty-six

TODD LEFT TO go to the grocery store only a few blocks away. Despite the cold, the sun was shining, and apparently the townspeople were taking the opportunity to walk and soak up some of the sun. Though he kept his eyes down, people stopped him. They didn't seem to know or care that *eyes down* meant *leave me the hell alone*. They were nice to him, too. Asking about his dog. A couple old guys invited him to a poker game, but he mumbled that he had things to do around the house.

This was awkward and uncomfortable. He was used to being ignored. Used to eyes that looked past him. As if he weren't really there.

In the grocery store, he headed to the dog food area. He picked up two small bags of dog food. He would see which one Baxter liked best before buying a bigger bag.

A pregnant woman who must have been in her early twenties was in the aisle, too. When he saw her take hold of a fifty-pound bag, he stepped in front of her and lifted it onto the bottom of the cart. She thanked him and told him she knew who he was already, the Marine who'd inherited Sarah Vardy's house, and she was sorry about his aunt.

Before he could thank her, she said her name was Amy, and her boyfriend was going to sing at the bar on Friday, and he should stop by and say hi.

He nodded, but there was no way he was going. He

avoided bars. Booze made him a crazy person, and he was already more than a bit crazy.

But he ended up walking out to her car parked in the small lot and hefting the bag into her trunk.

She gave him a hug, her pregnant belly pushing against his stomach.

"I'll see you at the bar!" she called before she closed the car door.

He shook his head as he walked home with his bags of groceries. He didn't know how he felt. A mix of nervousness and excitement maybe.

Trouble Bay was a very odd town.

"WE'RE IN TROUBLE." Grant's words spat out.

Vince stood in the bedroom of the Milwaukee hotel suite, looking out of the long vertical window. It was midmorning, the sunlight sparkling in the air. So different from LA. He planned on leaving tomorrow, and when he'd seen his father's name on the cell phone, he'd thought about ignoring it for two seconds. Two wonderful seconds. But not answering might lead to more trouble, so he'd picked the phone up.

He would face that trouble soon, but wasn't ready yet. Not until he found Dawn.

"What is it?" Vince asked.

"The bitch."

"Dawn." Vince stiffened. If she'd been found, this had been a wasted trip.

"Not her." Grant scowled. "Not the sister this time. It's Sunny."

Vince raised his eyebrows. The good sister turned bad? He wasn't surprised. She was a singer with a few bestselling songs and over a million fans. She had a pop star's ego. She wasn't stupid. She was just used to being adored and had taken Jarret at face value. By now she probably realized her prince was a frog who needed her more than she needed him.

"She called the police yesterday," Grant said. "It's on the news. The fucking news. This is an embarrassment. How the fuck could she do this to us?"

"She's a diva."

"Jarret should have married the younger sister. Turns out she was the one with the real talent."

"Sunny's the sister in the spotlight. The golden girl. You know if there's a choice between glitter or no glitter, Jarret is going for the fool's gold."

There was silence on the other end, and Vince looked out at the city again. Not speaking first. His father went for the fool's gold, too. The brassy blondes with the long legs and the big boobs. Vince's mother had been the exception. Dark-haired, sleek, and smart. She was class, and Grant went for the blond bombshells. But his mother had been too beautiful for him to resist. Too exotic. Too rich. Too sophisticated.

Too good for him.

Some men, when someone was too good for them, they had to dominate them. Bring them down to their level.

And if the woman didn't allow the degradation, these men had to destroy her.

"Never mind Jarret," Grant said in clipped tones. "What's done is done. The police couldn't find a reason to charge us with anything, but she convinced them to take her to our neighbor's house."

"*Our* neighbor?" Vince frowned. "The old rocker?"

A snarl came from the other end of the phone, either because of his father's disdain for the rocker or because the rocker was about the same age as Grant.

Vince grinned.

"I bet he was thrilled when she came over there," his father said. "He hates me."

"You tried to boot him out of his home."

"He has orgies. How does that look? A man in charge of a

flock of people, telling them how to reach Nirvana, living next to a guy who smokes pot every day and who knows what the hell else?"

"Maybe he's your nearest neighbor, but you're not exactly a casual walk away from his place." Vince grinned again, enjoying this conversation. "Especially since you'd have to climb a half mile up the road. *And* he threatened to shoot you or anyone from Nirvana who stepped on his property."

"That son of a bitch. He's lucky if I don't hire a marksman to take care of him for me."

Vince's grin flattened. It wasn't funny anymore. "I wouldn't advise you to do that."

"I didn't ask for advice," Grant snapped. "The hippie singer is probably laughing his ass off. I hate to think of him lording it over me."

"He is lording it over you. Literally, at least." Vince pictured the old rocker's house on top of the hill, and the Nirvana Now compound a level below him. When Grant had bought the land, he'd hoped to convince the old rocker into donating his land to Nirvana Now. He'd thought that his pot-smoking neighbor would be easy to convert. Instead, his charm had fallen flat on the rocker. And in the years that had passed since Nirvana's purchase, the rocker had become living proof that marijuana didn't kill brain cells.

A hissing sound came from the phone. Vince imagined his father was like the Wizard of Oz, with his head blowing up, getting bigger and bigger with each inhale.

Until he exploded into pieces.

"You need to get home now," Grant said.

"I've got a lead on the missing sister."

"Fuck the sister," Grant said. "It's Sunny who's important. She's carrying my grandchild in her belly, and your brother fucked up handling her. I need you. Get home as soon as you can."

He hung up.

Vince put the phone away. Apparently the golden son was not the favorite. Not today.

Their father had brought them up to regard each other as rivals. It had amused Grant. With a four-year difference in their ages, Jarret had been taller and bigger than Vince, and he hadn't hesitated on pushing him around when no one was near.

Vince had avoided him, knowing that some day he would get revenge. Some day he would be on top.

He wasn't sorry Sunny had left Jarret. He was only surprised it had taken her so long. She had an ego. She was, after all, a rock star.

Not like the younger sister. It was only after Dawn had disappeared that Vince realized how special she was. He'd known that she'd written the songs and the music. He's known she was smart. But she had been so quiet. Not timid but more of an observer than a participant.

That should have told him something right there. Told him that she was watching and making decisions in her mind.

Just the way he did.

He frowned. Like his brother and father, he'd seen Sunny in all her golden glory, and he'd been blinded by her light. Too blind to look hard enough at the sister in her moon glow.

He took three strides back to the window, his hands clenched behind his back, and stared out of the windows for a long time. His mind made up, he turned to go down and eat breakfast. After that, he had a three-hour drive, and it wasn't going to be to the airport.

He'd heard people talking in the lobby about a flu epidemic hitting the Midwest. As far as his father was concerned, he was about to have a bout of a very nasty flu.

Twenty-seven

TODD IS HERE! He is here!

Peering out the back window, Baxter jumped off the couch and stood in front of the door, his tail wagging furiously, his mouth open, his tongue out, his breath panting. He heard the car door open, then close.

Todd is coming! Todd is walking up the sidewalk!

It was the best thing that had ever happened. Todd had come home. Todd had come back to him.

Baxter had been afraid that maybe Todd had left because of the bad smell in the house. He'd been afraid that Todd had gone away and would never come back.

SUNNY SAT ON Ledge's poolside lounger, a big, half-circle thing that could fit three people easily, with an overhead canopy to block her face in case any paparazzi tried to take a shot from a helicopter.

A mix of hot emotions swirled inside her. She was angry at Jarret and his father. Angrier at herself.

Sad for turning on Dawn.

Thankful for Ledge. Thankful for the song Dawn had insisted she sing with him four years ago. Dawn had said Ledge had a voice like an angel. As usual, she'd been right. Their voices had soared together.

Sunny could hear the excitement in Dawn's voice now.

He's one of those guys people love. He fought for the truth and for the farmers and for the working people. He's a great songwriter, too. I want him on the song about the angel talking to him, and his reply. You can be the angel. People will love it.

Immediately Sunny had pictured herself as an angel. Though she'd wanted to be more with the younger and cooler crowd, and not yesterday's heroes, she'd agreed. After all, it was only one song.

It had turned out to be her best professional experience. He really was the coolest man, the kindest man. Their song had turned out to be the hit of the album. Their voices had woven together—hers soaring and his gruff—and somehow it had worked magic.

She'd appeared on all the important talk shows, and she'd gotten her first Grammy nomination for her duet with Ledge, the same year that Dawn had gotten her first songwriting Grammy for "Lonely Girl."

How odd that Ledge had turned out to live in the house above her father-in-law's house. How odd that Grant hated him and belittled him and had insisted that Sunny stay away from him.

And for the last five months, she'd stayed away from this man she revered.

Just because her husband had told her she shouldn't go up here.

Fool, fool, fool. She clenched her fists and her teeth, her face screwed up. She'd been a fool, just like Dawn had said.

Footsteps slapped on the patio. Ledge. She couldn't look, she just stared at the blue waters in the pool, the sun sparkling down on it.

He sat on the other side of the round lounge seat. He was a tall, rangy man with pure white hair pulled back in a ponytail. His face was thin and lined, yet he was still handsome. She glanced over at him. He wore baggy gray pants and a long-sleeved shirt with red flowers over a black

T-shirt. As if he'd grabbed the first thing from his wardrobe that had come to hand.

"Having regrets?" he asked.

"I'm having anger," she said, and heard the wobble in her voice. "I'm so pissed off, and I'm not just angry at my husband. I'm really angry at myself." Her eyes filled with tears. "I was so stupid. I can't believe how stupid I was."

"Sweetheart, we're all stupid at one time or another."

"You don't know... I wasn't just stupid about my marriage, it's worse."

"Angel—"

She broke into tears, her hands over her face. "I can't tell you what I did. I can't. You'll hate me."

A sigh came from him. She heard him stand up, and seconds later, she felt the dip of the cushion next to her. Then he put his arms around her shoulders, drawing her against his side. She turned and sobbed on his shoulder.

She didn't deserve his consolation. She didn't deserve his generosity and kindness. She'd been a bad friend and, worse, a very bad sister.

THE EXCITED SOUND of a barking dog penetrated Raine's sleeping brain. The sound of happiness.

Her eyelids snapped open. The barking stopped, but she was awake now. Immediately she knew she wasn't alone. That Chuck was with her. That they'd made love last night.

A smile tipped up the corners of her lips. Last night had been...better than good. She remembered screaming. She remembered his shout of exultation. She remembered him holding her tightly, and then...dreams. Melodies. A slow and sexy saxophone sound...

She sighed. The room was dim, the shades blocking the sunlight, though some rays had sneaked in. She wasn't sure what time it was, but she suspected it was midmorning. Chuck slept on his side facing her, his eyes closed, and his breaths soft and even. She rolled out of bed, careful not to wake him, then quickly pulled on her clothes.

Barefoot, she picked up her shoes and tiptoed out of the room. There was a song in her head. Music was thrumming and a jumble of words were inside her head, knocking against each other in their need to be heard, clamoring for her to write them, singing through her blood, along with the need to do this *now*.

Because if she waited for a more convenient time, it would all disappear like fairy dust.

THE PHONE RANG. Chuck groaned and he reached out—and there was nothing next to him. No warm body. Just an empty space and his palm flat on a cold sheet.

His stomach felt empty and cold inside, too.

The phone rang again. He rolled over. There was a tightness in his belly, and he felt cold inside.

The name on the display said *Mom*. His stomach settled. He reached for the phone on the nightstand.

"Yeah," he said.

"You're not in a good mood this morning."

He sat up on the side of the bed, his legs apart, leaning forward. He should have ignored the phone. "Can I call you back?"

"This won't take long. I have to leave in a few minutes for my yoga class."

He rolled his eyes but his shoulders relaxed. He liked it that his uptight mother was taking yoga classes. Liked it that she'd found a man who made her laugh after years of dating stick-in-the-mud types, and, even then, only occasionally.

She was happy now, and it wasn't just because of Nate Finkelstein, her professor boyfriend who wrote screenplays on the side. She was different even before Nate had walked into their lives.

"I heard about your new project," she said.

His shoulders and neck tensed. He grunted.

"Would you like to tell me about it?" she asked.

"Not now," he said. Maybe not ever but he kept his mouth shut. In his mother's carefully lived life, she had never jumped into anything like he'd done all too often. If anyone knew that he wasn't an ambitious guy, she knew that. She—

"Whatever you do," she said, "you have my support."

His jaw dropped. He heard a voice in the background of his mother's phone. Her boyfriend—if a slightly chubby man in his fifties counted as a *boy*. Next he heard a clump, perhaps a door closing.

"I'm off to yoga," his mother said, "and you know I don't like to talk while I drive. Chat later."

Chat later? His mouth dropped open. When did *chat later* become part of his mother's vocabulary of phrases?

And when did she say, *Whatever you do, you have my support?*

"Uh...thanks, Mom."

"Oh, and about that woman you were with last night..."

He stood, wary. Who had called her?

He quickly wiped that question from his mind. It could've been any of a few hundred people.

"Yeah?" he asked.

"I like the sound of her. She might be a keeper."

His jaw dropped again.

"Well, I have to go."

"Uh, okay." He was about to say *Chat later* to her when she clicked off.

He set the cell phone down, then strode to the bathroom. When he finished in there and put on some clothes—his jeans and sweatshirt from yesterday would do—he needed to find Raine.

She could be anywhere.

She could be gone.

Twenty-eight

SOMETHING WAS WRONG. Baxter didn't like the bad smell. It was getting worse, and he didn't like it all.

Todd plopped down on the couch, saying his stomach was sick.

Didn't he know it was the smell?

Baxter had been afraid to tell him. Afraid that Todd would think it was his fault.

Afraid Todd would take him to the city and leave him.

But now he needed to tell Todd. If he didn't tell Todd, something very bad was going to happen.

He nudged Todd. Already, Todd's eyes were closed, and he was making snoring noises on the couch. Todd mumbled something, but his eyes didn't open.

Baxter barked. Then he barked again. And again. His sharp bark. Saying that something was very wrong, and Todd needed to open his eyes. *Now.*

"Wha...?" Todd's eyes half opened, and they looked dazed. "I feel sick."

Baxter knew the word *sick.* He felt sick, too.

They needed to leave the house.

He barked again, and then he put his teeth on the thing that Todd wore. The protection from the cold for his hairless body. The material clamped between his teeth, he tugged.

"What's wrong?" Todd sat up, his feet on the carpet. He shook his head, then made a sick sound. He stared into

Baxter's eyes. "Something's wrong, isn't it? Something's wrong with the house."

Baxter let go of his jeans. With a sharp bark, he ran to the kitchen and stopped by the stove.

Here it is! Here it is!

Todd stepped inside. His eyes looked dull. "Shit," he said. "Shit. I think we'd better get the fuck out of here."

Baxter barked again, and he ran to the back door. Barking and barking and barking. *Let's go, let's go, let's go.*

Still Todd didn't go right away. He had to get his shoes on and his jacket, then he picked up his backpack.

And all the while, Baxter barked at him.

They left through the back door. They weren't far from the house when Baxter threw up. Then Todd threw up.

And then they ran, both of them, slow and zigzagged, their heads and their bellies still sick with the taste and the smell of the very bad stuff.

☂

I am liquid. I have no bones
Flying high in your embrace
Melting, melting, melting...
Racing, racing, racing,
racing to the top...
Don't stop, don't stop,
don't ever, ever stop....

Raine's fingers stilled on the guitar, the last note vibrating in the air as she sat in the chair in her second-floor suite. There was that noise again. The barking. It had started with a sorrowful edge that was just right for her song. Then it had changed. The sound sharp and biting. Even afraid.

Now it was different. Louder. Coming from outside. Behind the house. Behind the tree line.

It was getting closer.

She peered out the window. There was an odd misting snow outside, a rain and snow mix, with sloppy drops of snow dribbling down the window. The sky was dark, the clouds blocking the sun. It looked dreary, though her heart was still filled with the joy of last night, and now the joy of the song.

What had happened last night between her and Chuck was saved. Recorded in her breaking voice and the twang of the guitar. A song of desire and wonder and consummation.

When this was over—when she left Trouble Bay—when life turned angry and sad and scary and hurtful, she could bring that song out. Turn it on. See Chuck in her mind. Feel his warm breath on her neck, on her face, and then between her legs. She could—

She stopped herself. Her skin was heating, and she was breathing hard. She laughed softly. Breathlessly.

Her songs were her own secret diary. Some were silly. Some were rants. She'd even written a song about food, and it had been a mini-hit, and she'd gotten a couple of offers to use it for commercials.

She'd gotten them. Not Sunny.

And now she'd just recorded the most sensual love song she'd ever written, and a barking animal was interrupting this warm and wonderful feeling.

The barking came again. Louder. Closer.

She got up, unable to ignore it anymore.

As she headed down the hall to the stairway, she heard footsteps stomping up the stairs. Chuck. Immediately the blood sped in her veins and her skin warmed.

Around Chuck, she was like a teenager. She'd skipped that typical stage, too busy concentrating on things like...oh, survival. Finding food. And a place to stay that wasn't on a street where drug dealers hung out. Or prostitutes, though they weren't as dangerous as drug dealers. They weren't likely to break into their room and steal their meager savings.

"Morning." Chuck stopped halfway up the stairs below her.

"Morning." She heard the softness of her voice. And she wondered if he really was a good man or if she was like her sister, who had the world's worst taste in men. Anything with a pretty face and slick talk was like the chocolate bar with caramel and nuts that Sunny couldn't resist.

And when the pretty face came with money and lived like a prince in his Beverly Hills mansion—and then there was the hotel-sized home in the compound—with people talking about him in reverent tones, well, Sunny had been a goner.

"What are you thinking?" Chuck asked.

"How pretty your face is." And wondering if she were as susceptible as Sunny to a good-looking man.

He made a face. "Not pretty. Handsome, maybe. *Masculine.*"

She laughed, and it felt good. "Yes, very—"

The barks came again, stopping her. She tilted her head in the direction of the sound. "Do you hear that?"

"Hear what?"

"The barking..." She frowned. "There's a dog in pain. It's been crying for about five or more minutes now. I should have gone right away. I have to see if it's okay."

"I can't hear anything," he said, "and I have good ears."

She pushed past him, urgency tightening her chest, not even slowing to tell him that compared to her, most people were deaf.

"I'll go with you." His footsteps pounded after her, and a sense of relief rushed through her. But she didn't slow down. She didn't stop. If he wanted to go find the animal with her, he needed to move faster, because she wasn't waiting for any man.

In the back hall, they both grabbed their jackets. As they zipped and buttoned, another howl came, the sadness and woe in the voice making her shiver.

"I hear it now," he said. "It's from the back, toward the

north. Sarah Vardy's house. She died a few months ago. I heard her nephew and his dog moved in."

Another bark came. This one sharp. And even closer.

Chuck snapped around. "Something's wrong. You stay here, in case there's any danger."

The bark came again. Raine stilled, listening. She'd always been hyper good at sounds, hearing the nuances in words and the wind and storms and, apparently, even barks.

This dog was scared. Frantic.

Something was seriously wrong.

"I'm not staying anywhere. I'm going, too."

She hurried after Chuck, her heart thumping.

Twenty-nine

BAXTER SMELLED THEM. Humans. Coming for them. Their breaths huffing. Their voices edged with urgency. A man and a woman. The woman smelled fresh but not the man.

If only Baxter's tummy didn't hurt so much... And he was tired...so tired.

Next to him, Todd was puking again.

Baxter's throat still felt sick, but he'd thrown up and pooped and peed. And stuff was coming down from the sky. A cold, sloppy mess. Not snow and not rain but something in between. He just wanted to sleep. And he didn't want to wake up. Not for a long time.

Maybe he could lay his head down for a moment...

☂

CHUCK PLODDED ALONGSIDE Raine toward the tree line in back. At the last minute, he'd insisted she use a black umbrella hanging on a hook in the back hall. She held it over her head as they trudged through patches of wet snow as fast as they could. It was nearly as bad as walking through mud. He guessed the weather was in the mid-thirties. A fluke for this time of year. That balmy temperature wasn't going to last long, and it would soon drop down to freezing once more. If a sick dog was outside, they needed to find it fast.

Chuck cupped his hands around his mouth. "Dog! Where are you?"

No whimpers came.

He dropped his arms and kept trudging forward through the soggy mess.

"I know it's this way," she said. "The dog must be afraid."

Or too sick to reply, Chuck thought but didn't say.

Or too scared.

Or too dead.

Still walking, he cupped his hands around his mouth again. "Here, doggie! Here, puppy!"

She glanced over at him, surprise in her expression.

"What?" he asked.

"You have a great tenor voice. Do you sing?"

"Next time we're in bed together, I'll serenade you."

She laughed, her cheeks flushing.

"I'm a better lover than singer," he said.

Her face turned pinker. She looked forward. So did he. It was hard to see through the flurry of snow and rain. He put his hand over his eyes to protect them. At least the umbrella was keeping her glasses dry.

"There!" She pointed and started to run slowly through the slush. "Something is moving. A black dog, I think."

He started running after her. Ahead of them, a man in a gray jacket stumbled out from between trees, half bent, his head down. A black dog ran at his side.

"There's something wrong there," Chuck said. "You should go back to the B and B."

"Maybe *you* should go back," she said, her tone grim. "Believe it or not, I'm used to things going wrong."

He glanced at her as she ran clumsily ahead of him. It was clear that the man and dog needed their help. Later, he'd find out more about her life. After all, she already knew about his problems.

Some days it seemed like the whole world was a problem.

He surged ahead of her, and she ran faster so they were racing together, her breaths huffing. They reached the dog, and Chuck stopped. He didn't want her to be bitten, and the man stumbling toward them appeared too sick to harm her.

The dog stopped. Chuck crouched down and put his arms around the dog's shoulders and neck, its head down, its chest expanding and contracting, huffing sounds coming from its mouth.

"You okay?" he murmured, though he knew the dog wouldn't answer him.

A few feet ahead of him, Raine bent over the man, holding the umbrella over him.

"Something's wrong..." The man stopped talking to suck air in, then huff it out. "Smell..." *Huff, huff, huff.* "It smelled in there. Sulfur."

"Sounds like a gas leak." Chuck rose from his kneeling position. "You were smart to leave. I'll take care of it. You and your dog can stay at my place." He looked at Raine.

"Go." She nodded her chin toward the B and B. "Just go."

Chuck gave her one long look, then he turned and loped back toward the other man's house.

Raine called something after him but he didn't look back.

Thirty

"YOU SHOULDN'T HAVE let him turn off the gas at my place," Todd said.

Her face looked sad, her forehead creased in worry. "I couldn't stop him. And he's right. It's going to take too long for someone from the gas company to get there. Better to shut off the gas before your house explodes."

Todd didn't think the house would explode, but if it did while his aunt's neighbor was in there—someone who'd been a stranger to him—he would feel like a murderer.

This Chuck was a good-looking guy with a pretty girlfriend. In the one minute Todd was with them, he could practically see the air sparkle around his new neighbor and this worried woman. His brave neighbor had something to live for.

All Todd had to live for was his dog. He should have forced himself to get to his feet. He should have crawled back and taken care of the problem himself.

If anyone should die, it should be him and not Chuck.

"It's the least we can do for you," the woman said.

"You don't know me," he said. "You owe me nothing."

"You're a veteran. You joined the Marines to protect us. To serve us. The least we can do is to help you back."

"How did—" He stopped and looked down at the dog tags hanging over his sweatshirt. Maybe he should stop wearing them. But he put his hand over the tags. They connected him to a time when he'd been a better man.

When being a Marine had been part of his identity.

He looked away from her, needing to get his mind off of his gas-filled house. He focused on the living room in the B and B, where they waited for Chuck's return. The furniture was a mix of old and new. Against the wall was a table made of dark wood that looked as if it could have been in the White House. Against another wall was a rustic hutch, as if a long-dead relative had made it himself. The couch and two groupings of chairs were more modern, though traditional enough to blend with the older pieces.

"I suppose you're not up to eating anything," she said.

He shook his head. "I wish your friend would come back."

"He will," she said, but she looked behind her. As if she could see through the wall to the kitchen, and then see through that wall to the yard behind them, and then see through the line of trees that blocked his aunt's house—*his* house now—and see the woman's boyfriend inside the house turning off the gas, then running the hell out of there.

She jumped up to her feet. "I know what we need. I'll be right back."

While she ran up the stairs, he bent to pet Baxter, who lay on the carpet by his shoes, his feet in slippers that weren't his. Probably his helpful neighbor's.

Baxter lifted his head a couple inches. He was still lethargic, but he wasn't throwing up. After Chuck had left for the house, Raine had speculated that, since Baxter was smaller, the gas had affected him more. Todd told her he'd been at the grocery store a short time before, leaving Baxter alone in the house. Once again, he thanked her and her boyfriend for coming to their rescue.

There had been a moment of silence before she'd explained that she was a guest and had been at this place only a short time. It surprised him. They'd acted like lovers. Like two people who could have a conversation just by staring into each others' eyes. He would bet they even smelled like lovers.

But he kept his mouth shut. If she wanted him to believe there was nothing going on between her and her host, and they weren't generating sparks that could light up a night sky, he wasn't going to contradict her.

She clambered down the steps now, stopping his useless thoughts. In her right hand, she held a guitar.

"I'll play some music for you." She stood in front of him. "What would you like me to sing?"

"You sing and play?" he asked.

"My singing isn't the best."

"It has to be better than mine."

She plopped down on the couch and put the strap around her neck. She held the instrument against her chest as tenderly as if it were a baby. "Got any favorites?"

"A dog song," he said.

Her laugh had a sob in it. "Why not? I'll give it a try."

As she strummed the guitar, he sat back. She lowered her pretty chin, tilting her head, and started to play. The music was melodic, and he thought it had a hint of mournfulness, like an Irish ballad. The kind of music that wrenched souls. She began to sing in a low voice.

"Blackie was his name, but it never matched his heart.
He was lousy at foreplay, but he sure knew how to fart."

Todd laughed. He hadn't expected that. Then the back door opened. His laughter stopped at the same time as the music. He stood. It had to be Chuck, back safely.

Raine ducked to take the strap off of her and set the guitar down. Jumping to her feet, she glowed, her face radiant.

"He's here," she whispered huskily.

"Go to him," he said.

She remained standing; two small lines indented the skin between her eyebrows.

"*Go,*" he repeated.

"Okay," she said. "But not long."

She half ran into the kitchen. Todd watched her until she was gone, and then he sat down.

He thought again of the life he'd hoped for one day. With a wife, a job, a home, and children.

The life he would never have now. He was too broken. Most of the time now he could hold it together...until something switched inside him, and he would start to shake and want to hide. Crawl into a hole and never come up for air again.

At least he had the dog, which was enough for him to handle now. And since he hadn't heard an explosion, he guessed he still had a house. Not too long ago, he didn't have that much.

Anything more was too much to hope for. Too much for him to handle. Too good for someone like him.

Really, he was a lucky man.

🌂

"YOU'RE STAYING HERE until the pipes are fixed." Chuck stared at the former Marine with the scruffy beard and sad eyes and the dog lying at Todd's feet in his kitchen. The dog's head that looked big for his body had settled on Chuck's slippers that Todd wore.

Todd reached down to scratch the back of the dog's ear. Not even looking, his fingers finding the perfect spot to rub. "I can't."

"You can, and you will." Chuck's heart was still pounding. The house had stunk of gas. This man and his dog could have been killed.

While he was in the house, he could have been killed, too.

The guy from the gas company had already come and gone. He'd said the gas company lines didn't have a leak, and Todd needed to call a plumbing contractor. He'd wished Todd luck, petted the dog, then was gone.

They'd all stared after his gas truck driving out of Trouble Bay.

"He's as slippery as a politician," Raine had said, and Todd had nodded.

"Ray said he'll be here soon," Chuck said about Ray, the plumber who did gas lines, too, though that was something that Chuck hadn't had to deal with yet.

"I suppose it won't be cheap." Todd frowned.

"You don't have to go with Ray," Chuck said, "but I advise it. He's fair. These are old houses. Yours was probably built in the 1950s. I don't know how old your aunt's gas heater might be. The problem might be something simple, like a valve replacement."

"Or it might be the gas heater," Todd said.

"If you need money," Chuck said, "I could loan you some. Without interest."

"Or I could," Raine said.

Todd stepped back. "I won't need your money. I have my own."

"In that case," Raine said, "just suck it up and pay."

Todd stared at her, his lips flattened against his teeth. Chuck turned to look at her, too. He hadn't thought she would be so...sharp. This vet needed compassion, not criticism. And now she was lifting her guitar on her lap, putting the strap around her neck, then adjusting the strings, and, finally, strumming the guitar. Her voice low, she started to sing.

"Sometimes you get lucky,
Other times you get sucky,
Sometimes living is cheap
Sometimes the cost makes you weep
The cost of life is never funny
But, honey, it's just money.
So suck it up and pay."

She stopped strumming, her head up. "That's it. All I've got."

Something hoarse came out of Todd's mouth, making the dog's head lift. But Todd still stared at Raine as another hoarse sound came out of his mouth, then another and another.

Finally Chuck realized what it was. Laughter.

Laughter that sounded a lot liked sobbing.

He sat back. Depending on what the plumber said, whoever Todd chose, they might have a temporary guest, including a dog.

He looked at Raine, who was grinning at Todd, and he wondered what difference this might make to their new arrangement. He gave a mental shrug. Like Raine said, sometimes you got lucky. Other times you got sucky.

And some days you just didn't know which way it would go.

Thrity-one

TODD LAY IN bed in the room in the front of the B and B that faced the main street and was two suites away from Raine's. Chuck and Raine had fed him, and they were nice to him. Chuck had put clean sheets on his bed. He'd even offered Todd a bigger suite on the third floor with the whirlpool tub, but Todd had turned it down. They even let Baxter sleep in his room.

They shouldn't be so nice to him. Treating him as if he were special when he'd been homeless for so long. When the only good thing he'd done for a long time was to feed the dog and let him share his shelter.

That had changed now. Here, in Trouble Bay, he wasn't one of those homeless people whom people saw and turned their heads away from. Pretending they didn't see him. Their noses pinched so they couldn't smell him. Here he was someone who was good. Someone who'd helped the world.

He knew that was wrong, and he hadn't done anything to make the world better. But it still made him feel like someone worthwhile. After all, he'd tried his best. It was the reason he'd enlisted in the Marines.

Sometimes, though, it felt like the only reason people in one country fought people in another country were so politicians could get people all riled up and scared. When people were scared, they were more likely to vote for the politicians with the biggest mouths, and then the companies that made weapons would back these politicians, giving them money.

He shut those thoughts down. They were merry-go-round thoughts. He could go round and round and round with those thoughts, and he would end up angry and sad and a little crazy, and not one damn thing would change.

He would rather think of something concrete and useful. Like plumbing. The plumber had said his house would be fixed either the next day or the day after that. The plumber had taken care of the pipes, too, so they wouldn't burst. More money spent, but that's what money was for. Spending.

This made him think of Raine's unfinished song. Maybe he should get some colored markers and write it on thick white paper, then frame it.

> *Sometimes you get lucky,*
> *Other times you get sucky,*
> *Sometimes living is cheap*
> *Sometimes the cost makes you weep...*

A rhyming line came into his mind. *Life can't be too bad when you're loved by a black lab.*

He snorted. Wasn't that the truth?

Next to him, Baxter's head lifted from the mattress and turned toward the back of the house, tension in his neck and the stillness of his head.

Todd became still, hearing the creak of a door opening. Then came the sound of footsteps on the hall floor. Not shoes, but soft slippers. Heading down the stairs.

Grinning, he put his hand on the back of Baxter's neck. He bent to murmur, "It's okay, Bax. Raine and Chuck are going to make each other happy. Nothing wrong with that."

He kept petting Baxter until he heard her reach the first floor. He still smiled, glad for them. Maybe someday...

With a twist, he closed his eyes. Sometimes it hurt to hope that things were different. That *he* were different. His belly hurt. His head hurt. Most of all, his heart hurt.

Baxter whined and shoved his face against Todd's side.

Todd rubbed his ears. Obviously Baxter was the smartest dog in the county, reminding him that he wasn't alone anymore. Baxter belonged to him now.

And he was just barely smart enough to know he belonged to Baxter, too.

CHUCK WAITED IN the hallway for Raine. They hadn't said anything, but he'd hoped... She came down, wearing a T-shirt and black and purple yoga pants that made him smile. No sexy lingerie, but he didn't need lace and satin to desire her. If she wore rags, she would still look sexy to him.

The living room was lit with only one light. She turned from the stairway, and when her gaze met his, her face lit up, as if she glowed from the inside out.

He felt that same glow. He opened his arms wide. With a low laugh, she ran to him, leaping up at the last moment like a scene from an old movie. He caught her, taking a step back to get his balance and not drop her. She laughed again, and her legs clasped around his hips.

He pulled her against his chest and kissed her. A long and hard kiss, as if he was telling her everything with the kiss and the embrace. Letting her know without words how much he wanted her. *Needed* her. Then he spun her around, so he was facing the hallway that led to his bedroom.

She drew her face away from his and unclasped her legs, then slid down his front, her eyes lit with laughter.

"You're killing me," he said, and he heard the hoarseness in his voice. "You're killing me slowly."

"I don't want to kill you." She cupped a hand on each side of his face. "I want to love you."

He kissed her again, his body pressed against her. Then he bent slightly, and scooped her up as if she were a child.

She laughed again, her head falling back, freer and happier than he'd ever seen her.

He carried her to his bedroom, vowing that he would make her even happier.

AN HOUR LATER, Raine felt wonderful. Sated. Boneless and liquefied. They'd returned to the living room, where she shared a bottle of beer with him. She wore her yoga pants and a sweatshirt of his, and, for this night, she felt happier than in a long time.

"You're okay?" he asked.

She turned her head. She'd traveled from Los Angeles to the Midwest, and how odd that this B and B was the place that felt most like home. "What a strange day this has been."

"Are you sorry?" He looked down a few inches at her, his face movie-star handsome.

"I'm happy," she said, though she knew it was happy-for-now.

Chuck's eyes burned brighter, and she felt as if she was melting from the inside out. Then he kissed her again, and there were no words, only his mouth on hers.

With a sigh, he pulled back a few inches. "Today made me realize the unimportance of my art mart. It doesn't matter. *You* matter. *This* matters. *We* matter."

"*This* matters now, but in the long run..." She frowned, and she thought about her music. Was it more important than love? "In the long run, will it be important in a different way? We can't make love all the time."

He lowered his gaze to her mouth, and she could see the intensity in his face. She felt warmer, but she wasn't falling into that trap of believing that love conquered all. Love was wonderful, but there was no way she would stop writing songs. Even if she never sold another song, writing songs was a part of her. It satisfied her. Fulfilled her.

"Even teenaged boys can't have sex all the time," she said.

He looked away for a moment, and she could see his profile and the frown. She made a face at herself. She'd messed that up.

"What if it's too much?" he asked.

"You're talking about the art mart, right?"

He nodded, the move so slight that if she hadn't been watching him carefully, she would have missed it. "What if it's too hard?" he asked.

"Sometimes the best things are hard."

"And sometimes you're chasing a dream."

She frowned. If he didn't want to chase his dream, she wasn't going to push him into it.

"What do you think?" he asked. "Do you believe in me?"

"You're asking the wrong person the right question."

"Who's the right person?" His mouth twisted, then he turned to her. "*Me.* I'm the only person who can answer that."

"But not now." She held out her arms to him. "Answer it later, please."

He got up, turned to her, and drew her up. She stood on the tips of her toes, and he bent slightly, and they clung together.

"Sleep with me tonight?" she murmured.

"Yes. It's been a long day," he said. "You want to finish the beer?"

She shook her head, feeling the energy seep out of her. She wasn't even going to run upstairs and brush her teeth or put her nighttime skin lotion on her face. Later, she might find out his answer. For now, she just needed to sleep with him next to her. She just wanted to be safe. She just wanted to feel that someone cared.

Thirty-two

A DAMP, COLD nose against Todd's cheek woke him, then came the fast and hard sound of a dog breathing. He opened his eyes, and a pink tongue swiped his jaw and cheek. With a groan, he rolled out of bed. It was early yet, with the sky just lightening.

"Just a minute," he said, and strode to the suite's bathroom. It hadn't taken him long to become accustomed to indoor plumbing all over again. He was back in the bedroom in a couple of minutes. He pulled on his pants and sweatshirt, then put on his socks.

He had no bad feelings about being jerked out of a deep sleep. He understood that when you had to go, you had to go *now*, no matter what species you belonged to.

He started downstairs, where he'd left his shoes by the back door yesterday, though Chuck had said it wasn't necessary. Chuck didn't know the places where these shoes had been. The streets, the alleys, the garbage...

Todd wasn't much for lists—not having a need for them for a long time—but he added *shoes* to his mental shopping list.

After he put on his shoes and coat, he attached a leash to the collar he'd bought Baxter. In the weeks he and Baxter had been together, Baxter had stuck around him. But this was a strange place, and Todd felt a sense of responsibility for him.

Their *home* was here now. He needed to take care of the

home. Of Baxter. He needed to take better care of himself, too. He had to be healthy for Baxter, who stood a few feet ahead of him, doing what he needed to do.

They headed out to the back of the B and B. While Baxter peed, Todd squinted at the trees on this side of the tree line. He saw glimpses of his house. It still appeared intact, and no explosions had startled him awake last night.

What would have happened if Baxter hadn't barked at him, waking him from his stupor?

Thinking about it, Todd fought back the panic rising in his throat. Telling himself that he was okay now.

Baxter, who had been sniffing the grass, whipped his head toward him, looking at him for a couple of seconds, then ran to him, reaching him, butting his head against his thighs.

Todd crouched, then looped his arms around Baxter's neck. He held on until the shaking slowed, and he stood again.

"I'm going to be okay." He looked down at the dog. "And so are you."

He and Baxter turned back toward the side door, walking side by side. It was a new day. This was only his fifth day in this small town and already his new home was going to cost him more money than he'd planned, like it or not.

His answer was *not*. He didn't like it. Not one bit. But he was alive, and so was his dog. And he was pretty sure that was just part of being a homeowner.

☂

A SNOWSTORM IN Milwaukee had delayed Vince's trip a day. He'd been ready to start out when there was a pile-up of cars and trucks on I-43, the expressway that led to the northeast. Milwaukee's traffic was kindergarten stuff compared to southern California, but when snow fell, that changed everything.

His father had called three times, and each time Vince

claimed he still had the flu. The last day, he was packed and ready to grab his jacket to check out when the phone buzzed. He looked at it and saw the caller name. Jarret.

Now what?

Vince picked up his cell phone and clicked it on. Jarret didn't ask how he was. Instead, he dived right into complaining about his wife. She acted like a diva, manic one minute and sick and crying another.

"And now she ran away, telling everyone she was a prisoner." Jarret's voice rose into a whine. "This whole thing was a big mistake of Father's."

Vince could practically feel his brain cells sparking as he turned on *Record*. "A lot of men would think you were one of the luckiest men on earth to have married Sunny."

"What're you saying? You don't even like her."

Vince sat on the wing chair that overlooked the park-like square across the downtown Milwaukee street. Not a bad view, especially with the snow and the benches. Corny enough for a Christmas card. "Maybe I said that because you got the girl first."

"Oh, yeah?" Jarret's tone brightened.

"I'm not saying for sure, but maybe," Vince said. "What's the trouble? Is she still at the rocker's place?"

There was silence, and Vince pictured Jarret scowling. "*You're* the lucky one," Jarret said. "You missed a big mistake. Don't ever let Dad pick out your bride."

"So I'm right. She's still at our friendly neighbor's."

"She said she's not leaving." Nervousness edged Jarret's voice. "She's pregnant. When women arc pregnant, they start getting protective of that future person nesting inside them. It's the maternal instinct. That's another mistake Dad made."

Vince sat straight. "So Dad set her up?"

"He didn't *knock* her up, if that's what you mean." Jarret made a harsh sound that could've been a half laugh or a half cry. "Though if she'd given him any sign that she was interested, who knows what he would've done.

Sometimes I wonder if Dad really thinks he is God."

"Yeah." Vince hunched his shoulders. On this subject, he and Jarret were one. "He goes too far."

"Like the baby," Jarret said. "I wasn't ready to have a child. I told Dad that, but he insisted. And Sunny wasn't ready to be a mother yet. I wish to hell he hadn't bribed the pharmacist to switch her birth control pills for placebos. If he hadn't done that, I'm sure that Sunny wouldn't have run off."

Holy shit. One revelation after another.

Another day Vince would be chortling, but he unexpectedly cringed for Jarret. It wasn't normal for Jarret to confide in him, but who else could he complain to? Who else would know what he was going through? A grown man who kowtowed to a father who thought he was a god.

"And then there's our mothers," Vince said.

"What do you mean?" Jarret asked, but he was whispering.

"You know what I mean. Both wives killed in a fall... What are the odds?"

There was silence for long seconds. "I don't know what you're talking about," Jarret said. "I'd better go."

Vince got to his feet. "Just be sure that Sunny doesn't fall."

"Dad wouldn't harm the baby," Jarret said.

"Wouldn't he? If it suited him, wouldn't he?"

Jarret swore and hung up.

Frowning, Vince went to get his jacket. Things were about to happen. Bad things. Worse than he'd thought.

It was time to get the hell out of here.

IT TOOK NEARLY two hours to drive to Green Bay, the place where Vince was going to transform himself from businessman to sportsman with a change of wardrobe. He'd already rented a black pickup truck that looked like something a sportsman would drive. Or even just a regular guy, the kind who went fishing and hunting and hung around bars at night with the guys. He hadn't shaved in the last couple days, so he even had stubble.

Maybe none of this was necessary, but he had always been a careful man. When you're seven years old and your mother dies suddenly, you learn to be a careful kid, and you grow up to be a careful man.

He didn't want to blow this opportunity. It was the culmination of many years and many angry thoughts. He *needed* to make sure people thought he was the real thing. If he farted, he even wanted to smell like a farting winter fisherman.

No guns. He knew how to shoot guns, but for hunting guns, he'd need to get a license, and he didn't think that was necessary. Fishing seemed like a better bet. Not that he knew anything about ice fishing, but he had a story worked out: He was on a fishing vacation with a brother who was never going to show up. Who was always promising to be there the next day. The kind of brother who was a screw-up and had one excuse after another.

By the last day, he planned to have everything he needed and would be gone. Bye-bye, Wisconsin. Bye-bye, frigid weather and snow. Bye-bye, rustic buildings.

Hello to warm and sunny California.

He headed into a large sports store, and a salesman with an overlarge Adam's apple was happy to help him spend his money. An avid ice fisherman, the salesman talked about his favorite catches and places to fish in the town next to Trouble Bay.

After Vince stocked up on fishing equipment that he wouldn't use, the salesman took him to the other end of the store for boots that had soles for traction, telling him he'd need it on the ice. It turned out he also needed ice cleats, a waterproofed, insulated jacket with a hood, thermal underwear, and a red-and-black flannel hat with fake fur lining, ear flaps, and a chin strap. This new wardrobe was nothing near his normal white-shirt-and-black-slacks look. Suave and minimalist, his last girlfriend had called him.

None of the sportsman's attire was cheap, either. He was surprised how much money men spent on ugly clothes. All this for fishing that he'd never do but worth it. If Dawn was hiding in the town of Trouble Bay, she wouldn't recognize him.

With every item he bought, the salesman grinned wider. Finally, Vince said he thought he had everything, and the salesman sighed but agreed.

Since the salesman knew the town of Trouble Bay, Vince paid with cash and asked him about a place to stay.

The salesman said there were cabins for rent, a great B and B, or a resort.

"A resort," Vince said. Maybe that was where he'd find Dawn.

The salesman scribbled the resort's name and location on the back of a receipt. He looked pleased to help, his eyes bright as he handed Vince the receipt.

Vince pushed the shopping cart out of the store because he had too many items to carry. A cold wind cut across his face and ears, and he wished he'd put on the ugly hat. Yet he didn't flinch. Reaching the rental truck, he dumped everything in the backseat before he pushed the cart into the cart holder.

It was almost noon already. His mind was formulating plans, showing him choices. Soon he would be in Trouble Bay. He hoped Dawn had stayed in the town. And he hoped this Raine really was Dawn.

He was ninety-five percent sure she was, but the last five percent was always the killer.

Thirty-three

TODD RETURNED TO his aunt's house the next morning after breakfast, telling Chuck he would be okay without heat. That he'd been through worse.

He'd seen the sympathy on Chuck's face, and he knew that Chuck thought he was talking about Afghanistan. Maybe that was partly it. Maybe it was partly his fault. Maybe it was the military. There were a lot of maybes, and he didn't want to dwell on it anymore. He had his dog now. He had his house now. He needed to take care of both of them, and that was that.

In two hours, four people knocked on Todd's aunt's door. *His* door, which still felt unreal to him. Like a strange dream, and any minute he expected to wake up in his box in the alley again. Baxter barked each time someone rang their doorbell, protecting him, needing a calming hand on his neck before Todd opened the door. Two of his interruptions were by men and two by women. The two men came—at different times—to the front door. The two women came together to the side door.

That told Todd something about his aunt, the town, and the difference between men and women. The women gathered around the kitchen table here, but the men expected front-door treatment.

He wasn't sure what any of that meant, though the kitchen was homier. But he let them inside, and the first man brought a portable heater that he plugged in, ignoring

191

Todd as he said he appreciated it but he couldn't borrow it. It was too much.

"It's the least my wife and I can do for you." The neighbor, who'd said his name was Bob, looked like a human grizzly bear with his bushy grayish-brown beard, mustache, and hair. He was a couple inches shorter than Todd, but he gave the sense of being taller and wider. The kind of man who could fell trees with one stroke of an axe.

"You don't owe me anything," Todd said, knowing Bob meant his military service. Todd made a mental note to take off the dog tags. At the thought, his gut revolted, and he sighed. Apparently he wasn't ready to give up his dog tags yet. Apparently they were still his identity.

Bob socked Todd's arm hard enough to make him lurch sideways. Baxter barked sharply, and Bob laughed and bent to ruffle the fur on Baxter's neck.

"We're okay, buddy." He straightened with a white flash of teeth between his grizzled beard and mustache. "You got a good dog, here."

"The best." Just saying it made Todd stand up straight with pride. It seemed like all the good that had happened to him lately had begun after he'd befriended Baxter.

"What else can I do here?" Bob asked.

Todd shook his head. He wasn't even sure how long he would be here. Since Bob insisted he keep the heater until the gas was on again, Todd thanked him and said he'd bring it over to his place after the gas was on again.

By the time Bob left, the place was already warming. That's when the next neighbor stopped off with a six pack of beer. Though Todd didn't drink much, he thanked him, and nodded his head for the next ten minutes as his neighbor talked about fishing.

The two women came together, bringing cookies, brownies, and a flask of coffee. They were in their fifties or sixties, and they reminded him of his aunt, whom he hadn't seen for so many years.

For no reason at all, he wanted to cry.

They left soon but not before they found out he was single, and that he'd been living on the street. He wanted to come clean with these people. Let them know that they were dealing with a guy whose gaze normal people avoided.

Instead, they hugged him.

When they left, Todd took a deep breath, then looked at Baxter. "I don't know what's wrong with these people."

Baxter looked up at him with his trusting brown eyes. Todd crouched down and hugged him. A tear fell from each eye.

He didn't know what was wrong with himself, either.

CHUCK WOKE UP slowly, feeling the warm body next to him. Hearing the soft breaths.

Raine. Sleeping next to him. All night.

Joy spread through him. They'd known each other only a short time, and maybe it was crazy, but she was the one for him. He knew that the way he knew he breathed and she breathed. He'd known that when she'd walked into his house. He'd seen the hurt in her face, and he'd wanted to put his arms around her, to talk softly to her. To tell her he would be there for her. That he would make whatever was wrong better.

Only how could he make it better for her when his own life was a mess? When the people who knew him best didn't believe in him?

That's what had stopped him from going one hundred percent after her.

That's what had made him step back.

Because at some level, he knew the townspeople were right. He wasn't good enough. Not for the town. Not for her.

But that didn't mean he couldn't change. That didn't mean he couldn't make himself good enough.

That didn't mean that he was going to let other people's thoughts hold him back.

Only two opinions mattered. Raine's opinion and his own.

Careful not to wake her, he edged out of bed, then picked up last night's clothes from the floor and the chair in the corner.

It was time to man up.

It was time for him to prove he was good enough for her.

☂

RAINE FELT THE dip in the mattress and the sunlight on her eyelids. She knew it was morning, but she kept her eyes closed and her breaths even.

Last night had been...amazing. But she didn't want to replicate it this morning.

She heard Chuck's footsteps as he picked up his clothes that had been scattered on the floor. She kept herself from smiling. And then laughing. Joy spreading through her, inside and out.

She couldn't remember when she'd felt like this.

He wanted nothing from her. Not her music. Not her songs. Not to meet her sister or her manager.

He just wanted...her.

It felt like someone else's life.

Oh, wait! It *was* someone else's life. Raine's life, a person she'd made up. Not Dawn's. As if they were two different people.

The bedroom door clicked. Chuck leaving.

The heaviness of sleep still hovered over her, not completely dissipated. She sighed. Soon she would get up. Soon she would have to make decisions. For now, though, all she had to do was turn over on her side...and hide inside the dream of a life she knew would never come true.

How ironic. She wanted Chuck to grab hold of his life, to take control, but she was scared to grab hold of hers.

Instead of falling asleep, she waited until she heard him

in the bathroom across the hall, the water running. Then she rolled out of bed, pulled on her clothes from last night, and hurried upstairs.

She had things to do. The first was to fix what was wrong with her own life, as impossible as it seemed. Maybe she was stronger now, but she didn't want to run anymore.

Maybe she didn't want to hide who she was anymore.

She was ready to fight.

Thirty-four

BAXTER'S EYES FOLLOWED Todd. One of the two ladies had given Baxter a cookie before they'd left—which he'd chomped in one bite, then gobbled the chunks that had fallen onto the kitchen floor—and now another man was here, and he and Todd were heading down to the basement.

Todd was different now from when he had found Baxter in the alley. Baxter whimpered quietly, remembering the time he had been cold and hungry and scared.

And alone. The days long and cold and empty.

But now he had Todd. He jumped up to follow Todd and the man down the stairs. Baxter never wanted to be alone again. He loved Todd, and he didn't like it when Todd left him. Todd took care of him, and in return, it was his job to take care of Todd.

SITTING AT THE drafting table, Chuck finished his talk with Adam Donahue in Adam's contractor's trailer at the edge of town on the fenced concrete lot. Adam worked as a freelancer on just about anything to do with building. Year-round, depending on the weather. In winter, when he couldn't build, he plowed snow.

Adam gave him one long look. Something about him was different. It took Chuck a moment to figure it out.

Satisfaction. It seeped out of Adam's pores and in the brightness of his eyes.

If anyone deserved happiness and love, Adam did. He was a few years older than Chuck, and unlike Chuck, he'd married young. His first wife had died in a car accident, leaving him to care for their daughter, who was already a teen. He'd married again, a month ago, and happiness beamed out of him.

Chuck felt a twist of envy, but he pushed it away and looked down at the blueprint that Adam had sketched out for the two prefab pole buildings. One for the exhibits, and a smaller one for food and soda, with bathrooms on the side.

"You think that will do it?" he asked.

"I do, but I'm open to changes or suggestions." Adam stared at the blueprints. "Give me a couple days to make sure. For something like this, I recommend a chain link fence to protect the buildings from thieves. It's not cheap, but I think it's necessary. I can give you more advice if you want."

Chuck stood. "I want."

"You're all in then?" Adam stood, too, his face serious. "What if it doesn't work out?"

"I'm not looking at failure," Chuck said. "I know this can bomb, but I'm not turning my attention to what might make it a failure. I'm turning my attention to what will make it a success. I'm thinking now that we even have room for a couple more buildings."

Adam eyebrows rose. "You've changed since the last time you talked about this. What is it?"

A woman, Chuck thought, but he just grinned. "Maybe a sign from God."

Adam laughed and socked him on his shoulder. Chuck laughed, too. Because for all he knew, maybe Raine stopping off at the B and B was a sign from some divine being.

Or maybe it was just a cosmic accident. Maybe all of life was a cosmic accident.

Or maybe he'd just gotten lucky.

Or maybe this good stuff had been within his grasp all along, and maybe this was the first time he was reaching out and grabbing it.

☂

"DAWN!" HOWIE'S VOICE was harsh. "I expected to hear from you sooner."

Sitting cross-legged on the bed in her suite, Raine grimaced. When Howie sounded like a frog was stuck in his throat, that meant trouble.

"Why?" She had a sinking feeling that she wasn't going to like his answer. "What happened?"

"You haven't heard?"

"I've been avoiding the news."

"This has been on the front pages of the newspapers. You know Sunny's pregnant, right?"

"No!" She shook her head. "Sunny wasn't ready to have a child. Jarret told her his father wanted a grandchild right away, but she wanted to wait."

"Apparently she changed her mind," he said. "Or it could've been an accident."

"There's no way she changed her mind. Not about that. She had a plan for her life, and babies weren't part of it yet. You know how she doesn't like to deviate from her plans."

"Yeah, Sunny's almost as stubborn as Zola," he said about his wife. "It would take God rising up from the sea for Zola to change her mind. And even then, I think Zola would tell God to mind his own business."

Rained laughed, but it ended with a sob, and she closed her mouth.

"There's more to this than Sunny's pregnancy," Howie said.

"What?" Too nervous to sit on the bed anymore, she pushed off of it, onto her feet.

"It's on the news already. She fled her father-in-law's

compound. She and her pregnant belly somehow either walked or hitched a ride to Grant's nemesis."

"*Ledge*?" She shook her head. She and Ledge were friends before this, but she couldn't imagine Sunny doing that. Sunny liked to take the easy way. She wanted to be a star, wanted to be the center of attention, but Raine was the one who had always pushed her to the next level. "How did she get away?"

"Google it, my dear. I don't know the details. I'm not sure if anyone besides Sunny knows how she did it."

Raine frowned. "How long has she been there?"

"Two days now."

She stepped up to the window in the back and stared out of it, not seeing anything except patches of snow on the grass and the cold sky. She felt as if someone had slugged her in her belly with a hard fist.

How could this have happened without her knowing? She used to think that if Sunny was hurt, she would feel the pain. She would cry with her.

"I need to see her," she said.

"I'll call Ledge and ask him to let her know," he replied. "She called me the other day, and I scolded her. She didn't appreciate my point of view. You know how she is. I doubt she'll call me back."

Tears burned Raine's eyes. She had always thought she would know when Sunny needed her. She and Sunny had been a team.

Until they weren't anymore. Until Prince Charming with his capped-tooth smile and bright eyes had come courting.

But they were still sisters. Nothing could change that.

Not even a man. She might have run away from Sunny, but the tug was still there, telling her to go back and save her sister.

Thirty-five

THE PLUMBER LEFT and so did the gas service guy. Everything was fixed, the gas working, the pipes working, too, and Todd had turned off the space heater.

In the living room, Todd turned to Baxter, who watched him with love in his eyes. And not just love but trust, too. As if Todd were someone to be counted on to take care of him.

If only he could be as good as his dog thought he was. If only he could believe in himself.

He looked down at the space heater near the door.

Then he looked toward the kitchen. Though he couldn't see through the wall, he imagined the homemade cookies, and he could still taste them on his tongue.

And he thought about all the other people he'd met since the beginning of this journey. The lawyer, the trucker who'd driven them here, the woman at the V.A., his aunt, and Chuck and Raine.

While he'd thought of himself as worthless, they all thought he was a person worth saving.

He stood there, feeling a giant rise of emotion inside him. Like he was a volcano about to spit out all his hurt and fear and anguish.

Leaving him a void to fill up...any way he wanted.

It came to him that maybe he could do something in return. Maybe he could do something worthwhile.

He scratched the back of his neck, then looked down at Baxter. "What?" he asked. "What can I do?"

Baxter breathed hard, but he had no answer.

SUNNY WAS TIRED. Wiped out. Dizzy. She sat at the cement table on the patio beneath the umbrella. Jacinda, the new housekeeper, came to the patio to take away the dish for Sunny's eggs over easy, but she left the orange juice with the funny taste. Ledge had left early this morning for a guest gig on a talk show, and it was just her.

And the housekeeper.

She felt like a fool. She had been a fool. Dawn had tried to tell her, but she hadn't listened. She'd wanted the fairy tale, complete with Prince Charming. But instead of a prince, she'd married a daddy's boy.

Fool. Fool. Fool.

She'd tried to call Dawn the night before, but the phone still wasn't in service.

She'd emailed her. She'd messaged her. She'd done everything she could think of.

Dawn hadn't contacted her.

Sunny wasn't surprised. Dawn was in hiding, and Sunny didn't blame her. This morning, before she'd drunk her orange juice, she'd tried to call Howie again, but his number didn't seem to be working, either. Maybe because she was on the top of the hill. Maybe the phone service wasn't working. Maybe that's why she felt so lethargic, even though the housekeeper said there were special vitamins in the orange juice.

The vitamins couldn't have been that special, because they weren't working. All she wanted to do was to cry. She was pregnant, and she didn't want to be pregnant. She was married, and she didn't want to be married.

All she wanted was to be with Dawn. They'd been together for so long. Two peas in a pod. Now the pod had split open, and they were two peas that had fallen out of the pod.

It was her own fault. She'd been so stupid. Stupider than the stupidest person in the world. If she were to write a song, the lyrics would say, *I'm stupid, I'm stupid, I'm stupid.*

She was tired, too. So tired...

She picked up her glass but something was wrong with her fingers. They wouldn't hold on to it, and the glass slipped right out of her weak grip. The maid swore and jumped back. A piece of glass scratched Sunny's thigh, and she screeched.

"Shut up, you swollen-headed bitch," Jacinda said.

As Sunny gaped up at the woman, rough hands grabbed her from behind. She screeched as something wound around her chest, her upper arms, and her back, like a big bandage. She struggled, or tried to, but the bandages tightened, swaddling her like a mummy.

She had the impression of two men, and one grabbed her cloth-covered breast, his big hand trying to squish it. She cried out.

"Asshole," Jacinda said, and Sunny heard the sound of a slap. Not on her, on the man's face.

Sunny knew that sound from her mother. A sharp, stinging sound.

Then blackness shrouded her. One of the men slipping a thick hood over her head, jerking it down to her shoulders, cutting off the fresh air, making it hard to breathe, as if she were inhaling flecks of cotton. Suffocating her.

Help, help, help.

She was yelling in her mind, not with her voice. Her voice seemed to be taken away, along with her energy. She was falling...falling...falling. Slipping into nothingness...

A HISPANIC-LOOKING DESK clerk had checked Vince in. The man was at ease and confident, and it was clear to

Vince that he liked his life. That might have had something to do with the wedding ring on his left ring finger.

"Have you been working here long?" Vince glanced at the name plate, which said his name was August Reyes.

"Since I was a young teen." Reyes grinned. "My stepfather owns the resort. How long will you be staying?"

"At least a couple days," Vince said. "A friend and I are going ice fishing. He was supposed to meet me here, but something came up. He should be here in a day or two."

"That's fine," his host said. "You came at the right time. We're having a fish fry on Friday, with all the proceeds going to the schools for extracurricular activities. You're welcome to come. Your friend, too. It's only twenty dollars a person."

"Ah... Sure." Vince had to stop himself from stepping back. He'd been so tied to all of his father's schemes that something simple and generous like a fish fry to help kids blindsided him. Though perhaps he was wrong to be taken aback. Maybe this guy was going to keep the money for himself.

He took the key card. "Any other strangers in town?"

"Ice fishermen. That's it."

"Only men?" He made his voice casual, as if it were a throwaway question, but the host's dark eyes narrowed.

"As far as strangers go." Reyes' tone roughened, and he went from genial to guarded.

So, yes, someone was there, and he wasn't telling Vince who or where. Dawn could be at this resort. She could be anywhere in town. The IP address hadn't been wrong.

He thanked the host and turned. As he did, a small, redheaded girl ran around the corner toward Reyes, her eyes only on him, her arms out. Behind her a laughing redheaded woman in her twenties was half running, her eyes sparkling.

"I'm going to get you!" the woman called.

"Daddy will save me!" The sprite giggled, peeking back over her shoulder.

Vince stepped to the side to watch as Reyes, grinning widely, strode around the counter and scooped up the child. "I'll save you from your mean mommy," he said, affection in his voice.

"But who's going to save you?" The woman turned her head and sent Vince a dazzling smile. "You must be a new guest. Enjoy your stay here."

Vince thanked her, then strode to the elevator, ignoring the choking feeling in his chest.

So that's what a happy family looked like. He'd wondered if there was such a thing or if it were only a myth.

As he waited for the elevator, his phone pinged. He took the phone out of the front pocket of his duffel bag and clicked. The text was from his dad.

We got her, it said. *Come home now.*

He stared at it for a long moment.

Sunny. His father had to be talking about Sunny.

How had his father gotten her back?

What had his father done now?

The elevator dinged, the door opening. He picked up his luggage and stepped inside. He wanted to run home but not yet. Until he knew how to fix this, he wasn't going anywhere.

Thirty-six

We were two together
Then along came Mr. Charming
Who turned into Mr. Alarming
Now we're two apart.
Now it's a knife in my heart.

"Two Together"
Lyrics and music by Dawn Keighly

TODD WIPED THE soles of his boots on the back doormat of the B and B. He'd knocked and rung the doorbell. Someone had called for him to come in. Raine's voice, muffled, but when he stepped into the hall, no one was there.

As he unzipped his jacket and hung it in the coat room, he heard a man and a woman talking, their voices muted. He didn't know where they were.

He shifted from one foot to the other, not quite knowing what to do.

Acting like a normal person wasn't easy.

He finally walked into the kitchen. Spotting an open laptop on the counter, he realized that was the source of the voices. He tried to ignore them. To just stand there. But he felt awkward. He wished either Raine or Chuck would come to the kitchen soon. He wanted to thank Chuck for taking him in. And Raine, too, for being so nice to him. For treating him like he was someone worthwhile. Though he wouldn't say any of that to her. He would just thank her.

Unable to ignore the laptop anymore, he stepped to the counter and looked at an image of two women on the screen. One was blond and sexy with a Miss USA smile. A thinner, slightly shorter woman had long, pale blond hair and was playing a guitar while the sexy blond woman was singing a catchy song about flying like a bird.

The song sounded familiar. Oddly, the guitar player looked familiar, too.

As he leaned down, the images changed to a tall, thin man with shiny hair and a woman so thin that, if not for her expensive clothes and jewels, she could've been mistaken for a refugee from a third-world country.

"The big entertainment news of the day," the male speaker said, "is that Sunny Keighly is back at her husband's home."

"She's at their home in the Nirvana Now compound," the too-thin, dark-haired woman shot back at him. "It's in the hills of southern California, not their Beverly Hills home."

"The sister is still missing," the man said. "The Nirvana Now people aren't replying to our questions."

"Ledge has a few things to talk about, though," the woman said. "He claims that while he was lured away from his home on top of the hill above the Nirvana Now compound, someone drugged his housekeeper and kidnapped Sunny Keighly, who was taking refuge from her husband. We've spoken to the sheriff, and he was informed that Sunny Keighly is under a doctor's care."

"It could be true." The male speaker smiled at the camera.

"Dawn Keighly, Sunny's sister, is still missing," the woman said. "You have to admit, Ronnie, that this all sounds very curious."

Footsteps came from the hallway. At the same time, the blond singer and the woman with the guitar popped onto the laptop screen again. Leaning forward, Todd leaned forward to pause the video.

The woman with the guitar. He knew her. It was—

"Chuck?" Raine asked.

Todd snapped his head toward the voice and stared at her.

The glow on her face dimmed, though her smile remained. "Todd. It's you."

"It is me." He gestured at the frozen video, still gazing at her. "And this is you. You're the missing sister. You're Dawn Keighly."

She took a step back, her eyes wide.

He straightened and held up his hands. "I won't tell anyone. Don't worry. I didn't mean to—"

"It's okay," she said, but the paleness of her face and the fear in her eyes told him that it wasn't okay. "I have to tell Chuck. I have to—"

The back door opened. She turned toward it and so did Todd as Chuck stomped his boots on the small rug by the door.

Chuck's eyebrows quirked as he unzipped his jacket. "It stopped snowing out. The fish fry dinner is still on. You two are coming, aren't you? I'm paying. Dinner's on me."

There was silence for a moment, and Todd looked from Chuck to Raine, his forehead creased. "What is it? What happened?"

"I'm still a Marine," Todd said to her, not answering Chuck. "Not officially, but there's no such thing as an ex-Marine. Let me know what you need, and I'll do it."

She smiled but it was a sad clown smile. "I don't know for sure, but I'll go to the dinner tonight. It might be my last supper."

"It won't," Todd said, and something odd was happening. He just felt...stronger. "I won't let that happen."

"Is that a promise?" she asked.

"That's a vow." As Todd spoke, he stood straighter. Feeling strong again, at least for a moment.

A vertical line between her eyebrows, she nodded.

"I'll be back later." He headed toward the back door, his head held high.

"Wait!" she called.

When he turned, she looked from Chuck to Todd and back to Chuck again.

"I have something to tell both of you. My real name isn't Raine, and I'm hiding from a powerful man who might or might not be trying to kill me."

T

"WHAT CAN I do to keep you here?" Chuck asked. Todd and his dog had left, and it was Raine and him sitting in the living room on the couch. His arm was around her shoulders, and her head was leaning on his shoulder.

She looked up at him. Before Todd and his dog had left, she'd given both men a rundown on who she was and why she was in Wisconsin.

As she'd talked, she'd looked down at her feet instead of their faces. Chuck had glanced at Todd and seen his face darkening, his teeth gritting.

He'd guessed that Todd had looked at him and had seen the same darkening in his face, the same hardening of his features.

Now he twisted to see her head on his right shoulder. "Unlike Todd, I've never been a Marine. But I know how to shoot a gun and a rifle. I'm here for you. Whatever you need, I'll do it."

"Save my sister," she whispered, lifting her head.

He didn't answer right away. Then he nodded. "All right. I'll save her."

"I didn't mean for you to really do it. I don't want to put you in danger. But it's sweet that you would do it." She leaned forward and kissed him. No tongue, just a hard kiss.

Slowly, her mouth softened and she melted against him. He just held her, holding his own simmering emotions back, letting her take the lead. Not asking too much, but ready to give her whatever she needed.

He'd always been there for friends, but this was different. For her, he would do anything.

He would do everything.

He loved her. This fragile woman. This strong woman. This woman in pain.

"Let's go to the bedroom," she said. "We have time."

He nodded. She stood first, and she turned toward the bedroom upstairs.

"No," he said, and he steered her to the hallway, to his bedroom.

Just in case something happened. Just in case she left and never came back, every time he went to bed at night, he wanted to remember her there.

Naked. Tangled up in him, and him tangled up in her.

It had only been a short time since she'd walked into the B and B, but because of her, his life was changed.

THEY WERE DONE. Sated. Happy. Raine felt boneless, and Chuck's wild call of triumph still echoed in the bedroom.

They both lay on the bed, the sheets and covers half off of them, their bodies so warm they didn't need them. He didn't move, as if worn out. She felt the same way, empty in a good way. An amazing way. A way that might never happen to her again.

She closed her eyes, imprinting these last moments with him in her memory.

"I love you," he murmured.

Her eyelids popped open as he lifted his head.

"You don't need to say that just because I did." She held back a groan. She'd shouted out the three words during an orgasm that had gone on and on, and it had made him more wild. As if her words had been an aphrodisiac.

He slid his hand up and curved it around the side of her face. "I mean it. I love you."

"I have to leave tomorrow," she said.

"I understand. But you won't be going alone."

She wanted to argue, but it was hard to argue with tears welling up in her eyes.

"You're a fool," she whispered.

He smiled. The sweetest smile she'd ever seen, through her tears or no tears. "I'm a fool over you." Then he rolled off of her. "We'd better clean up. We don't want to miss the fish fry."

"No, we don't want to miss that." There was a sobbing laugh in her voice, as if she couldn't decide whether to laugh or to cry. Because if he was a fool over her, that made two fools in this bedroom.

She didn't know what had happened, or how it was that she, who was always so cautious and suspicious, had let down her guard while this man had stolen into her heart at the worst possible time.

And no matter what he said, she was *not* going to let him go with her. She didn't know how to stop him, but she would figure something out.

She had no illusions about the lengths that Grant Wellington would go to in order to get what he wanted. That was the reason she'd traveled to the northeastern corner of Wisconsin, using a fake name. Not hiding exactly but...well, yes, she was hiding. Using a different name, with a different haircut, wearing different clothes.

But it didn't *feel* as if she were hiding. Instead it felt as if she were in the right place with the right man.

A smile curved her lips as she slipped into the bathroom. *Definitely* the right man.

And she knew one thing for sure. She was not going to let him die because of her.

She didn't know how she was going to do this, but she needed to sneak out of Trouble Bay, and no one would know she was missing or where she was heading until she was long gone...

Thirty-seven

TODD HAD MONEY now. Not a lot, but to him it felt like a lot. He lived frugally. Dumpster food had been enough for him. At times, he'd felt that it was all he'd deserved. And now his aunt had left enough so he could pay the plumber and maybe have some left over for taxes at the end of the year.

Even before he'd heard from the lawyer, he'd had enough money to pay for a small apartment in a bad neighborhood, with heat in the winter and a small fridge for food and a small oven and stove. He could have had a bed with a mattress and covers. A kitchen table, a sink, and a bathroom. He could probably even have had a TV.

He could have paid bills. Filled out taxes. Reported to the VA Hospital.

Maybe the people at the V.A. could've helped him. Or tried to. Or blown him off. But at least he could have tried.

He hadn't done any of that. His mind had been in a scary place, keeping him from settling down. As if being in a small place, with the sounds of his neighbors seeping through the walls, would have been too much for him to take. Would have made him shake and given him screaming nightmares.

For a long time, the nightmares had plagued him. He still had them, but they were shadowy now. Muted. Maybe time had healed him a little. He'd never been too crazy. He'd just needed to be alone.

Until Baxter had come into his life. Todd wondered if saving Baxter from the cold and giving him food had saved him, too. He'd been a protector in the Marines. Maybe he'd needed to be a protector as a citizen, too.

The sky was darkening, and he went to the bathroom. After he'd left the B and B, he'd known what he needed to do. First he'd gone to the town's barber in a small white clapboard two-story, the barber shop on the lower floor where it housed three sinks and barber chairs. The barber, a chubby man with a nearly bald head, had trimmed Todd's hair, beard, and mustache. He'd even trimmed Todd's eyebrows as he talked about the fish fry dinner and how they could help the kids who had problems and needed help.

Todd felt odd to be in a place where people did this kind of stuff to help other people. It gave him an ache in his chest.

Maybe instead of feeling sorry for himself, he could help people who needed more help than he needed. Though his mental health wasn't anything to brag about, at least he had his physical health.

When he returned home, Baxter jumped on him, and Todd hugged him.

"I'll have to leave you again tonight," he said. The guilt was horrendous, but Chuck and Raine had been there for him. And now it was his turn to be there for them.

So he dressed in his jeans and a Green Bay Packers sweatshirt he'd bought in the grocery store. Not anything fancy, but it was clean, and so far Todd hadn't seen anyone dressing fancy in this place. Then he crouched in front of Baxter and petted him and kissed the smooth crown of his head while Baxter squirmed happily.

"I have to go." Todd got to his feet. "But I'll be back." He put on his jacket, and Baxter was on his feet, too, his whole body wagging, because he expected to go out, too.

Todd made sure his keys were in his pocket, then he grabbed the chew toy he'd hidden on the top shelf of the coat closet. He threw it.

As Baxter leapt to get it between his teeth, his whole being alive with joy and life, Todd strode to the front door and slipped outside, hunching his shoulders against the wintry wind.

He reminded himself once again that Baxter was safe in their new home, and right now Raine needed him. For bad or for good, he was a Marine. *Semper fidelis.* Dedication to Corps and country. Trained to protect.

Or maybe it was just payback. She had helped him; now he was going to help her.

No matter what happened.

He'd once been courageous. He headed to the B and B to drive to the fish fry with Raine and Chuck, ready to be courageous again. His shoulders up. Walking tall. Striding wide. Ready for anything.

☂

ALL AROUND VINCE, people were talking, though he sat at a table near the back by himself. A few women had come up to him, flirting. He'd told them he was married, and they'd backed off, wishing him an enjoyable stay.

The food was good, he'd say that for the charity fish fry. The local wine was decent, too, though he was taking small sips, keeping to the one glass. He wasn't here for food and wine. He was here as a means of retaliation.

He'd been waiting twenty-one years for this.

The door opened again. Two men and one woman, heading to a table two rows up from him. The blond-haired man was greeting people, the woman was nodding, her short and curly ash-blond hair bouncing with every movement. The other man was older, about ten years or so. He was stiffer than the others, as if he were ill at ease.

Vince turned his head away, toward the entrance again, but a niggle in his mind brought his gaze back to give a second, deeper look at the woman's pointed chin and the way she tilted her eyes and the slimness of her body beneath the slightly baggy clothes she wore. As if she were deliberately hiding her figure.

Dawn.

He started to push up to his feet but sat down again. Not here. Not now.

Maybe she'd seen the sudden movement out of the corner of her eyes, because her head turned toward him.

He swiveled around to the table behind him where two couples in their sixties or seventies sat, and he asked to borrow the ketchup.

The man grabbed the ketchup and passed it to him while the woman facing him said the bottle on his table looked full.

"It is full," he said. "It must be plugged up."

When he turned around with the extra bottle, Dawn and her two male friends were sitting two tables ahead of him, and he was looking at her back.

His heart was beating hard and fast, as if he'd run a mile through the sand and any minute his heart was going to burst.

He squeezed ketchup out of the bottle, then handed it back to the table behind him. His heart still beat too fast, but he forced himself to eat his dinner of fish, coleslaw, and fries as people talked around him. The man who'd checked him into the resort sat at the main table, with an older couple and the redheaded woman and child. People were coming up to them, chatting and smiling. They were obviously respected by the community.

But they weren't his target. He narrowed his eyes. The blond man was leaning toward Dawn. Twice he touched her arm. Then he rested his hand over the back of hers. A man who couldn't stop touching his woman. His lover.

That was not good. She had someone to watch over her.

She touched him back, too, though not as often. But she wasn't the demonstrative type. Vince knew a little about Sunny and Dawn's childhood. Sunny had come out of it more vulnerable, though she hid that part of her under a veneer of confidence. Despite her thinness, Dawn was tougher.

He didn't hold anything against Dawn—in fact, he admired her and Sunny—but it would have suited his needs better if she had been alone and vulnerable. He wanted her to lean on him and not this guy who looked like he should be the lead in a detective TV show.

Vince's brain was spitting out ideas, but nothing was clicking. He had to think of something. This was so damn important. So many years were leading up to this, and if he didn't play it right, he might lose it all.

That couldn't happen. He wouldn't allow it. He had to do something. Had to do it right now.

He grabbed a napkin, and he started to write.

A pudgy teenaged waitress with apple cheeks and a happy smile stopped by and asked him if everything was all right, and if he wanted coffee or anything to drink.

"You saved my day," he said.

Her eyes opened wide. "You need a drink that bad?"

Instead of answering, he signed his name, folded the napkin, then pointed at the table where Dawn sat. "Do you see the table two rows up with the woman in the purple sweater and the two men?"

"You mean Chuck and the guest at his bed-and-breakfast?" she asked. "And then there's Todd. He inherited his aunt's house, and he's new here."

"Ah, yes." He felt a little taken aback by the overload of information, but he held up the folded napkin. "Would you drop the note off to the woman?"

"Sure." She grabbed it and started to turn.

"Just a minute." He gave her a twenty.

She looked at it, and her eyes and mouth rounded. Then she rushed away, and in a few seconds, he saw her give Dawn the napkin.

But the waitress didn't leave right away. She leaned down to say something to Dawn while gesturing at his table.

Shit, shit, shit. He should have guessed the chatty waitress would do that.

Dawn's muscles in her cheeks twitched and her jaw stuck out. She stared at him as if she were spotting a venomous snake.

He held his breath, waiting to see if she'd tell the two who sat on either side of her. Both of them. Though he worked out almost every day, these two men looked as if they could beat the crap out of him.

All the talking in the room seemed to be background sounds, and he could have sworn he could hear Dawn's angry breaths and seen her thoughts churning in her mind.

And then...she opened the napkin, her head lowering to read what he'd written...

Thirty-eight

TODD HAD POSSESSED one skill since childhood that was worth nothing at all. It had never come in handy except for one time in an algebra class in high school when the smart girl in the row next to him had dropped her paper.

He could read sideways as well as upside down.

He would much rather have a better skill, like understanding computers or—when he was much younger—women. But he took one glance at the napkin that started out with *I promise not to hurt you. My father killed my mother, and the reason I've stayed with him all these years was to get evidence to prove this.*

Todd stopped eating the perch that had tasted pretty good up to now.

Looked like he was going to help Raine sooner instead of later.

FEAR TWISTED RAINE'S stomach with the first sentence and even tighter with the second one. Both Chuck and Todd stopped talking, and she felt their gazes on her. Knowing they would make sure she was safe kept her from jumping up and running out of the resort dining room as if the devil were after her.

It was the only reason she kept reading. As she did, the sounds of people talking around her seemed to move farther away. Her heart pounded against her ribs. Her skin chilled. Her fingertips numbed. As she continued to read, she felt frozen and fascinated and afraid and excited.

As a child, I rarely saw my father, and when I saw him, he mostly ignored me. My mother was everything to me. When I was seven, I knew she was having an affair. I liked her lover better than my father, so I never said anything. One night my mother told me that she and I and her lover were leaving for a better life.

The next day, my mother was killed in a fall that was similar to an accident that killed my father's first wife. Her lover disappeared. I believe he was murdered, too. All these years, I've stayed with my father to catch him doing something horrendous.

I know you want to save Sunny, and I think we can do this together. I know the compound. I know how to get inside it. I know how to get out of it.

I can help you save your sister.

Vince

She read the note a second time and a third time. She handed it to Chuck.

He read it once, then his eyes flickered to the top as he read it a second time, as she'd done.

She waited, breathing shallowly. Waiting for Chuck to finish.

Still holding it, he looked at her. "You know this man?"

"Not well. Vince didn't talk as much as his father and his brother." She let out a pent-up breath. "He reminded me of an enforcer in a spy movie. He seemed smarter than the others. He gave me the chills."

"And now? After reading this?" He held up the napkin. "Now what do you think?"

She wanted to cry. He'd *asked* her and hadn't told her. She wasn't used to men like that except, perhaps, in a professional way. "I still don't like him, but..." She swallowed and took a big breath. If it weren't for Chuck, she'd be out of here. She'd be running like the wind.

"If you want," he said, "I can beat him up for you."

She laughed, the sound surprising her. "No need. At least, not now. I think I should talk to him."

"Can I read it?" Todd's request surprised Raine. His voice was firmer than usual, and his hand was out, as though he expected her to hand it over.

She knew her eyes had widened, and she recalled that he'd been a Marine. She gave him the napkin.

He frowned as he read, then he lifted his head. "You didn't ask my opinion, but I believe collecting facts and evidence would be helpful to us."

"*Us?*" she asked.

His thin face, weathered by the sun that had scored lines around his eyes and his mouth, looked intense and alive. His dark brown eyes had sharpened as she'd never seen them before.

"Where is this compound?" Todd asked.

"Southern California. Near the Pacific Ocean."

"It's been awhile," Todd said, "but I knew some Marines from that area. I could contact them. See if they're around and are willing to help."

"Good idea," Chuck said. "We have a few vets here. I'll ask who they know in southern California."

"This is getting a little crazy." Raine looked from one to the other.

Chuck took her hand in his. "It's already gotten crazy."

She laughed, but there was a sob in it. She couldn't argue with that.

"The publicity..." She stopped. For her sister, publicity wasn't bad. And in this case, it might help save her. Besides, there was a small chance it wouldn't get out.

Taking a deep breath, she nodded. "Okay. Let's bring it on."

"Here?" Chuck glanced around, then back to her. "We're already the center of attention."

She sighed as she looked down at her plate. Half of her walleye was gone, but it had been a big walleye, and she was pretty sure she wouldn't eat much of anything else on her plate. Maybe the applesauce. "I think we should see what he has to say."

"Good idea." Chuck stood, and his face was hard with purpose. "I'll let him know."

Her gaze followed him as he marched over to Vince. His purposeful stride reminded her of a cowboy in an old movie ready for a gunfight.

A cowboy who was ready to save the girl.

She wanted to laugh and to scream. She wanted to tell him she could save herself.

But she wasn't sure if she trusted Vince. She *wanted* to trust him. What he'd written on the napkin seemed possible. Even plausible. She'd certainly wondered about both Grant's wives falling down the stairs. Only he would be so arrogant to kill both wives the same way. Or so stupid.

Yet he'd gotten away with it. And perhaps the first wife's death—Jarret's mother—really was an accident.

She curled her fingers tightly. She could prove nothing by herself. Nothing at all. For her sister's sake, she had to accept Chuck and Todd's help.

And maybe Vince's. The man who might or might not be his father's minion.

☂

CHUCK ESCORTED VINCE to their table. He was a dark-haired man about Chuck's age, average height. On the lean side, he looked like a runner, with a blade of a nose. He sat next to Todd, across the table from Chuck, but he didn't flinch from Chuck's narrow-eyed stare.

Perhaps he had nerves of steel, which didn't surprise Chuck as Vince mentioned his father, a man who seemed to think he was a demigod.

"My father wanted me to find you," Vince said to Raine. "It suited my agenda, so I didn't argue."

"You found me," Raine said.

Vince's story was getting to her, Chuck could tell. She probably empathized with Vince. Chuck knew by now that her mother had been selfish and probably addicted to drugs, and neither her father nor Sunny's had been in the picture.

It made him appreciate his own mother more.

His father hadn't been the best man in the world or the worst. He'd taken Chuck fishing a few times, and Chuck remembered his dad putting him on a bike and shouting encouragement, telling him he could do it. But other than those few times, he hadn't been around much.

His mother had always been there. She'd more than made up for his dad.

He put his hand on Raine's thigh under the table and squeezed. Her face sad, she turned to him. "It's all right," he said, his voice low. "It's going to be all right."

She blinked her sad eyes, then her lips curved in a slow smile. Vince said something to her, and she turned to him. Chuck removed his hand from her thigh. At least he'd made her smile, even if it had only lasted a few seconds.

The four of them talked for about five minutes, then they stopped talking. Stopped eating. Just sat there in grim silence, as they considered their options.

"We might need an army," Raine said.

"Army?" Chuck felt the hairs on the back of his neck rising, and he remembered what Todd had said about contacting his Marines buddies. "How about the Army, the Marines, and the Navy?"

He stood, even as he saw the startled look on Raine's and Vince's faces. Out of the corner of his eye, Todd was nodding.

"Hey!" he called out, and heads turned. "Anyone know any veterans in southern California?"

A strangled sound came from Raine. He looked down at her scrunched face, not sure if that was a cry or a laugh. She gazed up at him with a smile, yet tears dampened her eyes.

"I know a few former Marines in that area," a wood sculptor called out, and Chuck gave him his attention.

"And me." August stood.

"And me." A woman in her forties who painted on fabric stood. She was a newer resident and kept to herself usually.

One by one, other diners stood, including Todd, their ages ranging from the mid-twenties to the early sixties.

"What do you need?" August asked.

Chuck glanced down at Raine, then looked around. Ten men and two women were standing. He took a deep breath before speaking.

"I need your help to save a life."

Thirty-nine

TODD WAS GEARING up. Not weapons but his mental health. He'd come this far, and it had taken seven years to get here. He didn't want to fall apart again under stress or attack. He didn't know if he would get the shakes, the kind that came from his inside and worked their way to his outside. Didn't know if he could be around so many people without wanting to jump out of the plane.

He shut down those thoughts. Shut them down and locked them up tightly.

It was early Saturday morning. The first rays of the sun shimmered into his bedroom. And today he was about to go into a battle. War.

His entire body shaking, he got down on his knees in his bedroom, facing east like the Muslims did. He guessed that God didn't really care why he faced that way, but the window faced the rising sun, and it felt right.

His eyes closed, he felt the rays of sun against his eyelids as he prayed for the first time in many years. Maybe the first time since his mother had died.

He prayed for her. He prayed for his father. He prayed for the guys from his unit—the live ones and the ones who hadn't made it. He prayed for Raine and her sister and the baby growing inside Raine's sister. The baby was the reason he and the others were flying down to California today. After two hours of talking in August's house a short walk from the resort, he and the other vets, plus Chuck, Raine, and Vince, had mapped out a plan.

Throughout the years, Todd had kept the phone numbers of his buddies, not ready to give up the link that he'd had with the only family that had cared for him during his eight years in the Marines. In all this time, he'd never called any of them. Last night, after he'd come home, his hand had shaken when he'd dialed the phone. Only two still had the same number, and they'd both answered. They were both coming.

They both said they'd bring friends.

He prayed extra hard for all of them.

A whimper came from his side. Baxter leaned against him, as if trying to be one with him. A cool nose bumped his jaw. A tongue licked his cheek.

It took strength of will not to open his eyes. Took strength of will not to twist around and hug his dog right now.

Instead he prayed for his dog. Prayed that if anything happened to him in California, Baxter would find a loving home.

THEIR PLAN RAN like a military operation. Raine chartered a mid-sized jet, then called the others to tell them what she'd done. She told them to tell their friends in L.A. They had to act fast.

It wasn't until she and Chuck were leaving the B and B that he asked who'd chartered the jet.

"I did," she said.

He set his duffel bag on the front porch.

"I can afford it."

He locked the door.

"Does that bother you?" she asked.

He shook his head and grabbed his duffel bag. "I'm used to strong women."

She blinked, then everything happened quickly after that. Sue Jankowski, the middle-school bus driver, drove them and the other volunteers to the Sturgeon Bay airport, where she kissed her chubby, middle-aged husband goodbye. Ben Jankowski was a former sharpshooter in the Army, but now was Sue's father's partner in a small winery.

Before they loaded onto the airplane, Chuck asked Marsha Hauser, who trained and showed English setters for dog shows, to sit next to Todd. She could talk for hours about her dogs—boring most people to a head-nodding sleep—but Chuck asked her to befriend Todd. He looked lost without Baxter, who was staying with a neighbor who had two labs and a fenced yard.

Chuck and Raine settled in the back and put on their seat belts.

She closed her eyes and leaned her head on his shoulder. In a few minutes, her breaths were even with sleep.

He put his arm around her, and he wondered if this plan would work. He wondered if they'd be arrested. He wondered if Raine would be united with her sister and decide to stay in California.

By now, he knew that she'd taken care of her sister when they were younger—even though her sister was two years older. She might want to take care of her again.

If their plan worked. A big *if*. The men and the two women had called their military friends, and apparently they expected most of them to show up. He didn't know how many that would be. There were too many variables.

No one was ready to count. Nothing was for sure. There was no contract signed. There was no money changing hands. There were just a good number of good people who wanted to help a pregnant woman escape from an egotistical madman.

Chuck tilted his head against the top of Raine's. Nothing was ever sure in life. There was only moment by moment and second by second. He wasn't going to worry about the difference in their incomes. He wasn't going to worry about launching his art mart. He wasn't going to worry about Vince's father and his followers who wanted to kill in the name of a cruel egotist.

For this moment and the next and the moments after that, all he was going to think about was the way Raine leaned her head so trustingly on his shoulder. All he wanted to think about was the way she'd felt in his arms this morning. Beneath him. Above him. Her eyes darkened, her complexion bright, and the small sounds she made.

"I love you," he whispered, though she was breathing heavily with sleep. "We've only known each other a short time, but love doesn't need a clock."

Then he closed his eyes, his muscles relaxing and his breaths slowing as he eased into slumber.

TEARS WARMED RAINE'S eyes as she felt his head heavy on hers. He was sleeping. Really sleeping. Not pretending, like she had done, just closing her eyes to slow down an emotional overload.

Chuck loved her. Or he thought he did. She wasn't sure if she loved him, either, though she thought she did.

The only thing she knew for sure was that she trusted him. In her life, trust was better than love. She loved Sunny, enough to go back for her. Enough to risk her life. But after what had happened, she wasn't sure if she could trust her again.

If everything worked out, she would save Sunny's life. If necessary, she would die to save Sunny and her baby. But after that...

Nothing would be the same.

If they survived. Too many people were involved, and it scared her.

But she had to do this, and she couldn't make it happen alone. All she could do was trust and hope. Maybe praying wouldn't help, but it wouldn't hurt, either.

Please, God—or whatever or whoever might be listening. Please watch over Chuck. Please watch over every person in this plane and their friends who will be helping us. Please, please, please, please. Please save Sunny and her baby.

She wanted to name Chuck again, but if someone really was listening, he/she/they/it had heard her the first time. Just thinking about the possibility of Chuck being hurt—or something worse—made her chest hurt.

So maybe what she felt for him really was love. Who said love had to feel good?

Forty

THEY MADE IT to California on time, landing at a small airport just outside of L.A., Todd was glad there were no fires, no droughts, no earthquakes, and no floods. As they got off the plane, Todd had a view of the airport parking lot. He counted seven motorcycles, and also Jeeps, vans, sedans, and a few convertibles, foreign cars, and cars supposedly made in America.

Todd didn't know that they weren't, but he didn't trust many people, and he certainly didn't trust corporations.

Dogs were different. He trusted them. So did Marsha as she strode alongside him. He liked her. He liked women. On the whole, they were kinder than men. And he was heterosexual. Maybe...

He swallowed and shut down those thoughts. He didn't want to think about it.

She grabbed his arm. "I hope they have something good in the cafeteria. I'm starving."

He let her guide him. His pulse was jumping.

Inside the cafeteria, he only put a cheese sandwich, chips, a cookie, and orange juice on his tray. He liked coffee, but he was too nervous already and knew it wouldn't be a good idea.

"When this is over," Marsha said, as they carried their trays to a long table where some of the Wisconsin group was sitting, "maybe we can get together."

"Uh, get together and do what?" He wasn't sure where

they were going, but he sat down at the end of the table with her.

"Sleep together," she said, putting a paper napkin on her lap.

When he didn't reply right away, she looked at him, the thin brows on her roundish face arched up. "Have sex."

"Uh..." He swallowed. "Maybe. Sounds like a good plan."

She slapped him hard on his back. "You'll be happy you said that. You won't have to worry. I'll take good care of you."

He grabbed his orange juice and gulped half of it down. He felt like his face was burning, and so was his heart.

So far, he had a house, a dog, and now maybe he had a girlfriend. At least for one night, he might have one.

It had been a long time. A very long time.

Life was odd, but it was becoming more interesting. After all these years of knowing that one night or one day he might die violently, and not really caring that much, he now had one more reason to stay alive for a while.

AS THEY HEADED out to the parking area, someone was saying that more than fifty people, from their twenties to their seventies, were there. Raine looked around. Their small army was mostly men, with seven women, including the two from Wisconsin, and there were a lot of dog tags hanging around necks.

People were talking about the weapons they'd brought with them.

Raine shuddered, then she thought of her pregnant sister being held prisoner in the compound, and she stood up straight. They were warriors. She needed to be a warrior, too.

They reached the parking area, and Vince stopped and faced them, holding up his hands. Behind him were a variety of motorcycles, cars, SUVs, and one delivery truck.

The sun was bright, and it hit Vince's face, and it highlighted his eyes, showing their brightness. Their fervor.

"We had a minor miracle here," Vince said, and Raine shivered, though the sun was shining and the temperature was in the mid-sixties. She had been to one Nirvana Now sermon, and his voice was as strong and mesmerizing as his father's. "None of us posted on social media."

Laughter sparked around Raine. Even she smiled slightly.

Someone of the California group was handing out a map of the compound to everyone. Raine frowned. Vince must have been behind that. He had his own agenda, and she wasn't sure how she felt about it. All she wanted was to save Sunny.

He wanted revenge.

"You won't be allowed through the gates of Nirvana Now," he said. "Don't try to break through. Don't use your weapons. Their weapons are bigger and they have more of them. They'll kill all of us without any compunction."

"If we can't do anything," a tall, muscled man with a bushy beard asked, "then what the hell are we doing here?"

"You'll be a diversion." Vince looked around, and Raine tensed. In case one of the group was untrustworthy, Vince couldn't tell them what he'd planned. But they needed these men and women.

"What the hell do you mean by that?" the same guy demanded.

Chuck stepped up to stand next to Vince. "He hasn't told me what his plan is. But I'm going to guess that if you're in one place making a racket, that's where their attention will be."

"Yeah," someone behind Raine shouted out. "That's why it's called a diversion."

The husky guy shrugged, his expression sour. "I don't want to kill anyone, but I was hoping to get some action."

"I know what you can do to help," Vince said. "Who's good at taking videos?"

A dozen hands rose, a dozen or more held up cell phones.

"Can you do a live filming of the protest?" Vince asked. "When we get to the front gates, stream it on the social media sites. Say that we're here to save Sunny. A pregnant Sunny who's being kept prisoner."

Several people from all sides called out that they could do it, excitement in their voices. Excitement in the air.

"They won't let you see Sunny," Vince said, "but ask them to let Sunny speak for herself. Ask them if she's a prisoner. They'll say no, and they'll look guilty."

"And make sure you mention that you're military vets," Chuck added. "Maybe interview each other. Say what you did to serve our great country while guys like Wellington live in a mansion and keep a pregnant woman hidden. That's going to get us plenty of buzz."

The atmosphere changed. The stony faces brightened, smiles on most of them, showing teeth and sparkling eyes.

"If that's squared away," one of the women said, "I'm ready to roll. Anyone else?"

"Marines are always ready," a bald, medium-sized guy said.

"I've heard that about the Marines." A woman wearing tight jeans and a red top looked him up and down slowly.

He gave her an equally slow up-and-down gaze. "Hearing isn't believing. *Experiencing* is."

She laughed and strolled toward the cars, her hips swaying.

The Marine followed her.

Raine sniffed back tears and an overload of emotion. She had a sister to save. Like the woman said, she was ready to roll.

☂

"DID YOU READ this?" Chuck asked, showing her a pamphlet on the compound. He and Raine sat in the backseat of an Army-green Jeep. Vince was driving, and he'd chosen Doug, a muscular former Marine, to ride with them. In Doug's civilian life he was a wrestling manager.

"I've been there once," Raine said. "There's a full golf course, a large swimming pool, plus a mansion on steroids for Wellington and his family."

"There's another luxury-hotel-like building for the church's top ministers," Vince said, his eyes not leaving the road that seemed to be winding upward around a hill, though the land on the passenger side was flat, with trees, fields, and, once in a while, big homes.

The view was breathtaking, especially on the driver's side, where Chuck could look down and see the ocean. Though he preferred the flatter land in Trouble Bay and the tamer waters of Lake Michigan, he had no complaints about the seventy-degree weather in southern California.

"Isn't there a punishment building, too?" Raine asked. "Sunny mentioned it once, then she wouldn't say anything more. I asked her about it a couple times after that, and she told me not to talk about it. I could tell she was scared."

Chuck felt her hurt, and he squeezed her hand in his.

"She always looks confident," she continued, "but that veneer is thin."

"She's stronger than you think," Vince said from the front seat. "Look how she escaped."

"And you're here to save your sister," Doug said.

Chuck thought that this was sounding like a therapy session. Maybe that was a good thing.

"I am," Raine said. "I'll save Sunny, but I don't know if I'll ever fully trust her again."

She sat back, hand gripping his more tightly.

The silence lasted for about five minutes, until Vince spoke again. "We're almost there. On your maps, do you see the long building called the Happiness Center? It's near the north edge of the other buildings, and there's a stream between them."

The sound of paper snapping came from the front seat. Chuck frowned at the map he shared with Raine. "The stream has some kind of fence around it," he said.

"It flows through the Happiness Center," Vince said, his tone flat. "It's part of the recommitment progress. Another step up to Nirvana."

"Well, shit," Doug said. "I'm surprised everyone doesn't walk out of there."

Vince's laugh was bitter. "Once you're in Nirvana Now, you don't walk out. Not unless my father wants you out."

"That's easy for you to say," Raine said. "I doubt your father would put you through that. Not his own son."

Vince gave another bitter laugh. "Want to put money on that?"

"Shit." Doug turned his head toward Vince. "He did? That's sick."

"Did he make Jarret go through it?" Raine asked.

"No."

There was silence as he continued to drive.

"It sucks big-time that we can't kill anyone," Doug said. "Some people just deserve to die."

In the long silence that followed, Chuck took Raine's hand in his.

"I doubt he'll die for a long time," Vince said finally. "But at least we'll take his grandchild away from him. At least Sunny will be free."

Something in Vince's tone made Chuck stare at the back of his head. Made Raine suck in her breath.

"Once Sunny gets free," she said, "everyone will know about your father. Does that bother you?"

"I'm pretty sure he killed my mother." Vince's voice was so cool he could have been talking about the weather.

Chuck looked at Raine, and she looked back at him. They held each other's hand a little tighter.

"So, no," Vince said. "I wouldn't care if everyone knows. I hope he rots and dies. I hope it happens soon."

The Jeep slowed and he pulled off the road onto the

bumpy ground, heading straight toward a thick grove of trees.

"I think we're going down the rabbit hole," Raine said, her grip on Chuck's hand tightening.

Chuck wished it were rabbits they hoped to avoid, but instead it was the most dangerous animals on Earth.

Humans.

Forty-one

TODD LOOKED BEHIND them, and the Jeep wasn't following them anymore. He'd known this would happen. Vince had warned him that he needed to keep the others noisy and motivated, and not to worry about the Jeep. Todd's job was to make sure none of them broke through the gates. If anyone did, Vince said they would be harmed or imprisoned. Hidden where no one could find them.

Todd had told Vince he could do this, but even as he'd spoken the words, he'd started to shake.

A sigh came from his left, interrupting the thoughts whipping through his head. "It's going to be okay," Marsha said in the seat next to him, then her hand settled on his shoulder, and she patted him. Much as she'd pet one of her dogs.

His shoulders relaxed, and he gave a little laugh.

"Something funny?" she asked.

"I just realized it is true," he said. "Men really are a lot like dogs."

They were both laughing as the van turned around a curve, and they saw tall metal gates. Parked on the side of the road were a half dozen cars and what he assumed to be journalists and paparazzi, though they dressed more casually than they did in Wisconsin. A couple looked so young that he thought they should be in school.

"Looks like it's show time!" someone in the front of the bus called out.

They all laughed, except for Todd. He looked down at his cell phone. No messages yet. No matter. The four in the Jeep had their own agenda. Todd knew what the people in the bus were supposed to do. Keep the attention on them and not do anything stupid. When Todd had told the others he didn't want anyone to pull out a gun or a rifle, most of them had nodded, with only a few grumbles.

But in case the others started something, they were all armed. Including Chuck.

After all, an army without weapons was only a lot of people with big mouths and nothing to back it up.

Todd patted his right side, by his hip, and he felt the bulge of the holster and the gun that Chuck had given him before they'd left Wisconsin.

He felt nauseous but, at the same time, relieved. He was, after all, accustomed to war. And this was war in America.

🌂

THE FOUR OF them jumped out of the Jeep, stepping onto weeds and long grasses.

Raine was grateful she wore her hiking shoes and jeans. She and the other two men followed Vince down a hill to a four-passenger golf cart with a tan canvass roof and no sides.

The trees here were tall and leafy, hiding the Jeep from aerial views.

"Is this for us?" Raine asked after she hopped into the back of the covered golf cart. Chuck jumped in next to her, and Doug sat in the front next to Vince, in the driver's seat.

"It's always here," Vince said. "In case one of the lieutenants or captains wants to play a round of golf."

"Lieutenants or captains?" She snickered, and Chuck and Doug laughed, too. Not Vince, though; she could see the stiffness in his shoulders and neck as he started the engine.

"Gas engine?" Doug asked.

"This one is. We—I mean *they*—have electric cars, too."

"I've done some golfing," Doug said. "These babies don't come cheap."

Vince didn't answer.

Doug's eyes narrowed. "I'm starting to feel bad that I'm not going to shoot someone."

Next to her, Chuck laughed as Vince turned into a large tunnel.

"Holy shit," Doug said.

"Nothing holy about it." Raine leaned forward; it was getting darker by the second. "Where's this thing taking us?"

"We could stop a few places," Vince said, "but I'm taking this all the way to the mansion. I know my father. That's where he's keeping Sunny locked up."

"I didn't see this tunnel on the map," Chuck said.

"You won't." Vince didn't look back at them. "Only a few people know about it and have access to the golf cart."

"Gotta admit," Doug said, "this is kind of cool."

"Kind of freakish," Chuck said. "Like something out of a comic strip."

Raine made a face. "Sunny loved Grant's home, but it reminded me of a bad copy of Buckingham Palace."

For the first time, Vince laughed. And for the first time, Raine's doubts waned, and she believed he was telling the truth. That he did want to get revenge for his mother. And that he would do his best to help her and Chuck save Sunny.

"Won't there be guards around Sunny?" she asked. "She got away once. Sunny can be stubborn. If there's a chance to escape, she'll try again."

"That's why the others are in front," Vince said. "Chanting and showing off their veteran statuses. They'll be a distraction."

"People are watching us because we're veterans." Doug glanced around, lips flattened against his teeth, his facial muscles tensed. "Everyone is thankful for our service. Or so they say. Except when it comes to treatment and medical help and job help."

"All the things that matter." Raine noted that they were farther down the tunnel. The tunnel builder had put open spots in the tunnel roof, letting in enough light to see each other's faces and for Vince to navigate. "Are you sure they don't have the tunnel hooked up to an alarm?"

"No alarm," Vince said. "They don't want this tunnel on record. And right about now, the local deputies will be coming by the front gate."

"Uh-oh." She sat back. "That's not good."

"It is good. The sheriff and his deputies don't care for the Nirvana Now people. They don't shop in the nearest towns. And it works both ways. My father ordered his people not to recruit the locals. He doesn't want them to know too much."

"They don't want their converts to have friends near the compound who might help them." Chuck's voice was flat. "That's what you really mean."

"You're probably right," Vince said.

She shuddered, and Chuck covered her hand with his.

"And then what?" she asked. "Do you think your father and his other top lieutenant and captains or whatever"— she made a face—"will be running out to tell the protesters to leave?"

"They'll be in the war room. It's in the headquarters, a safe room in the basement." Vince twisted slightly to see them. "They have computers there that show views of the gate. That's what they'll be busy watching. Not us."

"You're sure about that? Sure they won't suspect us?"

"My father suspects everyone. Except me. He's known for his arrogance. He's never guessed that I've been waiting a long time for the chance to nail him. I highly doubt that they'll find us."

There was silence in the car. Raine leaned closer to Chuck, and her knuckles brushed against the holstered gun at his hip.

Cold sliced through her, and she wondered if this would work. Suddenly, she wasn't sure.

Another chill leaked into her veins as she suspected that everyone else in this golf cart was wondering the same thing.

CHUCK SAT STRAIGHT in the golf cart, peering around, ready for anything. He was in strange territory. Beautiful, yet he felt the evil.

For more than three decades, he'd lived in a small town, a place where he knew everyone. He'd traveled a bit, as much as someone could without a lot of money, but he hadn't felt a big urge to go far. He liked his town. He liked the people. He even liked the influx of tourists during the summer months.

He'd always thought he'd had a good life, and now, this winter, suddenly things were changing. First his Great Idea that he thought of with capital letters. And then the mass rejection by the people he'd thought would believe in him.

And he'd wondered if they were right. For years he'd felt that he'd been waiting for something. For the *right* something. The art mart had given him the *this is it* feeling inside his gut. The *right thing* he'd been waiting for.

Even after the mass rejection, he still believed in the art mart. He suspected his so-called friends knew it was a great idea, too, and that it wasn't the idea they didn't believe in. It was him.

Every rejection had felt like a knife in his heart.

And then *she* had come.

Now he knew that it wasn't the art mart he'd been waiting for. It was Raine.

He took her hand and squeezed.

She didn't look at him, but she squeezed back.

The erratic beating of his heart settled, and at the same time, he thought, *if necessary, I will die for her.*

But he'd much rather not die. He'd much rather stay alive and love her.

And though he didn't much care for killing, for both of them to stay alive, he would kill without hesitation.

Forty-two

"YOU NEED TO leave." The man with the shaved head and solid muscles on the other side of the iron gates looked like a giant to Todd. He had to be nearly seven feet tall.

"I could take him." Her voice low, Marsha held out her hands, her fingers curved like claws. "Get me close enough to his balls, and I'll make him scream for mercy."

The ponytailed, gray-haired guy from the California contingent who had told everyone to "call me Dude" laughed. The big guy glared at them through the bars, and suddenly Todd laughed, too.

Dude laughed louder.

Marsha laughed.

Everyone else started to laugh.

The tall, skinny guy behind the hairy behemoth raised a shotgun and shot into the air.

Todd stepped in front of Marsha, and he whipped out his gun.

Someone shoved him to the side. Marsha.

People on the other side of the gates yelled angrily, and their own people yelled back.

"Don't ever do that again," Marsha said to him, her voice steely.

He looked into her narrowed eyes, and he slowly nodded. "I won't." Then, not sure he would be able to stop himself, he added, "I'll try not to."

The shouting was still going on around them but her

posture changed. The tightness in her face eased, her shoulders lowered, her lips widened in a slow smile.

"You're sweet." She reached up and patted his cheek before she turned away.

He could feel the energy surging from her. She was so vital. *Alive.* All these years since his last tour, he'd been half-alive, knowing he could die anytime. And if it happened, he was ready for it. Life didn't matter. Life wasn't good. Only instinct, luck, and a naturally healthy body kept him alive.

Now, just being near her made him feel the same way he felt with Baxter.

Well, not quite the same way. He wasn't sure what that meant, but he wanted to explore it with her. He wanted to be her friend. And maybe her lover.

Most of all, he wanted to be alive.

He was waking up. It had started with the dog. It had expanded in Trouble Bay. And now...now, he didn't know. But he wanted to find out.

One of the guys in front of them called out, "Hey! We're on the news." He held up his cell phone, and Todd and Marsha and a few others nearest him stepped closer.

Mostly the image was of the people nearest the gate, and the guys on the other side. A news anchor with a deep voice spoke about the military veterans who'd come to the compound to protect the pregnant singer. He went on to say that the veterans believed she'd been kidnapped from the home of Ledge, an old rocker who had won multiple Grammy awards.

The whir of a siren came from up the road. Not one siren but two or three.

The cell phones turned toward the road.

Guns were shoved into holsters or put away on their side of the gate but not the other side.

"Free Sunny!" someone shouted. "Free Sunny!"

They all began to chant, including Marsha and Todd.

"Free Sunny! Free Sunny! Free Sunny!"

As Todd shouted, an ache grew inside him. An ache that had been inside him since Afghanistan.

Free me! Free me from despair. Free me from my memories. Free me from flinching at every storm and every firework, just like my dog. Free me, free me, free me.

Free everyone.

THEY REACHED THE end of the tunnel, stopped by a wall of solid dirt. Light spilled into the tunnel to the right, leading up to steps and a door.

"This feels like a scene out of a spooky children's movie," Chuck said, and Raine choked out a laugh.

"A children's movie with monsters." Vince stepped out of the golf cart and onto the first step. "The most monstrous is my father."

Chuck followed Raine out, thinking of his own father, who'd always had a smile for him, but was rarely home, more interested in drinking with his friends and, as Chuck had discovered in his early teens, women. A lot of women. So many women that his killer had never been caught, though the consensus in Trouble Bay was that it was either a jealous woman or an angry husband.

He knew that neither she nor Sunny had known their fathers, and her mother hadn't been a prize, either.

Raine would be a prize. The thought lit up in his head. Followed by another one. *I'm going to be a great father.*

The door opened. They were on the downside of a sloping hill with a row of bushes on the top. Vince was hunching down in front of the door. "Follow me."

They headed up the hill, stopping in front of the bushes, still bent low. Vince pointed. "The mansion is that way."

Through the branches on the green, leafy bushes, Chuck gazed at a stone and wood building that would make most mansions look undersized. "Is that where you live?" he asked.

"It's where I have a room," Vince said, and Chuck caught the difference.

"You can get us in there?" Doug said.

"If no one shoots us first."

Doug cracked a low laugh, and Chuck realized they'd been talking in hushed voices as tension thrummed through him.

"Are they watching us?" Raine glanced around.

"Once we break through the bushes, we might be on their radar." Vince gave all of them a keen look, straight in their eyes, radiating tension. "Right now their attention is most likely focused on our small army in front of the gates, but I can't guarantee they won't have someone watching the mansion, too."

There was silence. Raine broke it. "In that case," she said, her voice crisp, "what are we waiting for?"

Doug laughed again, and Vince gave her a humorless smile, his eyes dark, not giving away anything.

"Follow me," he said. "Stay low. Run fast. Don't shoot yourself." He turned and pushed branches away. His head tilted to protect his face, he barreled through them.

Doug went next.

"You go," Chuck said to Raine, gesturing at the bushes. "I have your back."

She blinked, leaned forward, and kissed him hard and fast. Before he could respond, she twisted around and followed the others.

It was his turn. He pushed the branches away, but a few snapped at his face as he hurried after her with his back bent, as close to the ground as he could get and still run. As he half ran behind her, he thought that if she was going to hell, he would follow her there, too.

Forty-three

WITHIN MINUTES OF the two sheriff's cars pulling up, Todd knew the deputies—two from each car—weren't going to arrest him and the others. He could tell they were on their side, and the bigger, older one had a military background. He didn't say anything, but it was just something about the way he stood. Tall and strong. Ready to serve. Ready to protect. And, if necessary, ready to kill.

Besides, there were the paparazzi—and maybe some people from legitimate newspapers and news channels, too. With so many witnesses, the deputies wouldn't arrest or shoot them.

It was also clear they weren't going to do anything to the Nirvana people. But neither were they going to leave two groups of people with guns on both sides of the gate. So they stood between them and the gate and tried to make both angry groups go away.

Todd thought that would be like separating two dogs who wanted the same bone.

"They better fix this soon," Marsha said, scowling.

"You okay?" he asked.

"I really have to pee." She laughed harshly. "Maybe if I shoot one of them, the deputies will take me to jail and I can use their bathroom."

He stepped up to what he'd silently named The Line of Contention. The angriest of the other group, and about four angry guys from their group. And, standing between them, the deputies.

"There's an easy solution to all of this," Todd said.

No one heard his words, but the four deputies turned to him, frowning.

"There's a solution," he said louder.

"Yeah?" one of the deputies asked, a husky guy with a beaky nose and short, graying hair.

The veterans quieted. The other side was still throwing angry words at them, but they ignored them. The sun still shone down on them, though it was lowering. Todd was glad he was wearing a cap with a bill to block the rays from shining into his eyes. "Why not ask Sunny if she was kidnapped or if she's here because she wants to be here?"

The other side had quieted enough to hear him. Now they yelled louder about trespassing and searching without just cause or a search warrant. Todd didn't know if it was true or not, but all the noise was making the nerves in his body jumpy.

There were a hell of a lot of people talking at once. And now he saw that the singer's husband was in the front by the gate, throwing around the word *sue*.

All Todd knew was that this Sunny was Raine's sister and Vince's sister-in-law, and she was pregnant and the reason they were here.

And Marsha had to pee.

To be honest, so did he.

Probably they weren't the only ones.

The thought oddly made him relax. Gave him the courage to turn back to the deputies. "If you suspect that someone was kidnapped, don't you have to check that out?"

"If you don't," Marsha said, "and you find out she was, you'll get sued for *not* checking."

There was a loud whirring noise in the air. Todd looked up at a helicopter hovering above them. It was annoying and made him jumpy. He fought an urge to whip out his gun and shoot it.

He turned back to the deputies. "Just think what the news outlets will say."

They all looked at him like they believed him. None of them knowing that a short time ago, he'd been sleeping in a cardboard box in an alley and eating food out of a dumpster. None of them knew he had been a crazy mess.

Or that, inside his mind, where no one could see, he was still a crazy mess.

He took a deep breath and looked from one deputy to the other. "What's going to happen if you don't go in, and you find out later that she's harmed by these people? What if she dies?"

"Yeah." Marsha raised her chin and her voice. "Listen to my friend. He's a smart guy."

Todd stared at her.

"If you don't go in now," she continued, "and she or the baby is hurt, you know that someone will sue the crap out of you."

The Nirvana people started yelling about sanctuary and religious rights—though he didn't know what that had to do with a woman being possibly kidnapped. If this were any normal situation, he was pretty sure the police would be storming in there.

"If this were a normal situation," Todd said, because, after a decade of rarely talking to anyone, he was apparently having diarrhea of the mouth, "you'd be crashing through the doors right now."

One of the deputies was on his cell phone, and the others didn't say anything, but they looked away, so he was pretty sure they agreed with him.

He hoped they would do something quickly. He hoped so for Raine's sake. He hoped so for her sister's sake. He hoped so for Chuck's sake, because it was clear as a cloudless sky that Chuck cared about Raine.

Lastly, he hoped that Marsha could get inside Nirvana Now and use the bathroom.

†

VINCE ENTERED THROUGH a side door that led to the kitchen pantry, using his own key for the door for Nirvana Now aspirants. "To get to the next level," he told the others, "you needed to clean and scrub and cater to my father."

"What crazies want to do that?" Doug asked.

Vince shrugged. He'd never figured out why these aspirants wanted to be like Grant. Since his mother's death, Vince had wanted to be anything but like his father.

"Now what?" Doug asked.

Vince looked behind him. They were surrounded by food items and provisions and cleaning supplies on open shelves. A movement caught his eye as Dawn grabbed a spray bottle.

"What are you doing, Dawn?" he asked as she sniffed it.

She held up the plastic spray bottle. "There's bleach in here. It will make a good weapon."

He frowned. He should have chosen one of the others instead of her. Someone familiar with a gun.

"Call me Raine," she said. "That's my name now."

"Raine." He nodded. It was too late to switch her with someone else. And Sunny might listen to her. "I'll take you up to Sunny's room. We can call the police from there."

"Someone will be guarding her," Raine said. "Let me go first. They'll recognize me."

"That's not a good thing." Vince held his voice steady with an effort. Why was she doing this now? When they were almost there? She was going to get in the way. "You aren't considered to be the best influence on your sister."

"Maybe, but they won't be afraid of me. I'll say that I'm worried about her and the baby. They'll be less likely to shoot me."

"What about the spray bottle?"

Her forehead furrowed. "I'll think of something."

He stared at her as Doug shifted from one foot to the other, impatient for action. And Chuck watched her, looking worried but not saying anything.

"We're going up the back stairway, right?" she asked.

He nodded. The focus of the guards would be in the front, but there would be at least a couple guards in the back.

"Good." Dawn—no, Raine—nodded, then stepped past Doug and then him, her shoulder and right arm brushing his arm. In front of him, she turned. "Stay behind me a little, so you'll surprise anyone guarding her room."

Vince tightened his jaw. Doug laughed quietly, but Chuck pushed ahead of Doug and Vince.

"Hey—" Vince slapped Chuck's shoulder. "I need to be behind her."

Chuck turned his head. "I've been shooting since I was a kid. I'm an expert."

Vince held back a groan. "Maybe, but like she said, whoever is up there will know me. They won't expect me to take them down. I'm the son of their leader. If I'm behind her, they'll at least pause before they shoot."

Chuck narrowed his eyes, his lips flattened, then he stepped back and gestured Vince forward.

One victory, Vince thought as he followed Raine. And one failure.

It had better be the last failure. They couldn't afford any more.

THE TWO GUARDS were talking, and Raine could hear the tension in their voices.

Good. They were worried. They were probably thinking this wasn't going to end well for Nirvana Now.

While the others waited in the stairwell, she strode down the hallway toward her sister's door, purposely making enough noise for the guards to look at her. She didn't recall their names, but they looked familiar, one tall and thin, one short and thin.

"Hey," she said. "What's going on outside?"

Their jaws dropped, they looked at her, then at each other, reminding her of guppies.

She kept walking, smiling slightly at them.

The guards turned back to her. "You're not supposed to be here," the shorter one said. He looked wiry, while the back of the taller one was stooped, his mouth still open.

Her gaze settled back to the shorter one. "They let me in. Sunny wanted me."

"I guess that's okay then." The taller one brought down his rifle, and he stepped back.

The shorter one remained in front of the door. "What're you carrying?"

"This?" She held up the spray bottle. "It's for cleaning. Sunny's allergic to dust."

"Well, maybe she is, but we didn't get orders to let you in."

She didn't let her smile waver. She didn't scream, though she wanted to. Wanted to badly. She kept walking. "Would I have gotten through the gates if there weren't orders to let me in?"

"Probably not." The shorter guy took his cell phone out of his pocket. "I've gotta call in about this."

At two steps away from him, she kept smiling as she said, "Just one minute."

He looked at her, still holding the phone but not pressing any numbers as, still smiling, she held out the bottle, pressed down the lever, and sprayed bleach at his eyes.

He screamed, the phone dropping from his hand.

The other guard stepped toward her. "Wha—"

She sprayed his eyes, and he screamed, his hands flying up to cover his eyes.

Behind her came pounding footsteps. She didn't wait for

the others. She stepped past the guard, who was holding his hands over his eyes and making odd noises. Pounding on the door, she called, "Sunny, it's me. Open the damn door!"

Forty-four

TODD'S CELL PHONE rang. He saw Chuck's name and held it to his ear. After listening for a moment, he turned to the deputies and stretched out his arm holding the cell phone. "Our friends are in Sunny's rooms. She wants to talk to you."

The deputy closest to him took the cell phone. He listened, then talked to the other deputies who'd gathered around him, his voice low so only the other deputies could hear.

As they stepped away from each other, the Nirvana Now group started yelling again. The husband was missing, but he'd looked to Todd like the kind of guy who would leave a sinking ship.

"I'll keep your phone for now," the deputy said.

"You're going in?" Todd asked, keeping his voice down. "You can keep my phone, but let us go in with you."

"Why should I?"

"Our friends are in there." Todd gestured to Marsha. "We care about them. We want to make sure they're okay. We won't talk to anyone or get involved with the investigation."

"We can't do that," the deputy asked. "You'll have to stay outside."

Marsha took a step closer to the deputies. "I'm an Army vet, an animal vet, and a woman. She's pregnant and upset and possibly drugged. She very likely needs my help. I could even give her medical help."

"Forget it." The first deputy handed him his phone. "We won't need your phone. Keep it, and stay out here."

As he turned away, the sound of someone yelling came from the phone, and Todd realized the deputy hadn't turned it off. He put the phone to his ear.

"Go away!" a woman was screaming. "Go away!"

"You're my wife!" a man shouted. "You have to do what I say!"

Todd jerked the phone from his ear, then held the phone out to the deputy so he could hear the shouts. "Her husband's in the bedroom. The man she ran from. You need to go there now."

The deputies looked at each other, then turned to the fence. "Open this *now*," the deputy he'd been talking to said to the Nirvana Now people.

"There's a woman being attacked in the house," the other deputy said. "If she gets shot, all of you are going to be arrested."

"You can't do that," someone yelled.

"We can charge you with obstruction of justice," the third deputy said.

"Or kidnapping," the fourth one said. "Is that what you signed up for?"

☂

"GET AWAY FROM my wife." Jarret's tanned face looked pale. "Get away now, or I'll kill you."

"Raine." Sunny's voice quavered as she turned to Raine. "Do as he says."

Raine nodded, even as rage built up inside her. Fury.

She was so sick of these men pushing her around.

She was not going to have it anymore. But she couldn't say that now. She moved away from Sunny, toward Chuck, Doug, and Vince, all three of them aiming guns at Sunny's husband, who was carrying what looked to her like an assault rifle.

"And you three." Jarret waved the assault rifle at them. "Put them down *now*."

"Ain't gonna happen," Doug said.

Vince stood straight, his dark eyes burning. "Don't do this, Jarret."

"She's my *wife*," Jarret said, his face sweating. "I'm warning you. You need to leave or die."

Raine looked at Chuck, who stood still, not saying anything, just staring at Jarret, as if studying his every move.

"One," Jarret said as he raised the scary-looking rifle, his gaze going from Doug to his brother, not bothering to look at Chuck or Raine, who he obviously considered not to be a threat. "Two."

Raine lifted the bleach bottle, her index finger on the pump. As she lifted her foot to step toward Jarret, she saw Chuck's arm move, then heard a gunshot.

Fear froze her. In her mind, she screamed, *Chuck!*

Another scream echoed around her. Jarret. In what felt like slow motion, he dropped the rifle. As he did, Vince dived forward, sliding to catch the assault rifle before it reached the wooden floor.

"My arm!" Jarret cried, on his knees, staring at Chuck. "You shot my fucking arm!"

Sunny rushed to Jarret's side, and Raine gaped at her. She couldn't believe Sunny was going to embrace him. Not after—

"Bastard!" Sunny kicked him in his face. "Fucking bastard." She kicked him again and again and again as he screamed again and again and again.

Vince handed the rifle to Chuck, then stepped forward, put his arms around Sunny's breastbone, and hauled her back.

"Don't," she shouted, fighting him. "Don't stop me."

"I have to, honey," he said. "Deputies are coming. You don't want them to catch you beating the shit out of him."

She stopped struggling. When he dropped his arm, she twisted around and glared at him. "Right now, I don't give a damn."

"Shh." He pulled her against him, her chest against his, then he rubbed her back with his left hand. "Shh. Everything is going to be all right now. I'll take care of you."

"Promise?" She lifted her face to his.

He nodded. "I do."

Raine watched them with her jaw dropped. The deputies barged into the room, and she blinked and shook her head. Behind the deputies were Todd and Marsha.

Two of the deputies immediately headed to Jarret, still on his knees, holding his arm and sobbing. Another deputy strode straight to Chuck, who was holding out the assault rifle. He nodded his head toward the sobbing husband. "This was his, not mine."

The other deputy stepped over to Sunny, with Vince still holding her.

"Jarret was going to kill them with the rifle," Sunny cried out. "This man"—she pointed at Chuck—"saved their lives, my sister's, and then mine and the baby's."

"I'll say." The deputy holding the assault rifle whistled. "This baby could take out a train."

"Arrest his father, too," Sunny said. "He's the mastermind behind all of this. He's the one who drugged and then kidnapped me from Ledge's place." She put her hand over her belly that still looked flat to Raine. "I don't know what the drug has done to my baby."

"Where is your father-in-law?" the deputy asked.

"Ask *him*." She glared at Jarret, and her leg kicked up behind her.

Raine knew her sister wanted to kick him. She didn't blame her. If the deputies weren't here, she'd want to kick him, too. *After* she sprayed bleach into his eyes.

And then she would stomp on his injured arm.

And she would kick him in the balls.

She was sorry she hadn't thought to do that before the

deputies had stormed into the bedroom. That would be even better than bleach.

An arm curved around her back. Chuck. With a sigh, she rested her head against his shoulder. He would let the deputies take care of the creep. She supposed the deputies would thoroughly question Chuck about the shot in Jarret's arm, but they were all witnesses that the jerk had been threatening them. Chuck might get in trouble because he didn't have a gun license in California—Raine wasn't sure about that. But the sheriff's department was going to be embarrassed by this whole thing, including their reluctance to protect Sunny in a timely manner. She would bet the sheriff had received plenty of complaints about Nirvana Now that his department had ignored. After this, former church members would be filing lawsuits and complaining on social media and talk shows.

Besides, Chuck could have killed Jarret, and he'd only wounded him.

Jarret had gotten off lightly.

Todd and Marsha came over to them. "Is there a bathroom around here?" Marsha asked.

Raine drew away from Chuck. "I'll show it to you."

As they headed out of the room, she half expected one of the deputies to call out to them, but it was Sunny who asked where they were going.

"The bathroom," she said.

Sunny drew away from Vince. "I'll go, too."

A deputy took a step after her. "I'm not sure—"

"All the action happened in this room, not the bathroom." Sunny stepped away, not looking back, her expression determined. "I'm pregnant, and I have to pee. If you have a problem with that, then you'll have to arrest me."

No one tried to stop them. As they turned into the hallway, Marsha said, "I'm sorry but I have to go first."

It wasn't that funny but they all laughed. Then Sunny started to cry.

Watching her, Raine's eyes filled, too. She'd been strong

for too long and scared for too long and worried for too long. Holding the emotions at bay, because if she hadn't, they would have overwhelmed her. Now they rushed over her, and her eyes heated with tears that dripped down her cheeks. Whimpering sounds came out of her mouth as Sunny threw her arms around her. The whimpers turned into a full cry, and they held on to each other, sobbing, as Marsha hurried past them into the bathroom.

They were still crying together as Marsha left the bathroom, and Todd stepped inside it.

And they cried as another flush came from the bathroom, and Todd left, giving them a wary look and hurrying past them.

And then then they were alone, and Sunny lifted her head, sniffing, with tear tracks showing on her reddened face.

"I'm sorry, I'm sorry, I'm sorry. Will you forgive me?"

"You're my sister. I love you." Raine sniffed, too, and let go of Sunny. "I'll even forgive you. But I think it's time for you to look at songs from other songwriters. And I'm going to ask Howie to send my songs to other singers."

"I deserve this." Sunny stepped back. "It's all my fault. I was an idiot, and I don't care about the songs. I missed you. And now—" She stopped, looking down at the floor.

"Now what?"

"I don't know. I guess now I go to the bathroom, and then I don't know what else will happen. Will you stay with me? At least until this is over?"

Raine heard a sound from the hallway. She knew before she turned that it was Chuck. She saw the tension in his face, and she knew that he'd heard his sister's question.

"I'm sorry, Sunny." Though she was speaking to Sunny, she kept her gaze on Chuck, and he kept his on her. "I'll be here for the trials, but I think I'm making a small town in Wisconsin my home base."

ONLY TWO DEPUTIES were left in the front room with Vince and his brother. Doug and Chuck had left to find a bathroom, too. Vince had directed them to the one in the back. Without the others, the room felt empty. Or maybe he just felt empty after purging years of hatred out of his soul today.

"We need to find my father." He gazed down at his brother and felt no pity. He was sure Jarret knew or guessed what their father had done to both of his wives, Jarret's own mother and Vince's. But as long as he was Daddy's favorite, he didn't care.

The apple not falling far from the tree was true for Jarret. Not Vince. All these years later, Vince remembered his mother, who had loved to dance and laugh and love.

All these years later, he'd stayed with his father, waiting for him to do something so horrendous that he could nail him for it.

Now it was done. Now he could live for himself and not for revenge. He hadn't been able to prove that his father killed his mother, but at least he was showing the world what his father was really like. He guessed that former members of Nirvana Now would crawl out of their safe places and tell their stories, too.

One of the deputies stood. "Grant Wellington isn't in the house."

"I know a few places to look," Vince said.

"Wait!" Jarret shouted. "If I tell you where he is, will you give me immunity?"

The deputy stared at Jarret for about five seconds before turning back to Vince. "You were saying?"

Vince told the deputy about the hidden room in the headquarters, and another hidden room in the house. His father's safe room. He also told him about the tunnel and the approximate place where Grant would exit onto the road.

As a couple deputies dragged Jarret away, he yelled at Vince to call their lawyer. Vince watched him, then sagged onto the sofa, his head back, his energy drained.

The worst was over.

Sunny came into the room. "I'm so tired, but I won't sleep here tonight."

Vince opened his eyes. "You can stay at my place."

She stared at him for a long moment, then her lips slowly curved into a smile. "I think I'll sleep at Ledge's place tonight."

"It was broken into," he said. "It could happen again."

Her eyebrows rose. "Are you threatening me?"

"No." He shook his head. "Your sister and her boyfriend can come, too."

She looked at him, and he saw the sadness in her face. "We'll see," she said. "We'll see."

He nodded, hearing low laughter, Dawn—no, *Raine*—and Chuck, coming from the other room. Then the voices of Marsha and Todd.

"We'll see," he repeated her words. He felt...tired. Twenty-one years of hate. Twenty-one years of waiting for vengeance.

It wasn't over yet. There would be a trial. A long one. But in the end, his father would go to jail. Jarret would go to jail.

He'd need a new life.

And Sunny carried a new life inside her.

"Dawn is moving back to that little town in Wisconsin," Sunny said.

"I can see why. I'm not crazy about the weather, but it's a nice place to live."

"Seriously?" She stared at him.

"Maybe," he said. "Maybe I feel another big change coming on."

Forty-five

TWO MONTHS PASSED. The days felt longer than normal. April already.

Raine hadn't returned with Chuck after all. Her sister needed her. Chuck hadn't argued or tried to dissuade her. It wasn't in him to tell her what to do. It was her choice, and he respected her for it.

He'd let her go.

But her absence was an ache that wouldn't leave him. A piece of his heart had remained in California.

One thing had changed after he'd returned home. Artists and craftsmen—and craftswomen—called him or just came over to the B and B, wanting to be part of the Trouble Bay Art Mart. At first, he hadn't understood, then he'd realized why they trusted him now. He'd proven himself in their eyes. They believed now that he was a stand-up guy, and he would be there until the end. He would make the art mart work.

All of this because he'd shot a man to stop him from killing the woman he loved. It had been all over the news that he could have killed Jarret instead of wounding him—or dived behind a piece of furniture and stayed out of the whole mess.

He wasn't angry. He didn't hold grudges. Before this, he'd never taken control of anything. He'd never committed to anyone or anything. He'd been content with his easy and fun life. Statistically, one-third of his life was over, and he was finally showing initiative and ambition.

As he'd told Raine on one of their morning, noon, and night phone calls, shooting someone had showed he could be serious.

They'd both laughed, but not long. If he had to do it again, he would do it. But he hoped it would never happen.

He missed her so badly. She'd ended up staying with her sister temporarily at her condo, though they'd stayed at Ledge's for the first month, and now she and Sunny were staying at Sunny's villa in a gated community.

Raine's condo had been ransacked by the Nirvana Now people, though that couldn't be proved. Furniture had been broken. Files were missing.

But that wasn't the reason she stayed in Los Angeles. The reason was her sister.

While they stayed at Ledge's, she'd written songs for him while Sunny regained her confidence.

Every time Chuck talked to Raine, she swore that she would be back to Trouble Bay soon.

He believed her.

He *had* to believe her.

He loved her. As simple as that.

The trial had started two weeks ago. Because Jarret had cut a deal with the prosecutors and was testifying against his father, Chuck wasn't required to be at the trials.

Raine wasn't supposed to talk to him about the trial, but of course she did. Besides, reporters and bloggers sat in the trials, and they'd immediately shared the details. Chuck had been sorry not to go. He wanted to be with her, but she didn't need his support.

His mother was still in Madison. She and Nate were talking about marriage, though she was reluctant to give up her freedom.

Chuck knew his dad's infidelities had hurt her. Sometimes it was hard to shake off something like that, even when decades had passed. Even when your life was good now. Even when you had plans for the future that excited you. And you had friends and your health, and you told yourself every night that you were content.

Except for the missing piece of your heart.

I love you, I love you, I love you.
I love your face. I love your kisses. I love everything about
you.
I love your laugh. I love your smile. I love your shining eyes.
I even love your tantrums. I even love your tears.
I'll love you more with every year.
This love, this huge, giant, all-encompassing love that makes
my heart sing,
It will never go away.
I love you, I love you, I love you.

I Love You, lyrics and music by Raine Keighly

HOME.

Her heart was singing and playing a happy song that had guitar music and a sexy sax.

She pulled up her rental car in front of the bed-and-breakfast.

Cars were in the parking lot, half filling it. The unofficial opening day for tourist season was May first, but stores were stocking up on their merchandise, redecorating was done, the sun was shining early in the day, and most women were wearing cotton instead of denim. Driving through Sturgeon Bay, Raine had even seen girls and women wearing shorts.

In April, Chuck had said, the earth came alive in Wisconsin and so did the Door County communities.

Everything had a cycle, she thought, as a song shimmered for a minute in her mind. Normally, she would grab a pen and paper or type it in her cell phone—because those ideas that slid into her mind had a way of slipping right out again. But this time she let it go.

This time words and music weren't what caused an ache in her chest.

It wasn't because of her songs that she felt joy.

Everything about Trouble Bay today echoed her life. A new life was beginning.

The trial was over. She'd moved out of Sunny's condo.

Vince had moved in.

Raine had a good feeling about this pairing, though only time would tell if it would work. And she wasn't going to be her sister's keeper. Not anymore.

She had her own life to live. Good or bad. And she could only see good ahead of her.

A man stepped out of the front door. Blond hair, wearing jeans and a long-sleeved T-shirt and what looked like work boots.

And a big smile.

Happiness that felt like sunlight filled her. Arms open, she ran to him.

Arms open, he ran to her.

Laughing. Both of them laughing.

And crying. Tears tracking down her face.

They kissed in the front yard, and someone honked. So did someone else.

"Get a room!" someone yelled.

"Yeah!" someone else called as they clung to each other. "Get a room."

More laughter and guffaws came. He pulled away, his forehead slanted on hers. "My heart is whole again."

More tears filled her eyes.

He smiled, and it was the best smile in the world because it made her want to kiss him again.

She blinked away the tears. "Is there room to park?"

"I'll always make room for you. But the car can stay in front for now. Let's get your suitcases in."

"You're in a hurry?" She pressed a button on the key ring to open the trunk.

He pulled one suitcase out of the trunk, and she took the other.

"You see how this is," he said. "Someone just advised us to get a room, and it so happens that I have one."

☂

THEY HEADED STRAIGHT to his room, and their clothes seemed to fly off, and she didn't care where they landed. She only cared about connecting with Chuck in the most basic way. Flesh to flesh, chest to chest, lip to lip, and best part below as her body lit up like fireworks.

They made love and shared love and became love, until he collapsed next to her and she felt like a river. A wonderful, happy, contented, fulfilled river.

"Marry me," he said.

She turned her head slowly. When she spoke, her voice was languid. "Okay."

He laughed, and she smiled as her heart sang the "I Love You" song.

Forty-six

"I'M PREGNANT."

Todd stiffened and swallowed and shook a little. He and Marsha were sitting at the kitchen table while Baxter was lying on the tiled floor with Marsha's two English setters.

"I'm sorry," he said, and his voice came out in a croak.

"I'm not."

"You're not?" He was shaking now.

She put her hand over his. "I wanted this. You might be angry, but after we came back from California, I stopped using birth control."

"You *wanted* my baby?"

"Yes. I waited nearly four weeks, just to make sure. But I knew on the airplane flying to California that I wanted you to be my baby's father."

He stared at her wide face that was now a little sad.

"I could see right away," she said, "that you were healthy, despite the life you lived so shortly before you came here. And I knew you'd passed the mental, intellectual, and physical tests to get in the Marines. You told me you hadn't had sex since you got out, and I believed you. Basically, you were pretested."

She laughed, but it didn't sound like a real laugh.

"That mental part didn't always work so well," he said.

"Some things are so awful that they break down people. The same way my Allie shakes during thunderstorms. We're animals, just like dogs."

266

"I'm not so sure about the intelligent part, either," he said.

"I am," she said, her voice firm. "And I have to be honest, I wanted your baby because of your physical attributes."

"Huh?"

"Your face. You have a nice-looking face. It's not round like mine." She grimaced. "And my mom before me, and my dad. And look at your body." She waved a hand toward him. "You're tall and lean."

"I scrounged for food," he said. "I ate food that restaurants threw away."

She leaned over the table. "Quit putting yourself down. You had horrible things happen, and you survived. You healed yourself. You're the perfect father for my child."

"*Our* child," he said. "Mine, too."

She sat back. "I wasn't planning on putting any burden on you. To be bluntly honest, I don't want to get married. I'm happy sleeping in my own bed and waking up to my own dogs. I'm happy having dinner with you in the evenings. Happy making love to you. And I'm happy, too, when you go home." She put her hand out to his shoulder. "I hope the baby doesn't change that."

"That's okay. It's just..." A choking sound came from his throat. "A baby. I'm going to be a father." Tears burned his eyes, and he wept. He turned his head away from her, but he heard the scrape of the chair, and he heard the tap of dog feet, then Baxter whined at his feet.

Todd tried to stop his tears, but it was like trying to stop the rain.

Marsha stood and curved her body over him then pulled his face against her breasts. "Oh, honey. I didn't mean to make you unhappy."

He lifted his head, letting her see his tear-stained, tear-reddened face. "These are happy tears. For so many years, I thought I'd never have children. I thought I'd be alone for the rest of my life."

She twisted and leaned down to grab a napkin, handing it to him.

He thanked her and blew his nose as she stepped back. Putting the napkin down, he stood, too. Facing her. "I have money saved from the Marines. I have a house. I know it's smaller than yours, but it's something. I have money from my aunt. Not a lot, but enough. And I work part-time at the humane society now."

"I make good money with my bookkeeping business. I don't need yours."

"Then I'll save it for the baby's college education. I can do that."

She nodded, and her face was turning red, as if she was going to cry, too.

He lifted his hands to the sides of her face. "You're wrong about your face. You're wrong about your body. Your face and your body are beautiful. I thought so the first time I saw you, and I've thought so every day since then."

"You're such a liar." She laughed at him, but now she blinked away tears.

"It's my truth. You're beautiful, inside and out. And we're having a baby together."

She leaned her head against his chest, and he put his arms around her. Baxter rubbed his head against his leg.

Todd knew he wasn't healed. He wasn't the man he used to be before the Marines. But maybe in some ways he was better.

A dad. He was going to be a dad.

He could hear the rain start outside, and he thought of Raine and Chuck.

He and Chuck were both lucky men. The luckiest men in Door County.

THE TEARS AND Todd's shaking voice had scared Baxter. But it was okay now, and he could feel Todd's happiness. It was like Todd felt after playing with him. The kind of happiness that came from just being.

Still, he watched Todd and Marsha for another minute, then he went back to the two dogs that Marsha called Sleepy and Happy.

Life was good now. All good. Todd loved him. So did Marsha. So did the other dogs—even when he stole their food.

The best part was that he and Todd were together almost all the time.

He put his head down. All was well. He and Happy and Sleepy were lucky dogs. They must be the luckiest three dogs in the world.

Excerpt from

Christmas Redemption
LOVE & MURDER, BOOK 5

Edie Ramer

One

"WARNING TO ANY Michiganders who might be listening. First, you had to watch out for the water. Now, you have to watch out for the modern-day Bonnie and Clyde. Yep. You heard me right. They change their hair color. They change their cars. They change their names. And you know what else they do, peeps?"

In the Buick's front passenger seat, Sylvia looked at Nate, her eyebrows up. His eyes were on the traffic, but he must have felt her gaze because he smiled, his cheeks pouching up. Her slightly chubby teddy bear with his curly gray hair, protuberant nose, and ready smile.

"Aren't you sorry now that you didn't listen to NPR?" he asked.

She laughed. After living in a small town in Door County, Wisconsin, for the first fifty-three years of her life, she relished her new life in Madison with the concerts, the plays, the art exhibits, and often National Public Radio. Still, it felt good to be going home for Christmas. This Christmas would be tamer than the last, she was sure, and glad for it.

"They murder." The DJ's smooth voice regained her attention. "You heard me right. I said murder, and that's what they do."

Sylvia supposed the DJ meant to be humorous, but she shuddered, and it wasn't because of the twelve-degree temperature outside or the meteorologist's snow warnings.

She'd had enough of murder, and none of it had been funny. Especially since some of the murders had involved her.

She had killed three people and hadn't been caught.

Yet.

She planned on the *yet* to mean *never ever*.

At least she hadn't killed maliciously. Except, perhaps, once.

She'd been younger then. Ice-cold outside; boiling hot inside.

Crying inside.

Screaming inside.

Feeling like the world's biggest fool.

Worrying about what would happen to her son.

Worrying about what would happen to her.

There had been no pre-nup. Charley would have claimed half of the bed-and-breakfast she'd grown up in. The bed-and-breakfast that had been in her family for generations.

And from Charley...? He would have given her nothing. And nothing for Chuck, their son.

Even now the memories made her clench her jaw tightly. She forced her jaw to relax and reminded herself that Chuck was almost thirty-two now, with his own plans for a business. An amazing man. Engaged to a wonderful and talented woman who made him light up every time he looked at her.

A big difference from his dad. At Charley's wake, she'd overheard one of his bar friends saying, "I'm sorry he's gone but not surprised. If any man was born to be die with a bullet in his cheating heart, that man was Charley."

Perhaps she should have waited for someone else to kill him, but she was never the type to wait for other people to do her dirty work.

And the other two murders...well, there were reasons for those, too.

In one case, she had saved lives.

Her other victim had ruined lives.

But Charley's murder... As much as she told herself that he had deserved to die, it haunted her.

Her hands shook, and she clenched them. She was not the same person now. She needed to let go of the past. She needed to be happy. She needed to forgive herself, though years later now—*decades*—the hurt was still there. A raw wound that had never healed.

She took a deep breath. She was just here for the Christmas holidays. She and Nate would be staying until after New Year's while Chuck and his fiancée visited her sister and her sister's baby in Santa Barbara.

When this holiday was over and Sylvia and Nate returned to Madison, she could work on forgiving herself and releasing the closed fist that was squeezing her heart so tightly.

For a beginning, she could let her fingers open.

She could let her heart beat steadily.

She could breathe deeper and slower.

She could accept Nate's marriage proposal.

She could allow herself to be happy.

Sitting with her back straight, she felt better now that she had a plan. A goal. Until the time was right to put her thoughts into actions, she would enjoy the holiday and help give the two couples who had booked suites at the bed-and-breakfast a Christmas they would never forget.

THE DJ PROMISED to play the new Adele song after the commercial. Julian reached forward to lower the sound then turned to the driver. "You know what I like most about Wisconsin?"

"Cheese." Avery steered the car along the Upper Michigan highway, the heater on high, snow and pine trees on both sides of the road. "And beer."

He glanced sideways. One thing Avery did well was drive. His mother had preferred to be driven, and so did he.

And Avery had money. He liked that. Liked that very much.

He took after his mother that way, too.

And Avery liked going down on him. He liked that very much, too.

A memory flashed in his mind. He was ten years old, and it felt as if he weren't thinking of something in the past but reliving it. Hearing guttural sounds coming from his mother's bedroom. Sounds like someone was dying.

He hurried down the hall. The door was open, and he stopped and stared. His mother and Carl, his second stepfather, were naked on the huge bed, his mother kneeling between Carl's legs, her head curved down.

Watching them, Julian drew his breath in, nervous and excited and mesmerized.

Carl's croaks became louder and louder, until he let loose with a roar, his hips slamming up and down between his mother's hands, smashing against her face. Julian was still staring when his mother rolled off of his stepfather and flopped down on the bed next to him, the side closest to the hallway.

Then she turned her head and looked at him, her eyes dark.

A small smile appeared on her face. She opened her mouth, and he could see the shininess inside. He was old enough to know what that was.

He ran to his room, closing the door, shoving his hand down his pants.

In the car, he shut down those thoughts.

Even before that night, he'd known he was different from other people. He'd celebrated the difference. The others were lemmings, and he was a shark.

His mother had been a shark, too. He'd give that to her. The kind of a shark who liked to bite her son. Showing him she was the one in charge.

Avery was a shark, too, but a smaller shark. He was the biggest shark. The smartest one. So when Avery said foolish things, which she often did, he let them go by. After all, he never did like women with brains.

Women like his mother.

"What I like about Wisconsin," he said finally, "is that no one will expect us to strike there."

Avery giggled again. He sat back with a half smile, dismissing his memories. They were part of yesterday and had no meaning to him. Shakespeare had been wrong. The past wasn't prologue. The past was dust.

Santa was coming to the town of Trouble Bay, and Julian was going to get a very big Christmas present. He knew that because he was giving the present to himself.

He touched the car's digital screen, switching to another station. Then he sat back, the corners of his lips curling as he listened to his favorite holiday song, "You're a Mean One, Mr. Grinch."

About Edie

USA Today bestselling and multiple award-winning author Edie Ramer loves dogs, cats, family (the human kind), and readers. A Wisconsin native, she has been to the Door County peninsula quite a few times. She and her husband once stayed in a Sturgeon Bay bed-and-breakfast for two nights. It was research, of course.

Before she was a writer, she was a reader. Her favorite books make her care about what happens to the characters, and that's what she wants readers to feel when they read one of hers. She's proud of every book she's written, but the Love & Murder books are her favorite, containing all the elements she enjoys in a book. She hopes you enjoy them, too.

To learn more about her, visit www.edieramer.com. While you're there, check out her Search For Happiness blog and sign up for updates of new books on her newsletter. You can also sign up for Edie's author page on Facebook and follow her on Twitter and Goodreads.

Acknowledgments

I love good music and lyrics, and I've written a few books with music as an important part of the book. I'm inspired by many great songwriters, musicians, and singers. An offhand remark by author Elle J Rossi, a former professional country singer (under a different name), was the inspiration for my heroine's profession and the plot. Much gratitude to Elle, who is also a wonderful author, digital artist, and friend.

www.ingramcontent.com/pod-product-compliance
Lightning Source LLC
Chambersburg PA
CBHW060900250626
47159CB00008B/2817